W

A Regency Romance

MARTHA KEYES

OTHER TITLES BY MARTHA KEYES

Isabel: A Regency Romance (Families of Dorset Book Two)
Cecilia: A Regency Romance (Families of Dorset Book Three)
Goodwill for the Gentleman (Belles of Christmas Book Two)
Eleanor: A Regency Romance

Wyndcross: A Regency Romance © 2019 by Martha Keyes. All Rights Reserved.
All rights reserved. No part of this book may be reproduced in any form or by any electronic or mechanical means including information storage and retrieval systems, without permission in writing from the author. The only exception is by a reviewer, who may quote short excerpts in a review.
Cover design by Martha Keyes.

This book is a work of fiction. Names, characters, places, and incidents are either products of the author's imagination or are used fictitiously. Any resemblance to actual persons, living or dead, events, or locales, is entirely coincidental.
Martha Keyes
http://www.marthakeyes.com
First Printing: July 2019

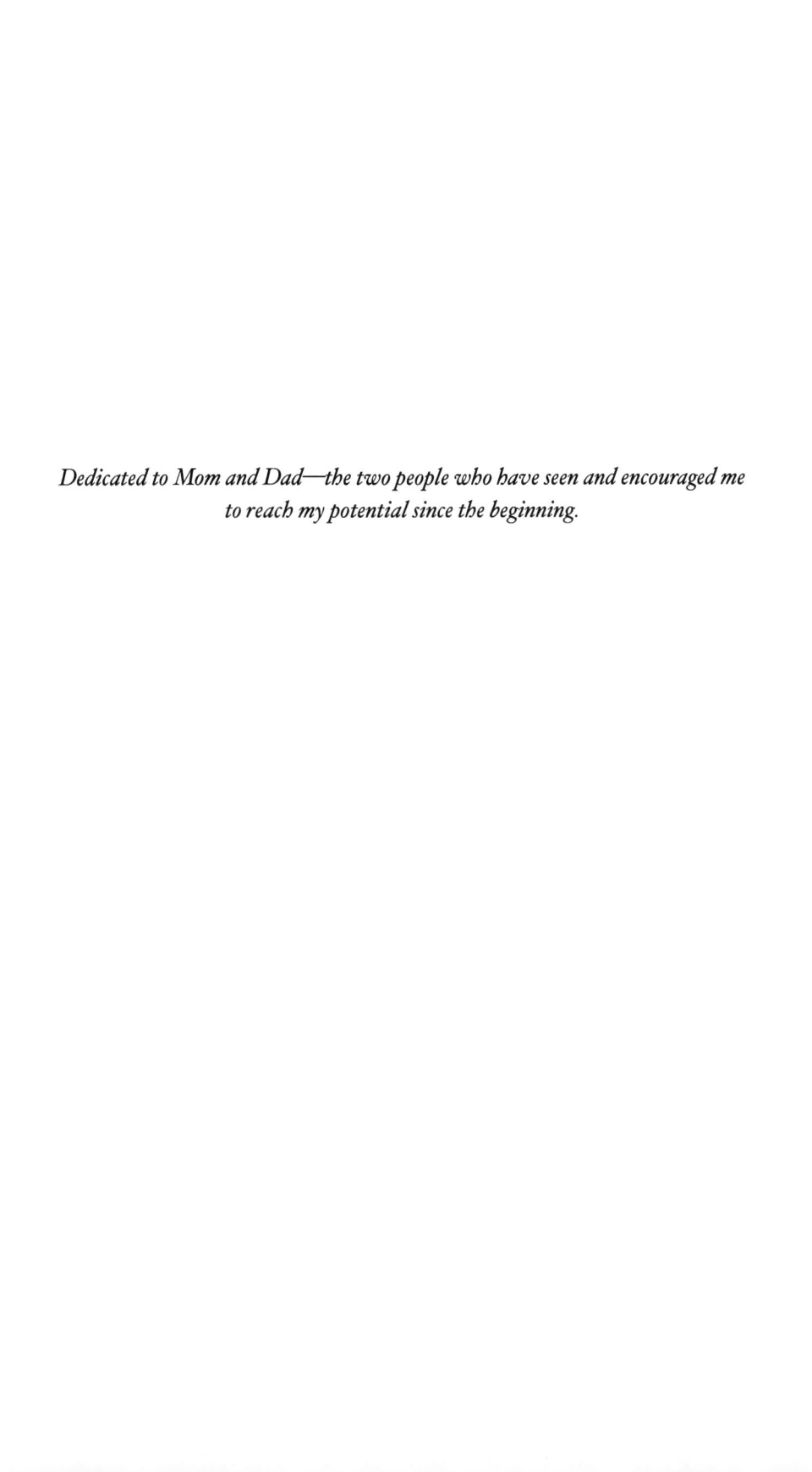

Dedicated to Mom and Dad—the two people who have seen and encouraged me to reach my potential since the beginning.

I

Kate Matcham thumbed the threadbare crimson reticule sitting on her lap, feeling the reassuring presence of the letter inside. Her eyes shifted to the numerous ball guests surrounding her and her aunt Fanny.

"For heaven's sake, Fanny," she pleaded, "keep your voice down."

Nearby, Charlotte Thorpe whispered to the woman next to her, and Kate's jaw clenched. If Charlotte Thorpe overheard, all of London would know in a matter of days. Kate was already regretting telling her aunt of the letter.

Lady Fanny Hammond guiltily covered her mouth with a hand, but she couldn't dampen the excitement in her eyes. "Do you even know your stepfather's worth?" she half-whispered, leaning over in her seat toward Kate.

"No," Kate admitted, rushing on before Fanny could enlighten her, "but it is immaterial. His brother stands to inherit, and I am certain that he will be found alive and well."

It was certainly what Kate hoped would occur. It would be much easier if the choice not to accept the fortune was made for her. She smiled and inclined her head at a passing acquaintance.

"But he might well be dead," Fanny said optimistically, smiling at the same acquaintance. "People die in the West Indies quite frequently, I believe."

Kate looked down at her young aunt with a mixture of consternation and amusement. "How very morbid you are."

"Perhaps," Fanny said, her wide, blue eyes scanning the room, "but a little morbidity might not be uncalled for when twenty thousand pounds are at stake."

"Twenty thou—" Kate's eyes widened. She took a steadying breath.

Whether it was twenty pounds or twenty thousand pounds, she could never accept money from her stepfather, Mr. Dimmock. Nor did she believe he would give her the chance.

"It's neither here nor there," she said. "My stepfather detests me and always has. He would surely find a way to ensure that his fortune couldn't pass to me."

"Well," Fanny huffed, "I'm sure I don't see why. Hateful man."

Kate smiled at Fanny's offense on her behalf. She had long since ceased trying to curry favor with her stepfather. Nor did she waste energy trying to understand the dislike for her which he took no pains to hide.

Fanny continued, "I'm sure you are the most unassuming and pleasant stepdaughter one could wish for."

Kate leaned over to kiss her aunt's cheek. "And you are the most wonderful chaperone one could wish for—not to mention the most beautiful and young and charitable and long-suffering."

"The most beautiful?" Fanny said, ignoring the other epithets in favor of the one she most prized. "Do you really think so?" She touched her honey curls with a cupped hand in the gesture Kate had come to know well.

"Without question," Kate said with feigned gravity, hand over her heart. Hoping to keep Fanny's mind off the letter, she continued, "In truth, you are more in need of a chaperone than I."

Fanny scoffed. "I need no chaperone. I am a widow, besides being fully two years older than you, my dear." She stretched herself high in her seat, though Kate's tall figure still eclipsed her.

Kate smiled and shook her head as she looked off into the groups of people dancing and conversing. The brightly lit ballroom was peppered with Fanny's admirers. "I have tried my best to keep the fortune-hunters at bay, but one can only do so much, you know." She sighed melodramatically and then turned to wink at her aunt.

Fanny collapsed her fan and rapped Kate's knuckles with it. "Nonsense," she said, but her blush-tinged cheeks betrayed the pleasure she took in flattery.

Kate spotted Mr. Walmsley on the other side of the room, making his way over to them in his characteristic waddle. "Not all of them are fortune-hunters, thankfully," Kate said pointedly.

The portly but kind-hearted aspirant to Fanny's hand was sweating profusely as he tried to navigate his way through the crowd holding two drinks. His plump figure made him look all at once older and younger than his thirty-three years.

"No," Fanny said. "Walmsley is decidedly not a fortune-hunter. He is more likely to be hunted for his own fortune, you know. But I am not at all sure if I shall accept his offer." Fanny bit her lip as she tracked his movement toward them. She turned to Kate with a conscience-stricken expression. "The truth is, I have so much enjoyed being widowed."

Kate's eyes lit up with laughter, and Fanny rushed on, "I know it is an awful thing to say, but I married so young. I never had a real Season. Naturally Lord Hammond was very good to me," she added quickly, "and I had no reason to complain of my treatment at his hands. But he preferred spending most of the year in the country."

She said the last word with a touch of revulsion and then looked around the room with an air of melancholy. "London is my home, and I'm not sure that I'm ready to give this life up all over again."

Kate could readily believe that Fanny would be loath to abandon her current lifestyle. Her schedule consisted of one social engagement after another, and her wealth and widowhood made her an object of gallantry.

Mr. Walmsley came before them, handing one drink to Fanny and the other to Kate. "Too many people here, I tell you." The skin under his chin trembled as he shook his head. "I could barely get my hands on these drinks. Was nearly obliged to call a fellow out! The jackanapes tried to cut in front of me for these last two."

"Oh dear," breathed Kate. She lowered her head and turned it to the side, hunching her shoulders and hoping to avoid the attention of the gentleman heading in their direction.

"Not to worry, Miss Matcham," Walmsley reassured her in ignorant bliss. "I didn't *actually* call him out. Only tempted me for a moment. I'm afraid my dueling days are long past. My circumference, you see, provides much too wide a target for my taste." He looked down at his belly and rubbed it with fondness.

"No, not that," Kate hissed, biting her lip to keep from laughing at Mr. Walmsley's words. But it was too late. She had been recognized. She straightened hastily in her chair, pretending that she had been picking something up, and contrived a smile at the man approaching them.

Sir Lewis Gording stopped and bowed. His thin lips were stretched in a smile, though the lines above them betrayed the slight contempt they most often wore. Had Kate been standing, she would have come eye to eye with Sir Lewis. Despite their matched height, he always managed to make her feel as though he was looking down upon her.

Unlike so many of the young women who tolerated his aggressive flirting to placate their hopeful mothers, Kate had always found his company uncomfortable and paid him only the attention that civility required. Unfortunately for her, Sir Lewis seemed to find her company more desirable as a result. He was impervious to her subtle snubs.

"Good evening, your ladyship. Walmsley." He bowed and turned toward Kate. "Miss Matcham, might I have the pleasure of the next dance?"

She groaned inside but maintained the same contrived smile of civility. Out of politeness and the desire to be a credit to Fanny, she would not refuse him, but the feeling of obligation chafed her.

"Of course," she replied, with a bow of her head.

Helping her up from her seat and tucking her hand into his arm, Sir Lewis led her away from Fanny and Mr. Walmsley. Kate turned her head back toward Fanny with a look of helplessness. Fanny smiled at her and bobbed her head up and down in encouragement, failing to recognize the distress signal.

"I've changed my mind," Sir Lewis said, and Kate whipped her head back around, afraid he had witnessed her attempted call for help. "Let us instead take a turn about the room."

Before she could respond, he had guided her away from the dance floor. They passed through two groups of chatting women, the sound of organdy, muslin, and silk skirts brushing against one another. Kate envied the merry voices of the women they passed. If only she could disappear into one of their circles. Instead she was being guided firmly toward the brocade-draped windows lining the room.

Sir Lewis was clearly used to being in control. It was part of what she so disliked in him.

"As you please, sir," she said, clenching her teeth behind her smile. She felt his eyes studying her.

"You are the picture of perfection this evening, if I may say so," he said. His eyes moved from her head down to her slippers.

Where other ladies might blush at such a high compliment, or at least at his unabashed scrutiny, Kate's nostrils flared in consternation. "I'd prefer you didn't say such things, Sir Lewis, as you well know that I'm not fond of your exaggerated compliments. Or of such compliments in general."

"Every woman loves compliments," he said with his characteristic certainty.

The retort which rose to Kate's lips was cut off as she felt a tap on her shoulder and heard a man clear his throat. She turned.

The gentleman she faced bowed slightly. When he rose to his full height, he was a few inches taller than she. His brown hair was long enough to curl but had been brushed away from his face, though a few curls seemed to be attempting a revolt. Small lines at the corners of his eyes revealed a tendency to laugh, but as he met eyes with Sir Lewis, his pleasant expression flickered.

"Sir Lewis." He nodded.

"Good evening," Sir Lewis said, raising his brows in a gesture both questioning and dismissive.

"Forgive the interruption," the gentleman said, and he smiled at Kate. "I believe this belongs to you, Miss."

He held her crimson reticule in his outstretched hand. One of the strings—evidently the one which she had wrapped around her wrist—

had finally broken. "You dropped it a moment ago back there." He gestured with his head behind him.

Her eyes widened, and she looked at him with dismay. Had he seen its contents? Her arm shot out for the bag. Only when her hand reached his did she realize how peculiar her behavior would seem.

She looked up at him with warm cheeks and a sheepish smile. His brows were slightly raised, his head tilted to one side, and his eyes twinkling as he watched her reaction.

"It is indeed mine," she said, taking it from him gently with a relieved smile. "Thank you for returning it to me."

A smile played at his lips. "Yes, well, I admit that I was hard-pressed to give it up. Crimson is particularly good with my complexion, I'm told." He sighed. "But alas, it was not to be. My conscience won out in the end. I wish you joy of it."

Kate took her lips between her teeth to suppress a smile, and his eyes danced.

Sir Lewis's voice cut in on the exchange. "And now that you have returned it, we will trouble you no longer."

The gentleman's smile tightened, and he looked at Sir Lewis as if he had a rejoinder on his lips. Kate wished he would say whatever it was, but he bowed, shot another glance of shared enjoyment at her, and walked away.

Kate took a deep breath as she watched him walk off, feeling she had been undeservedly lucky. If he— (who was he? Sir Lewis had been disobliging enough not to introduce him)—had not seen her drop the reticule, who might have happened upon it? The person would have been required to look inside to determine its owner, and who knows what they might have seen, how much they would have read, or what information from the letter they would have decided to pass along to their acquaintances.

The last thing Kate wanted was for anyone else to take the letter's contents as seriously as Fanny had done.

"Where were we?" Sir Lewis said. "Ah, yes. I had just complimented your ever-increasing beauty."

Kate gripped her lips together, wishing that the interlude with the handsome stranger could have lasted longer. Any reprieve from Sir Lewis's attentions was a welcome one.

"Please don't," she said, feeling fatigued at the thought of continuing to fend off Sir Lewis.

His lopsided smile appeared again. "Would you really deprive me the opportunity of expressing the thoughts that fill my head?" His eyes were at odds with his words, almost mocking her. How many women had he flattered in the same way?

"Perhaps," said Kate, striving for a light tone, "if the thoughts are kept within they will diminish altogether in time, though I doubt they are as pervasive as you claim."

"I disagree," he said, coming to stand in front of her and blocking her way. "They demand to be given expression, Kate." He said her name slowly, looking into her wary green eyes with his cynical gray ones.

"Forgive me, sir," she said with a bite to her voice, "but I have not given you leave to call me by my given name." She moved to walk around him, but he caught her arm. She stopped but didn't turn her head to look at him. She had, in the past, done her best to put him in his place with gentle civility, but with each meeting, he seemed to grow more aggressive.

"No, perhaps you have not," he acknowledged, looking at her profile and gripping her arm with his teeth bared in a false smile. "But you will do so shortly, I feel confident."

"Your confidence is misplaced, sir," she said. She glanced at the group of people nearest them. The gentleman who had returned her reticule stood between two women. His intent gaze was on Kate.

She tore her arm from Sir Lewis's grasp, feeling a pressing need to make it plain that she was not a willing recipient of Sir Lewis's attentions. She looked back to Sir Lewis, her gaze hard and direct. "If you will excuse me," she said.

He grabbed her by the wrist and leaned in toward her. His lip turned up on one side. The smirk made her hair stand on edge. "You would have everything you could want living under my protection, you know."

She reared back, and her eyes glinted dangerously. "You dare offer such a thing to a lady?"

His smirk morphed into contempt, and the grip on her wrist tightened uncomfortably. "A lady? You are the daughter of a social climber and the stepdaughter of an unscrupulous tradesman." He blew out a derisive puff of air. "A woman with connections such as yours cannot be so particular about whom she accepts and on what terms, Kate." He drew out her name, as if to mock her.

She felt the blood rush into her cheeks, betraying her embarrassment and anger. But before she could think of a suitable reply, they were interrupted again.

"Excuse me."

Kate turned with a suppressed sigh of relief, meeting eyes with the same gentleman who had brought her reticule just minutes before.

Kate was conscious of her angry, red cheeks, and she tried to control the way her chest heaved with furious breaths. The gentleman had impeccable timing.

"I hesitate to deprive you," he said, "of the exalted company you somehow find yourself in, Sir Lewis, but I come to claim a promised dance." He wore a congenial grin, but his eyes challenged Sir Lewis.

Sir Lewis dropped Kate's wrist and looked at her as if to verify the man's claims.

She raised her brows at him in a similarly challenging gesture. She was more than happy to disregard that she had never promised the stranger a dance.

The gentleman shifted his eyes to Kate, the challenging glint gone. He wore a soft smile as he offered her his arm. She smiled at him gratefully, made a quick, icy apology to Sir Lewis, and walked away on the arm of her deliverer.

She looked up at his profile beside her. The man's expression was unreadable, and he looked straight ahead as though nothing out of the ordinary had occurred.

Kate drew in a deep breath, feeling her cheeks cool.

"Thank you," she said. Her brow creased. "Or my apologies. I'm not sure which is appropriate, to be honest."

He looked down at her with an amused tilt to his mouth. "Why should you assume either is necessary?"

"Well," she said matter-of-factly, "either you recognized my discomfort and intervened, perjuring yourself in the process, I might add; or," she shrugged, "you have mistaken me for a lady who had indeed promised you a dance, in which case I apologize for the misunderstanding and simply feel grateful that it occurred."

His smile grew. "I only did what I wish someone would do for me whenever I find myself in Sir Lewis's company."

A laugh escaped Kate. "I will endeavor to return the favor if I ever see you in his presence."

"The prospect of being in his company suddenly becomes more enticing," he said.

She glanced at him. Was he flirting with her?

But he was looking toward the dance floor where a set was forming.

"Shall we?" he said, motioning to the dancers.

Kate hesitated. She couldn't deny that the prospect of dancing with him was appealing. But they hadn't even been properly introduced.

"You realize," he said, watching her hesitation, "that if you refuse, I will have doubly perjured myself tonight. And you will bear some responsibility for the second instance."

How did he manage to look so censuring and playful at the same time? Kate suppressed a smile and shot a glance in the direction of Sir Lewis. His eyes were on them. She found that she was gripping the gentleman's arm harder than was merited and loosened her hold.

"How could I possibly refuse after such a compelling argument?" she said, looking up at him with a smile.

They took their places among the set on the dance floor for a lively country dance. She had danced with gentlemen after only a brief introduction, but never had she danced with one whose name she didn't know. The knowledge that they were complicit in defying etiquette brought a shade of pink to Kate's cheeks which had nothing to do with the heat of the room. There was something exhilarating about it all.

Her partner was skilled but droll in his dancing, and Kate found that her cheeks began to ache from smiling and laughing. There was hardly time for conversing amongst the energetic movements of the dance, and yet Kate felt carefree with her anonymous partner. His hand was light yet sure, and she felt a thrill each time the dance required them to stand shoulder to shoulder or join hands.

Before she knew it, though, the set had ended, and they were bowing to one another.

He offered her his arm, his breathless grin matching her own. "Where shall I convey you, madam? Back to Sir Lewis?"

"By all means," she said with a threatening lift to her eyebrows, "if you wish my specter to haunt you the rest of your days."

He threw his head back in a chuckle. "That prospect is not nearly as horrifying as you seem to think it."

"Well before you convey me to my aunt—" she emphasized the word and indicated Fanny whose back was turned as she conversed with Charlotte Thorpe "—perhaps I should at least know your name?"

He drew back with a scandalized expression. "When we haven't even been properly introduced? What an appalling suggestion." A smile twitched at the corner of his mouth for a moment, and he continued walking her toward Fanny.

She pulled back on his arm, preventing their progress. "Perhaps it is. But we can hardly ask someone to introduce us after they have seen us dance together. Besides, what if someone should inquire from me after you?"

He clucked his tongue, shaking his head. "What a dilemma for you."

"For me? Why only for me?"

"You have no way to know my name," he replied.

"Nor do you know mine," she countered.

"Ah." He raised a brow enigmatically. "But I will discover it, all the same."

He pulled her gently along toward Fanny who was still too occupied with Mrs. Thorpe and two other women to remark their presence.

The gentleman shot Kate a half-smile as he bowed, then leaned in and whispered, "My name is William."

And then he walked away.

Kate watched the gentleman stride off, feeling both frustrated and captivated.

"Miss Matcham?"

The voice, full of excitement and surprise, broke in on her thoughts.

She turned around to face the owner of the unfamiliar voice. A young woman stared at her with round eyes and a large grin.

Kate hadn't any idea who she was, though there was something familiar about her. With flaxen hair, rosy cheeks, and large blue eyes brought out by the lace-covered powder blue gown she wore, it was a face Kate was sure she would have remembered.

Her bewilderment must have been apparent, because the young woman laughed.

"It's me, silly! Clara. Surely you can't have forgotten?"

Confusion morphed into recognition and astonishment, and Kate's face lit up with a large smile. "Clara Crofte? But of course!"

The two embraced quickly, and a strong aroma of lavender met Kate's nose. Clara pulled away, holding Kate out at arms' length, a hand on each shoulder. "You are quite as grown up as I am," she said. "More so, I suppose, since you are older. And so very lovely. When I asked Mary Thorpe who you were, she said, 'Why, that's Miss Kate Matcham,' and I couldn't believe it. So of course I had to come to you immediately."

"I'm very grateful you did," Kate replied. "Indeed, I am in shock to be talking to you. I've often wondered about you and your family this past decade and more, and here you are in front of me after so many years. How is your family?"

"They are well, thank you. My mother is here with me tonight, though last I saw her, she was walking with Lady Carville." She scanned the room, looking for her mother. "I don't see her at the moment, and unfortunately, we cannot stay much longer. My mother is under orders from the doctor not to be to bed too late. May we call upon you tomorrow, though?"

"Yes," Kate said with enthusiasm. "Please do. I'm staying with my aunt, Lady Hammond, in Berkeley Square. We would be delighted to receive you."

Clara beamed. "Wonderful!" She glanced away and then put a hand on Kate's arm, her eyes still fixed on whatever had caught her attention. "Oh, I'm afraid you must excuse me. I see Lord Cartwright thinks I have forgotten that I promised him this dance,"— she shot him a coy glance —"but I shall see you tomorrow." She embraced Kate again, and, with a suppressed squeal of delight, left to favor Lord Cartwright with a cotillion.

Kate turned back toward Fanny with a dazed expression, excusing herself as she bumped into one of Fanny's friends.

"Good heavens, Kate," said Fanny, "you nearly knocked over poor Mrs. Orritt. So unlike you!" Her words censured Kate, but they also contained a hint of curiosity. Fanny was always quick to perceive when someone was full of news.

"Now, your ladyship," said Mr. Walmsley, with a kind smile at Kate. "I'm sure she didn't intend to knock Mrs. Orritt over, did you?" He paused, and then added as an afterthought, "Though, even if she *had* intended it, I can't say I'd have blamed her. The last time I was invited for dinner, I'm devilish sure she had the wine watered down."

Fanny waved an impatient hand at Walmsley, dismissing his hypothesis and looking expectantly at Kate.

"I'm sorry," said Kate. "I'm only distracted with surprise. Do you know who I just spoke with, Fanny?"

Fanny looked exasperated. "Well, really, Kate. With half of London here tonight, how am I to guess which one person you spoke to?"

Kate threw off her preoccupation with a shake of her head and a laugh. "Of course you could never guess. It was Clara Crofte."

Fanny looked none the wiser, staring blankly at Kate, who was obliged to provide more information. Once Fanny made the connection, Kate informed her aunt of the Croftes' plans to call the next day.

"Oh no!" said Fanny with a look of dismay. "Surely you didn't tell them they could call tomorrow? I've been promised to Lady Carville for a sennight."

"I had entirely forgotten." Kate apologized, looking deflated before perking back up. "Well, if you aren't opposed to it, I could receive them on my own?"

Fanny readily assented to the plan.

"Oh, Fanny!" Kate sat up straight in her chair. "I must ask you—" she scanned the room "—to tell me who a particular gentleman is." She blinked rapidly. The man was nowhere to be seen.

"Who?" Fanny said, her curiosity piqued. She followed her niece's eyes around the room.

Kate's brows drew together. "I don't see him anywhere. Perhaps he left." She went up on her toes for a better view of all the ball guests. He was tall enough that it shouldn't have been difficult to find him.

"His name is William," said Kate, still surveying the crowd.

Fanny scoffed. "He and half the men in this room, I imagine."

Kate plopped down in the nearest chair, disappointed. The charm and novelty of London had long since worn off for her, but her encounter with William had made her feel lively again for the first time in longer than she could remember. How would she ever discover his identity?

2

When Kate arose the next morning, it was with a full mind. She had been too busy at the ball and then too fatigued afterward to apply herself to all that had happened.

Between the letter from her mother, her troubling exchange with Sir Lewis, her intriguing interaction with the mysterious William, and the surprise of seeing Clara Crofte, she didn't know how to feel.

Fanny would be anxious to convey all the gossip she had acquired over the course of the night, but she never rose until well into the morning after a late night. She was promised to Lady Carville for the early afternoon, so it was unlikely that Kate would have the opportunity to talk with her before dinnertime.

She walked into the library and inhaled, smiling at the scent of dust and books, and settled into her favorite worn, wingback chair in the library, hoping to give her mind a respite. She had only read three pages when she was interrupted by one of the footmen.

"You have a visitor, ma'am. One Mr. Simon Hartley. I've shown him into the morning room."

"Oh, thank you, Griffyn." Kate looked at the clock. It was early for visitors, but Simon Hartley wasn't just any visitor.

When she entered the morning room, she saw Simon standing at the far wall opposite the door, hat in his hands.

No matter how many times she told him not to stand on ceremony with her and Fanny, Kate always found him the same way when he visited: standing stiffly as he awaited her invitation to sit.

He looked even more rigid than usual. She could tell that he had something particular to say to her.

"We looked in vain for you at the ball last night," Kate said as she shut the door.

"Yes," Simon answered, his lips forming the same straight line they always did. Smiles were as rare for Simon as they were common for Kate. "My mother didn't wish me to attend."

Kate smiled wryly, motioning for him to take a seat. "Still convinced that I have designs upon you?"

Simon grimaced as he sat on the edge of the seat. "I'm afraid so. She is sending me to Weymouth for a fortnight."

Kate sighed, sinking into the sofa resignedly. "To your aunt, I presume? The one who doesn't enjoy good health?"

Simon nodded, and she couldn't resist a smile. "Or rather the aunt who enjoys not enjoying good health. Well, we shall miss you here. I will do my best to help your mother understand that you are in no danger of being kidnapped and swept off to Gretna Green by me."

As the niece of Mrs. Hartley's archenemy, Kate had never been a likely favorite of hers. Circumstances had combined, though, to ensure her place in the woman's black books.

When the first dance of Kate's first Season arrived, she had been overlooked by all the eligible gentlemen in favor of debutantes with fortune or better connections. She had faced the mortifying prospect of sitting out her first dance when Simon had arrived on the scene, asking Fanny for an introduction and leading Kate to the dance floor.

It was only as she came to know him better that Kate understood how uncharacteristic Simon's kind action had been. It had entailed two activities he never engaged in: disobeying his mother's express orders, and dancing.

"What will you do when the Season ends?" Simon asked. "Does

Lady Hammond plan to stay in London? Or will you return to your mother and stepfather in Birmingham?"

Kate blew out a puff of air. "Fanny will go to Brighton, and I will likely join her to avoid Birmingham for as long as I can—until she and Walmsley marry, I suppose. I must decide on some path, though. I am as good as on the shelf already."

She pursed her lips as she thought of all the points she had working against her in making a good match. "Having a mill owner with questionable ethics as a stepfather has been every bit the obstacle to marriage that I anticipated it would be. Your mother isn't the only one who assumes that my only goal is to climb the social ladder." She thought of Sir Lewis, and her jaw tightened.

"Anyone who knows you wouldn't believe such a thing," Simon said flatly. "If you can't find it in you to have Lady Hammond continue as your chaperone, perhaps you could find a new one—some spinster in need of companionship?"

Kate laughed aloud. "A spinster in need of companionship! You seem to be foretelling my own future." She rubbed the embroidered white flowers on her muslin dress. "In any case, I cannot afford another Season."

Simon pursed his lips. "Can your stepfather not provide you with the means to stay in London another Season?"

Kate's wry smile appeared again. "Between my pride and my stepfather's selfishness, it is impossible. He sees me as an obligation— a waste of his money. And even if he would give me the money, I couldn't bring myself to take it. I would rather work for my keep than accept it from him."

"Your pride doesn't serve you," said Simon, shaking his head. "You can't survive without money."

"I know." She sighed then shook her head. "But if you could see how he treats us—my sisters and me—I think you would understand. I never visit but what he laments the expense of bringing me home and the fortune he feels he has squandered on my education. Do you know what he said to me on my last visit?"

Simon shook his head.

"He said that it's as good as highway robbery to charge for the education of a woman—that it's throwing good money after bad." She breathed in and closed her eyes, exhaling quickly. "I promised myself that I would free both him and me from my being beholden to him as soon as I could. And that is still my plan."

It was a plan she had done little toward accomplishing. She found that she had only changed benefactors once she left the seminary. Fanny was good-natured enough not to view her niece as a burdensome charge, but in some ways this fact made Kate feel all the more guilty. Being so good-natured, Fanny would likely allow Kate to trespass on her charity indefinitely.

Kate was determined not to let it be so.

Simon was silent, reflecting on her words.

"I suppose I have one more option," Kate said, almost to herself, "though it's one I can't even bear to think on." She shuddered then looked up at Simon. "Sir Lewis sought me out last night."

"He usually does, does he not?" Simon said, brushing off a spot of dust on his sleeve.

"Yes," Kate said, hesitating before she continued. "But last night he offered—" she tilted her head "—offered is perhaps too generous a word. Assumed? Yes, he assumed that I would become his mistress."

Simon's brows snapped together. "Surely not! Even such a rake as Sir Lewis wouldn't be so brazen."

Kate shrugged. "He is precisely that brazen and abominable. But perhaps that existence would be preferable in many ways to one where I have to work for my own support?" She recoiled even as she said it. It didn't bear considering.

"Miss Matcham," said Simon, shaking his head.

Kate raised her brows at him. He would insist on addressing her formally, even though she insisted on calling him Simon when they weren't in company.

"You had much better marry me than ally yourself with Sir Lewis." He cleared his throat and scooted even further toward the edge of the chair. "I have been thinking on the subject for some time now."

Kate laughed. "As if I would saddle you with the likes of me! Even such a kind soul as yourself would strangle me within the week. I'm sure I wouldn't blame you. And let us not even think on what your mother would say to a marriage between us. I shudder at the thought."

"My mother would come around in time," he said. "I am in earnest, Miss Matcham. I am not romantically attached to anyone—Indeed, I don't believe I am the type of person to form romantic attachments. You are not attached to anyone. You must marry. I must marry." He shook his head as he raised up his shoulders. "It is a sensible option."

Simon was always concerned with doing the sensible thing. Kate stared at him, her eyes glazing over.

He was her dear friend, but she had no desire to marry him. In fact, she had little desire to marry at all. But necessity required it. And while time was not something she had in abundance before a decision about her future must be made, she couldn't steel herself to make a decision. Not yet.

He watched her, and then added, "I leave today for Weymouth. Here is my address." He handed her a card. "I don't expect you to give me your answer now, but if you come to see the sense in allying ourselves in marriage—if you have a change of heart or mind—all you need do is write and tell me."

She nodded absently as she looked at the card in her hand, and Simon took his leave. She rubbed the card, thinking what a strange visit and proposition Simon's had been. Well, not strange, perhaps. But unexpected, certainly.

When the Croftes were announced, Kate was still sitting in the morning room, lost in thought. Her stomach growled as Gryffin let the Croftes into the room. Kate had completely forgotten to eat breakfast.

"How wonderful," she said, setting down Simon's card and shaking off her stupor as she rose from her chair to greet the visitors. "Lady Crofte, you look well."

The aging process had treated Lady Crofte kindly. While her figure wasn't as trim as Kate remembered it being, it had not become full like the figures of most women her age. She carried her head high, just as she always had.

"Well, there," said Lady Crofte, looking Kate up and down with an admiring expression. "If it isn't little Kate Matcham. Not so little anymore. How the years fly by!"

"Isn't she beautiful, Mama?" said Clara.

Kate shook her head, a slight blush stealing up her cheeks. She did not admire her own beauty, especially in company such as Clara Crofte's. "I'm afraid I may be taller but otherwise every bit the little dirt-covered thief who looted your gardens for roses."

Lady Crofte's shoulders and chest shook with laughter. "Was it you who did that? I had always suspected Henry. He was such a troublemaker."

"Then I owe an apology to Henry—or Mr. Crofte, I should say. How is he? Has he little troublemakers of his own yet?"

"Henry is very well," Lady Crofte replied. "Not married yet, but I have hope he will settle down in the near future." said Lady Crofte with a warm smile.

"And what of your family, Kate?" said Clara. "It has been an age since I saw any Matchams. Of course, we see your uncle now and again, since he took up residence at Coombe Park. But I know nothing of your life since you left Dorset. It seems an eon ago."

It seemed an eon to Kate, too. Life now bore little resemblance to her years at Coombe Park. "Yes, well I was only eight when we left, so an eon isn't too far off. Let's see," she said, casting her mind back to that time. "Once we left Coombe Park, we went to stay with my grandmother in Surrey. Then—but perhaps you already know—my mother remarried a man, Mr. Dimmock, from Birmingham, and she has been living there ever since."

"Oh yes!" said Clara, her eyes alight. "Mr. Dimmock of Dimmock and Sons, isn't it? I have heard that he is absurdly wealthy."

Kate suppressed a smile, and Lady Crofte shot a disapproving glance at her daughter. "For heaven's sake," she said, "don't be vulgar, Clara."

"I believe he is quite comfortable," said Kate, rising to ring the bell for tea, "though I admittedly know little of his affairs. My mother sent me to a seminary in Bath once they married. I returned to Birmingham for some holidays, but I spent the majority of my time in Bath. After, I returned to live with Grandmama in Surrey to help care for her until her death. I have been living with my aunt ever since, for the past two years." She came back to her seat, tucking one foot under the other. "But all this is quite a bore. Tell me, how is Sir Richard doing?"

"Oh, Father is well, of course," said Clara, brushing off the question. "But then you were not brought out until you were nearly 20?" Her eyes were wide in astonishment verging on horror.

Kate smiled at her, accustomed to such reactions to her peculiar story. "Yes, it was quite out of the ordinary, to be sure, but unfortunately, circumstances prevented it happening any earlier."

It had almost not happened at all. It had required many conversations to convince her stepfather that it would be worth his money to finance such an ordeal. "I don't mind in the least, though," she said. "I have had more than ample opportunity to experience all the gaiety London can offer, I assure you."

"From what I know of Lady Hammond," said Lady Crofte, wearing a knowing expression, "I would imagine you have been up to your ears in gaiety. She is so full of vivacity! Such a taking little thing."

Kate nodded. "I find it hard to keep up with her most days. She has been so very good to me and a wonderful chaperon and companion, with never a complaint about being saddled with such a burdensome charge as myself. And for longer than she had anticipated, to be sure."

"Oh, don't be silly, Kate," said Clara, dismissing Kate's concern. "She is fortunate to have you. Which reminds me...." She sat on the edge of her seat, her hands clasped in front of her chest and her shoulders raised, as if she was trying to contain her excitement. "Mama and I would like to invite you to come stay with us at Wyndcross."

Kate blinked twice. "I...."

"Please say you will," cried Clara, jumping up and grabbing Kate's hands. "Father is away from home, but Mama vowed she wouldn't let that stop us from entertaining. Do come!"

"Clara."

Clara stopped in her tracks at her mother's stern voice.

Lady Crofte's expression morphed into a smile. "Do give her space to think and breathe. She won't want to come to Wyndcross if she worries she will be suffocated all summer."

"Such a generous invitation," said Kate, still looking bewildered. "Naturally, I will need to speak with Fanny, but what a lovely prospect."

Her countenance brightened as she considered it, and she laughed. "Now I am taken up with visions of possibility. If Fanny refuses, I may fall into a decline."

"Then it's as good as settled," said Clara with a final nod of her head, "I feel sure Lady Hammond could have no reason to refuse." She squeezed Kate's hands. "It will be exactly like old times."

3

As Fanny was still out with Lady Carville, Kate had to while away the hours until dinner alone.

It was not the fashionable time of day for a ride in the park, but the day was cooler than it had been for the past week, and Kate wanted some fresh air. She had her mare Cleopatra brought to the house while she changed into her riding habit.

The mare Kate's father had given her as a spirited filly a year before his death was now well into her middle age. Kate had grown extremely attached to her over the years.

She was a handsome buckskin mare with black markings around her eyes. Her father had remarked that she looked like Cleopatra, and the name had stuck.

The horse had been one of Kate's greatest treasures, affording her the very small measure of adventure to be had in town. A solo ride through the park, while heavily frowned upon, could hardly be considered high adventure, but it was a delight to Kate, nonetheless.

She would likely incur Fanny's censure for it, but she comforted herself with the fact that she wasn't a young lady fresh out of the schoolroom; she had nearly two full Seasons of experience, besides being a few years older than most of the debutantes. Surely, she deserved a little leeway.

As she rode through the park, humming to herself in contentment, she realized with dismay that a visit to the countryside would mean leaving Cleopatra behind.

She could apply to her stepfather for the money needed to have the mare brought to Wyndcross Manor, but it could take two weeks for that communication to occur, and it would go against the independence she was working toward.

She sighed, patting Cleopatra's neck. "Sorry, girl. I would take you with me if I could."

When Kate arrived back in Berkeley Square, it was only half past three. Instead of losing track of time as she usually did on her rides, the clock seemed to tick at half-speed. After changing her dress, she went back to the library to continue her reading.

Her eyes soon glazed over, and her thoughts turned to memories of the Dorset countryside. Rolling green hills checkered with dark hedges, ending abruptly at precipitous white cliffs which dropped into a deep blue ocean.

Her heart skipped a beat at the prospect of returning. Her childhood in Dorset was such an idyllic part of her life. It was the place where she had felt carefree; before she had come to know pain, separation, and the weight of duty which made up the fabric of her life now.

Kate was expected to make a great match to further the interests of her younger sisters, and she wished to do everything in her power to help them. She still had some time, but Phoebe was in her last year at Miss Monaghan's seminary. Saddling Fanny with bringing out yet another Matcham daughter was out of the question for Kate.

Perhaps her visit to Wyndcross would be an opportunity to clear her head and decide upon a future for herself, away from the distracting hustle and bustle of the city.

The clock struck the hour of six. She had been lost in thought for the past two hours. She marked her progress—a mere two pages—with a bookmark of pressed lavender and made her way upstairs to dress for dinner.

Fanny was full of news from her day shopping with Lady Carville.

Kate preferred not to talk to Fanny about her visit with the Croftes until the servants had left, so she didn't interrupt Fanny's stream of talk: a log of her purchases with Lady Carville and the gossip she had acquired at the ball the night before.

"...And that wretched Charlotte Thorpe came up to me as you spoke with Sir Lewis, and do you know what she said? That you had better not be choosy with the gentlemen who take an interest in you since you are practically on the shelf."

Kate took another bite of dinner, meeting Fanny's fury with calm indifference. "Sir Lewis said nearly those exact words."

"Well," Fanny continued, a smug look replacing her outrage, "you can imagine that I wasn't about to let that scheming wretch get away with such a slight to you. You should have seen the look on her face when I casually mentioned that you were set to inherit twenty thousand pounds. I wish I could have bottled up her expression."

Kate's fork dropped with a loud clank on the dinnerware. "Oh, Fanny! Please tell me you jest."

Fanny straightened herself in her chair, lifting her chin as she cut her potato with a firm hand. "I was never more serious in my life. It was a masterful set-down, and no one could be more deserving than Charlotte Thorpe, believe you me."

Dismay was etched into every line of Kate's face. Her mind reverted to the ball. The looks and whispers which had tracked her, she had ascribed to those who had witnessed her intense conversation with Sir Lewis. Or had they rather been due to the quick work of Charlotte Thorpe's infamous tongue?

"I would not for the world have had you tell such a thing to Mrs. Thorpe, Fanny. She must have told the whole of London by now!"

"So much the better," exclaimed Fanny, impervious to Kate's consternation.

"But Fanny, it isn't true. The likelihood of me receiving any money is negligible, at best. And even if it were to happen, I told you that I don't feel I could accept any money. Indeed, If I must accept it, I am determined to—" she sputtered a moment "—give it to the church, or to some other worthy cause."

Fanny let out something between a laugh and a snort and covered her mouth in embarrassment at the inelegant noise. "What utter nonsense. Now it is you who are jesting."

"Not at all." Kate's face stilled, her eyes wide and grave. "I am very much in earnest. If you knew my stepfather and the mortification I've endured at his hands, I believe you would feel the same way, Fanny. And even if that weren't a concern, I don't wish to be tolerated or courted for my fortune."

She spent the next few minutes disabusing Fanny's mind of a vision of Kate being wooed by the most eligible bachelors in London. It was not easy work. Kate's reasons and concerns were ones that Fanny neither shared nor understood.

Having learned of Fanny's misstep, Kate was even more anxious to leave London behind for the summer. When she finally told Fanny about the invitation to stay at Wyndcross Manor, Fanny didn't seem at all surprised.

"When do you leave?" Fanny asked as she ate a walnut.

"They hope to leave within the next few days," Kate said, "which doesn't leave much time at all."

"No, it doesn't, but we shall manage." Fanny scooped a bite of tart into her mouth.

"Fanny!" cried Kate. "Admit it—you are positively excited to be rid of me." She cut into the glazed pear tart on her plate. "Though I can't say I blame you. Two years is an eon to be saddled with me."

"Don't be a ninny, Kate." Fanny dabbed at her mouth with a napkin. "Of course I'm quite cast down at the thought of you leaving me, but only for my sake, not yours. You need a change of scene. I know you don't thrive off town life as I do, and I am so grateful to you for indulging me by coming to all the parties, picnics, plays, and balls I've wanted to attend. How will I manage without you?"

She reached her hand across the table to Kate who smiled genuinely and squeezed Fanny's hand.

Kate's expression changed to one of faux innocence. She pushed the food around on her plate. "I suppose you might acquire some kind of permanent companion who shall be forced to escort you all around the town and care for you in sickness and in health, to love and to cherish til death do you part."

She looked up, feigning deep thought. "Now, where might you find such a companion...?" The sliver of a smile twitched at the side of her mouth.

"Oh stop," said Fanny, though she couldn't suppress a smile. "It's different. Walmsley is so..." she struggled to find the word.

"Masculine?" offered Kate.

"Yes!"

Kate's mouth broke into a full smile, and her eyes twinkled in merriment. "And so much more capable of securing your comfort than I. I am convinced he will make you very happy. He dotes on you, Fanny. And I know you care for him much more than you let on."

Fanny straightened her back and assumed an expression of exaggerated gravity. "A lady doesn't wear her heart on her sleeve." Her strict teaching face disappeared, and she stared ahead at nothing before saying, "I suppose I shall accept Walmsley." Her face brightened. "At the very least, that means you will be forced to return for the wedding, so that I shall be sure to see you again."

"Oh, Fanny," Kate said, "you are the one being ridiculous now. I'm going to the Croftes for a visit; not to die or to abandon you. Indeed, before you know it, I shall be back ringing your bell, forcing you to put me up for another two years."

Fanny looked doubtful. "In which case I shall be pleased. At any rate, we must make sure you are looking smart for your visit, since, from what I know of the Croftes, they are quite fashionable and frequently host parties."

4

The next three days were filled with shopping and preparing portmanteaux. Kate had a few dresses needing replacement due to the heavy use they had seen over the past two seasons. She could ill afford to buy any and maintained to Fanny that it was silly to buy new dresses to wear in the country. But Fanny insisted on making her a present of two dresses and a bonnet.

"Fanny, how in the world shall I ever repay you?" cried Kate on the way back to Berkeley Square, loaded with bandboxes and guilt.

"Nonsense," Fanny said, looking elated at the success of their shopping expedition. "I never gave you a proper coming out present, and I can't possibly allow you to return to your childhood home in shabby dresses when people know you've been staying with me. You see, it's quite selfish, after all."

Kate laughed and shook her head. Fanny's generosity was crushing, and she already felt beholden to her.

"Besides," said Fanny with a little too much nonchalance to be believable, "who knows but what the Croftes' son or some other country gentleman might take a fancy to you. I'm sure it would be no wonder if one did."

"Oh, my dear Fanny," said Kate with an appreciative smile. It was impossible to bring Fanny to understand that Kate's options for marriage were fast dwindling. Fanny would insist on believing that Kate could look as high as she pleased for a husband.

But she was alone in the belief.

<hr />

THE JOURNEY TO DORSET WAS MUCH MORE PLEASANT THAN KATE had anticipated. The weather was charming, and the roads were good, not having seen rain for nearly two weeks. Kate, Clara, and Lady Crofte spent the night comfortably in Andover at the King's Arms where they had an enjoyable evening dining and reminiscing.

"It is so long since I've been in Dorset that I'm sure things have changed," said Kate.

"Oh, I assure you that things are every bit as slow and mundane as they have always been," said Clara. "However, Weymouth has become quite a different place, thanks to the King's visits. It could never compete with London, but shopping has become much more tolerable than it was before. And some of the things we get here in the south would make Londoners crazy with jealousy to see. Did you see the lace I was wearing at the ball? Straight from Alençon."

"What a pretty penny that must have cost," Kate exclaimed. "Fanny has a dress of the same lace, and she told me that it would cost a fortune now with the import taxes."

A satisfied smile stole over Clara's face as she served herself from a plate of roast duck. "Oh no, it was quite an economical purchase."

Kate wrinkled her brow. It was quite rare to see new gowns featuring authentic French lace. Not only was it costly in the extreme, some people would not wear it on principle due to the ongoing war.

Clara's smile grew mischievous as she remarked Kate's reaction. "You will find that living on the coast has its benefits." She winked.

Kate's heart dropped, but she managed a perfunctory smile.

Had she agreed to the visit prematurely? Clara's thinly veiled implication that her lace was had by virtue of smuggling made Kate uneasy. She had been under the impression that the circumstances of her father's death and his views on smuggling had been well-known to the

Croftes. But the conversation moved on, and Kate was obliged to leave such thoughts for a later time.

※

Wyndcross was already shrouded in darkness when they arrived. The travelers were all anxious for their beds and bid one another goodnight shortly after Kate was shown to her room.

She awoke in the morning to the sun pouring into her room. The summer days were long, which meant that it was still very early. But she had always been an early riser, and she couldn't lie in bed when there was so much she wished to do. While it had been years since she had spent time with Clara, Kate felt tolerably sure that she was not an early riser.

Lindley was accustomed to her mistress's habits and had pulled back the curtains to let light in. Kate rose from her bed, curious to see what view her window offered. Her room in Berkeley Square faced the street and the small adjacent park—a wonderful view for London. She pulled back the curtains with a contented sigh and smile. Between two hills, she could see the sea—a sight she hadn't seen in fifteen years. It was an even more majestic blue than she had remembered. In the distance, she could see scattered white lines where froth gathered at the head of the waves.

Much was familiar at Wyndcross, if somewhat surreal. It was strange to walk the halls she had skipped along as a young girl, to see the aged faces of the few servants who had remained. The scale of the manor felt much smaller, whether due to her own height or to her experience with many other large estates, she couldn't be sure. But she found herself looking with great anticipation through the manor windows at the surrounding gardens and countryside, wondering when she would have opportunity for exploring them.

Lady Crofte kept to her room, fatigued from the journey and convinced that she had a spasm coming on, so Kate and Clara were left to entertain themselves after breakfast. Kate followed Clara's lead, unsure what to expect as a visitor at Wyndcross and not wishful to be anything but a pleasant guest.

Clara was eager to show Kate her generous wardrobe, and it was clear to Kate that Clara was rarely denied her wishes. As she ran a hand along the smuggled French silks and lace, she had to remind herself that Clara's admiration for such things was naive and thoughtless, not a willful slight to the memory of Kate's father.

THE NEXT DAY SAW THE ARRIVAL OF MR. HENRY CROFTE to Wyndcross Manor. Clara spotted him riding in on his horse as she and Kate walked the grounds.

"Henry!" shouted Clara. She covered her mouth with a guilty hand and hunched over, looking back toward the manor. "Mama despises yelling."

Henry spotted them and guided his horse in their direction. He was a handsome bachelor, with an athletic build, blue eyes like Clara's, and curly hair tending more toward brown than blonde. He was the eldest of the Croftes and the heir to his father's baronetcy. It was strange to see the rascally young boy she had known, now a grown man. How much of the unruly little boy would be left over?

"You'll never guess who's here," Clara said as she gestured for him to hurry.

Henry's gaze flitted toward Kate and back to Clara. "What? Have you finally found a friend, then?"

Clara scowled playfully. "Not for long, if she is forced to spend time around you and your bad manners." She abandoned the scowl, unable to resist breaking the news to him. "Do you not recognize her?"

Henry stared at Kate, eyes narrowed in thought.

"It's Kate," Clara interjected. "Kate Matcham."

His brows went up and he scrutinized Kate's face, as if searching for the 8-year-old version of her. There was a glint of recognition in his eyes and he said, "By jove, I believe you're right! How could I forget those little green eyes that always used to glare at me so?" He scrunched up his face into a childish scowl.

Kate laughed. "Yes, I'm afraid that I wasn't very fond of you most of the time."

"Well," Clara said in a rallying tone. "Times have changed, Henry, and now Kate and I are quite capable of paying you back for all the horrid things you did then." She turned to Kate. "You know he hasn't changed at all. He still tricks and teases me as much today as he did then."

Kate clucked her tongue in disapproval. "For shame, Mr. Crofte."

"Mr. Crofte?" Henry said, laughing. "It's Henry, thank you very much." His brows suddenly shot together, and he looked at his sister. "Do you know why Mama summoned me home, Clara? It's always best to be prepared if I'm to be subjected to one of her dashed sermons."

Clara picked a honeysuckle, not meeting his eyes. "You had better ask her yourself, Henry. You haven't done anything wrong, but she has a very particular reason for wishing you home."

Henry snorted. "In Mama's opinion, I am always doing something wrong."

***

THAT EVENING, THE FOUR OF THEM PLAYED AN ENGAGING GAME OF whist following dinner. Kate was hardly the most skilled card player of the group, but no one seemed to mind.

"Oh, I had forgotten to tell you, Kate," said Clara, playing a card. "I received an invitation today from the Cosgroves. They live down the road—you wouldn't remember them, though. They moved in some time after you left. They have planned an expedition for Saturday, and they would like us to join them. Well, that is to say, the invitation was addressed to Henry and me, but that's only because they didn't know we had a guest. I know they will be delighted to add one more to the party. We shall ride to St. Catherine's Chapel for a picnic."

Though an expedition was tempting to Kate—and a riding one at that—her pride balked at not only intruding on an expedition she had not been invited to, but at relying on the Croftes to provide her a horse as well. She did not share Clara's confidence that the Cosgroves would welcome an added stranger to the party.

"That sounds delightful," she said. "Only, I'm not sure if I should join. I have no mount for riding, and I don't wish to intrude. I shall be quite content here, though, I assure you." She smiled to ensure that her protestations would not sound like a plea for pity.

"Oh, fuss and nonsense, my girl," said Lady Crofte, peering at her cards with squinted eyes. "You will take one of our horses, of course."

"Mama's mare is quite tame, you know," said Clara. "And naturally, you are always welcome to ride my Rosebud if you should wish to do so when I am not in need of her myself. She could use the exercise, as Avery continually reminds me. Though she is quite difficult to manage, I warn you."

"Well, now that's rich, Clara!" cried Henry, slapping his knee in amusement. "You make it sound like a sacrifice. We all know you hate riding." He leaned toward Kate. "Ain't keen to have mud splashed on her precious riding habit. Though why she should bother buying 'em in the first place if she don't mean to ride is beyond me."

"I do ride," Clara insisted, her rosy lips pouting. "Only I am still teaching Rosebud to mind me, and I have no desire to be thrown."

"Well it is very generous of you," said Kate, trying to prevent further sibling debate, "but will you not need your horse for yourself on Saturday, Lady Crofte?"

Lady Crofte laughed. "Bless you, Kate. I rarely ride. Among us, Henry is the only one who rides frequently. As Clara said, our own horses are in great need of exercising, and both we and the stable hands would feel nothing but gratitude to you for taking them out anytime you should wish to. I'm sure Henry would be quite happy to take you around the area if you were desirous."

Henry looked at his mother with an eyebrow cocked.

"You are too kind." Kate said, greatly relieved that her use of their horses would not be a burden. "I admit that I dearly love riding and am grateful for any excuse to do so."

"It is settled then," said Clara with a smile at Kate. "I am quite impatient for it to be Saturday now."

Henry looked at Clara with mischief in his eyes. "Was an invitation for Saturday extended to his lordship, the great earl-in-waiting?" He said the words with a flourishing hand gesture as he peered over his cards at Clara with feigned innocence.

"How should I know?" asked Clara, avoiding Henry's eyes as she discarded.

Henry snorted with laughter. "Of course you know. Admit it, Clara. You're not above forging the invitation yourself."

Kate listened, intrigued by the implication that Clara had a love interest.

"I would never!" protested Clara, but she was unable to suppress a grin. "But if you must know, yes, he was invited, and he has accepted, of course. He and Lady Anne."

"I hope you will remember to act with decorum, Clara," said Lady Crofte with a hint of sternness.

"Of course, Mama," said Clara docilely. She perked up. "Henry is taking me to Weymouth tomorrow to buy a new pair of half boots, Kate. I saw the most lovely pair in London, and I'm determined to have some exactly like them. Will you accompany us?"

"How kind!" Kate said. "I think that I should stay behind, though. I haven't yet written to my aunt or my family, and I assured Fanny that I would do so as soon as I was settled." She felt guilty that she was already hankering after time on her own, though she truly did need to write to Fanny and her family.

"How insipid to be stuck indoors writing letters," Clara said.

Kate only nodded. In fact, she had no intention of staying indoors.

5

Wanting to make the best use of her time alone in the morning, Kate made her way to the stables once Clara and Henry had left. The old groom Avery's reaction at seeing Kate was warm and welcoming, though he put his foot down when he learned of her intent to go out riding alone.

"It won't do, Miss," Avery said. "Lady Crofte would have my head if she knew I had aided ye in such a notion. Let me saddle up my hack, and I shall accompany ye."

While she had felt inclined to argue the supposed danger of a solo ride, she decided against it. She had no wish to land Avery in trouble for neglecting what he felt was his duty. A ride with him in tow would be preferable to no ride at all.

She changed into her riding habit with the help of Lindley, and then instructed her to go in search of a basket, paper, a quill, and some ink which could be packed for her intent to write letters during the excursion.

Lindley had eyed her doubtfully upon being given these instructions.

Kate smiled at Lindley's hesitation when she returned with the requested items. "I know it is strange, Lindley, but why would I care to be cooped up writing letters when I could be doing so outdoors?"

"You and your strange ideas, Miss. Only take care you don't go spilling that ink while careering all over the countryside on an unfamiliar horse."

"I shall take every care," Kate promised, "and the ink shall stay safe in this basket the entire ride." She patted the basket gently.

Lindley pursed her lips.

Once mounted on Rosebud, Kate felt a surge of excitement for the possibilities of her ride. The day was warm with a slight ocean breeze and interchanging sun and clouds. A perfect day for a ride.

"Avery," Kate said as they started on their way. "Is there a place nearby where I can give Rosebud full rein?" She couldn't remember the last time she had a proper gallop.

"Aye, Miss," Avery said through a crooked smile. He was riding, as promised, at a discreet distance behind her. "Around the turn down the road, there's a nice, level field on the left. She'll be glad for a gallop." He indicated Rosebud with his head.

"As will I," Kate breathed.

As they reached the field, she slackened her hold on the reins, leaned forward, and signaled Rosebud.

The feeling was exhilarating. The ground flying swiftly under Rosebud's feet made Kate feel as though she were gliding. The wind swept past her, tugging on her bonnet, tossing any of her hair that peeked out, and making her eyes sting. The experience was so familiar, and yet her life in London had been frustratingly bare of such thrills.

As they approached the other end of the field, she reigned in Rosebud to a trot, stroking her warm neck, and praising her. She turned again to Avery, unable to school her expression into anything but a wide smile.

"Thank you, Avery. You can have no notion how much I've longed to do that this past age."

He looked at her approvingly. "She responds to ye, Miss. Miss Crofte has been trying to train her for months now, but the filly will have none of it. Tossin' her head fit to break her neck."

Kate said nothing for a moment. "She needs a gentle, confident hand, I think. She reminds me of my mare. Spirited, but loyal once she's won over."

She would have been happy for yet another gallop, but, remembering her promise to write letters to Fanny and her family, she instead asked Avery if there were a place she could tie up Rosebud in order to write.

Avery considered her question for a moment, chewing on a piece of wheat. "I think I know the place for you, Miss. Follow me, if you please."

He took her over a shallow stream and up a small hill. When they reached the top of the ridge, he told her to look down the other side. Sitting between two hills with only a small dirt road connecting it to anything were the ruins of an old abbey. Its roof was missing, the grass and weeds grew long around it, and the walls were overgrown with ivy and creeping vines. The morning light bathed the hard gray stones and deep green leaves in a warm glow, casting long, soft shadows on the tall grass.

"It's perfect," Kate murmured with near reverence. For a moment, she pictured her childhood family walking the path up to the opening where the church doors would have been. Her father had been a religious man, and all her fondest memories of church involved him.

They rode down the hill, and Avery tied the horses to a tree away from the ruins, giving Kate her privacy. He sat down and reclined against the wide tree trunk to relax.

With her basket of supplies in hand, Kate walked around the abbey for a time, admiring the age and beauty of the building, and wondering what its history must have been before falling into such neglect and disrepair. She ultimately came to a spot at the meeting of two ruined walls, suitable enough for a back rest. She hummed through delighted lips as she removed the contents of the basket and gazed at her surroundings.

Lindley, bless her forethought, had packed a book to be placed under the paper, and Kate silently thanked her for it, realizing that, without the book, she would have only had the unforgiving jagged stone walls to use for a desk. She placed the book on her lap, dipped her quill in the ink before setting the well next to her, and began.

The first letter she addressed to Simon. It was short, simply letting him know that she was also, ironically, in Dorset and providing him her address there. She paused before signing the letter but decided against mentioning their last visit.

The second letter she addressed to Fanny. Kate knew she would be anxiously waiting to hear all about her stay thus far, even though she had arrived a mere two days ago. Fanny was always impatient for news, and she would particularly relish in all the details about the personalities and wardrobes of Kate's Wyndcross Manor friends.

Kate's writing was unusually slow. She paused frequently to look at her surroundings, savoring the stillness of the countryside, the smell of grass and fresh air. Quiet moments in London were few and far between, and Kate's thoughts and feelings were enhanced in such tranquility.

Avery was far enough off that only a loud call would be heard, and she noticed with a smile that he had dozed off, hat covering his face, back against the tree, and the horses grazing next to him.

Once her letter to Fanny was complete, Kate set it aside and placed a clean paper on the book. She picked up the ink well and dipped her quill, wondering what to say to her sisters when, seemingly out of nowhere, she heard the pounding of approaching hooves. She startled, causing the ink well in her hand to jolt and send drops of ink flying around, onto her face, her dress, and all her belongings.

"Oh, bother!" she cried softly, setting down the ink and the book so that she could stand. She looked down at her brand new, ink-soiled dress and touched a finger to her cheek. It came away black and wet.

Realizing the ridiculous appearance she presented and aware of the ever-advancing hoofbeats, she looked around frantically for a place to hide. She snatched her things and ran around to the other side of the abbey wall where she stopped to listen, her heart beating loudly in her chest.

The hoofbeats softened, changing from a canter to a trot, and then to a walk. She furrowed her brow in confusion. The dying hoofbeats seemed to be going back in the direction they had come from. She strained her ears further, but the sounds died off completely.

She waited, listening intently. Nothing.

Peeking her head around the wall, she saw Avery in the distance, still sound asleep. Like Fanny, he seemed to have the ability to sleep through anything.

She chewed the tip of her thumb nail, thinking. She should wake Avery so that they could return to Wyndcross where she could clean up and change. Lindley would be beside herself to see the new dress covered in ink, particularly after she had warned Kate against taking it.

Kate sighed.

Putting off that encounter to spend more time in the serene environment of the abbey was tempting.

The matter was decided with the knowledge that she still had one more letter to write and enough time to do so before Henry and Clara would be home. She checked the inkwell which, in a stroke of good fortune, still contained enough ink for a short letter.

The silence continued, reaffirming her decision.

She sat down and arranged her things once again, ready to compose the second letter. She pictured her sisters together at Miss Monaghan's in Bath and smiled fondly. They would be so excited to receive a letter from her twice in the space of two weeks. Receiving correspondence at the seminary had always been a special treat. Letters were always shared amongst the seminary girls—a link to the outside world. She hummed quietly, dipped her quill, and began writing.

"Excuse me..." a polite voice said, once again startling her so that the quill stroke jerked across the page.

Her head snapped up. A gentleman stood at the end of the wall she leaned against, looking at her with apologetic eyes, a piece of paper in his hand, and the hint of a suppressed smile.

William.

Their eyes locked, her expression a mixture of surprise, consternation, and embarrassment; his a mixture of sympathy, curiosity, and humor. As she noted the suppressed smile and hint of humor in his eyes, her cheeks grew hot.

How must she look? A grown woman, sitting in a jungle of grass, in the act of writing a letter using the same treacherous ink well that had just splattered her with its black contents. It was absurd. A look down at her ink-covered dress and hands only confirmed the picture in her head.

Her eyes moved to the paper in his hand, and she recognized her letter to Fanny, covered, like herself, in blotches of black ink. She must have forgotten it in her haste to hide.

"You," she said.

His mouth twitched. "Me. As I was passing by, I noticed this paper escaping and assumed that the owner must be nearby, seeing as the man whom I presume to be your groom was...erm...resting his eyes not far off."

Kate glanced toward Avery who was fast asleep, head bobbing on his chest. "Thank you, sir," she said stiffly, standing and brushing off her dress.

Feeling an explanation was called for, she said, "I'm sure my appearance must be extraordinary. You'll have to forgive me, as I was startled in the middle of writing the letter you hold in your hand by the sudden, deafening—" she emphasized the word "—approach of what I can only presume to be you and your horse." What business could he possibly have in such a secluded, abandoned place?

His mouth twitched. "Indeed, you'll have to excuse my half-witted horse. His training has been sadly lacking. I am still working with him on the art of the silent canter so as not to frighten any ladies catching up on their correspondence behind abandoned abbeys."

Only a spasm at the side of his mouth and a slight twinkle in his eyes belied the gravity of his words. The way his eyes twinkled was as irresistible as it was familiar.

Unable to deny the ridiculousness of her accusatory tone, a smile tugged at the corners of Kate's lips, but, still resenting the situation she found herself in, she quickly forced it into what seemed to her a proper expression of stern dignity.

He hadn't missed the twitch, though, and continued on. "I only came to return this so that—" he looked down at the letter splattered generously in ink "—the recipient might not be deprived of the beautiful piece of art—or did you say it was a letter? —you have created."

She made a move to snatch the letter from his hand, but he pulled it away. "Perhaps," she snapped, indicating both him and his horse with her head, "you should both add your signatures to the end, as I can no longer claim responsibility for the entirety of its contents."

"It's only fair, I think," agreed the gentleman, nodding his head in agreement and inspecting the letter. He looked at her thoughtfully again. "However, between the letter and your person, I admit to wondering whether any ink remains?"

She let out an unwilling laugh, relenting to the sense of the ridiculous building inside her.

"You may well wonder," she said, rubbing at a large ink stain on her habit. "I suppose I should be thanking you for rescuing my letter, though I doubt it is worth keeping."

He had been making as if to hand her the letter but withdrew it once again.

"Doubt it is worth keeping?" he said incredulously. "When I've just told you it's a work of art? I find you offensive, madam." He held out the letter to inspect it again. "I am convinced it is every bit as good—indeed better than—most of what I saw the last time I was at the British Museum in London. Allow me to buy it from you. I feel sure it will sell for hundreds of pounds in a few years' time and you will live to regret your disdain of it."

He held the paper behind him with one hand, as if to make clear that he had no intention of returning such a valuable piece to one who did not appreciate it.

Kate shook her head, laughing softly. "My only real regret for this day must be that I was found in such an unlikely place, covered in ink. Not, as you state, for discounting the value of that," she said, indicating the paper in his hand.

He chuckled, and she found that she liked the sound of his laughter. "The combination of an ink-covered lady of quality, writing letters in the ruins of an old abbey is quite charming, I assure you, and not something to be regretted in the least. I concede that the mishap with the ink is somewhat unusual, but I believe that is well-compensated for by your delightful humming."

Kate mentally flogged herself for the habit. It was one that her mother, Miss Monaghan, and Fanny had all tried to rid her of with no success at all. It was not something she did consciously, though, so how could she be expected to curb the habit?

The sense of embarrassment which had begun to dissipate returned in full force, and she felt pride and resentment flare up again. "And do you make a habit of sneaking up and eavesdropping, sir?" she asked, hoping to put him in his place.

"Naturally," he said with no trace of a smile.

She laughed again, caught off guard by his nonsensical response.

He smiled at her laugh, as if he took pleasure in bringing her down from her high ropes.

"And, so that I may know who to attribute the work of art to when I inevitably sell it for personal profit in few years," he said matter of factly, "may I know the name of the artist? Erm...or the author?"

Kate crossed her arms. "So, you didn't discover my name after all?"

"Or," he offered with the quirk of an eyebrow, "I am testing you to see whether you will be truthful."

She looked at him through narrowed eyes. "In that event, you would be deserving of dishonesty. Why should I tell you my name when you refused to tell me yours?"

"But I didn't refuse," he argued. "I told you my given name."

"Yes," she said sarcastically, "what a clue!"

He pulled out his quizzing glass to inspect the letter. "I suppose I may simply look at the signature at the bottom for your name." He attempted to make out the signature, rotating the paper from side to side. "'*All my love, Kite.*'" His brow furrowed playfully. "No, I'm sure that can't be right." He looked up at her with feigned interest. "Or is your name truly Kite?"

She wrested the letter from his hand.

"Alas," he chuckled. "Even the signature fell victim to the ink."

It was obvious that he was enjoying himself immensely.

"If you must know," Kate said, "my name is Catherine Matcham."

"But I already did know," he said with a half-smile. "I recognized your aunt, Lady Hammond, and it was easy enough from there to discover your name."

"How resourceful of you," Kate said sarcastically. "However, I am still in the dark about your identity."

He considered her, his arms crossed, and his mouth twisted to the side. "Shall I make you discover it on your own?" He shook his head. "No, it would be far too easy now. William Ashworth is my name."

The name struck a chord somewhere in the recesses of Kate's memory; too deep in the recesses to be helpful.

"What brings you to Dorset, Miss Matcham?" he said.

"A visit to old friends. I am staying at Wyndcross Manor."

His smile flickered, and his brows knitted together. "Staying with the Croftes?"

"Yes," she said slowly, confused by his strange reaction.

"Ah," he said with something like a grimace.

A cloud obstructed the sun, casting shadow on the landscape and drawing Kate's attention to the sky. The sun had moved west, and she realized with surprise and then guilt that she had lost track of time.

It was past midday. Clara and Henry might well have arrived home. Avery should be helping in the stables with their return, and here she was, depriving her hosts of their groom. She didn't want to leave, but surely prolonging a conversation with a gentleman while her chaperone slept was every bit as improper as a solo ride in the park.

She began hurriedly gathering her belongings, saying, "Oh dear. I fear that I lost track of the time. I must return to the manor. Allow me to thank you again for your help in rescuing my sad letter." She held it up gingerly with two fingers, blew on it in hopes of drying any remaining wet ink, and placed it in her basket.

"It was my pleasure, Miss Matcham. Perhaps we shall meet again?" He raised his brows and wore a half-smile.

"Yes, perhaps so," she said in distraction, fitting the last items in the basket.

Having all her belongings in hand, she smiled at him with a little nod of her head and walked briskly through the tall grass toward Avery who had begun to stir, having woken himself with a particularly loud snore.

"Good morning," she said, using a low-hanging branch to help her onto her horse.

He yawned. "Sorry, Miss. I dozed off." He rubbed his eyes and sat up, using the tree to help himself to a standing position.

"Yes, I know, Avery," she said, with a laugh in her voice. "It is no matter. Let us be on our way. I have stayed longer than I intended, and I'm afraid that we shall arrive after Clara and Henry. I don't know the way from here, so you will have to lead."

Still wiping the sleep from his eyes, Avery mounted his horse and obediently led the way.

Kate heard the hoofbeats of William's horse and turned to see him galloping up the hill at full speed. Her eyes lingered as he disappeared over its crest, and she suppressed a sigh.

Avery led the way toward Wyndcross, leaving Kate to her thoughts. Her cheeks grew hot just thinking on having been found in such a situation. And though she had blamed Mr. Ashworth, she was at fault. But instead of handling the situation with a delicacy meant to mitigate the embarrassing position she found herself in, he had joked her into a better humor in spite of herself.

She didn't know whether to be grateful or upset. Had he ridden on, she would have been spared the mortification. And yet the thought of foregoing the entire episode made her sorry. She had enjoyed the sparring. And now she knew his name.

She wondered what Clara would think of the unlikely encounter. Though Mr. Ashworth knew Kate's business in Dorset, in her haste to leave, she had not had the chance to discover what brought *him* there. She knew nothing but his name. Much against her will, she was attracted to him and his sense of humor. He seemed to know the Croftes, so perhaps Clara could answer her growing list of questions.

He had asked whether they would see each other again somehow. She had doubted it, but she now recognized that, despite the unlikelihood, she wished it. It was a strange and novel feeling. Aside from Simon, she was, at best, apathetic toward all the gentlemen of her acquaintance.

She recognized, though, how ridiculous it was to feel anything at all about someone she had only spoken with for a few short minutes and danced with one time. She gave herself a mental shake for being so simple.

Their arrival back at the courtyard of Wyndcross took her by surprise. As Kate had feared, the carriage was already back at the stables, and one of the stable hands, on seeing Avery, called to him urgently. He walked quickly over to the boy where they stood in discussion.

Kate dismounted and, feeling no desire to keep her hosts waiting or wondering about her any longer, looped Rosebud's reins around a branch on the nearest bush for Avery or the stable hand to take care of.

Still wrapped up in thought, she entered the manor, heading for the morning room in hopes of finding Clara. Clara's voice sounded from within, and Kate opened the door to glance in.

The conversation within immediately halted.

There were multiple people in the room, and all of their heads were turned toward the door to see who could be entering. To her disbelief and chagrin, Kate saw not only Lady Crofte, Henry, and Clara, but Mr. Ashworth himself as well.

Mr. Ashworth, smiling at her in recognition, looked to be enjoying a joke, which immediately reminded her of that important reality which she had forgotten in her distraction of thought: she was still covered in ink.

"Forgive me, I did not know you had visitors," said Kate, ducking her head back out and closing the door behind her, hoping that her peek in had been brief enough that no one had noticed the state of her.

"Kate!" she heard Clara call.

Holding the doorknob behind her back, Kate closed her eyes, shook her head, and chuckled quietly at herself for being so mindless. She took a moment to compose herself, opened the door again, and stepped into the doorway. Already suppressing laughter due to her own heedless entrance while covered in black splotches, she was nearly put over the edge by the looks on the faces of the Croftes. Mr. Ashworth seemed to be enjoying the situation immensely, a fact that did not escape her notice.

"What happened?" Clara couldn't have looked more surprised if Rosebud had pranced into the morning room.

"I am afraid," Kate said, directing a quelling look at Mr. Ashworth, who was clearly trying his best not to laugh aloud, "that I mistakenly believed that letter-writing could be safely carried out in the great outdoors. I had an unfortunate accident, though, as you can see, and will not make the attempt a second time."

It was really too bad of him to sit there and laugh at her like that when, if it hadn't been for him she wouldn't have found herself in such an embarrassing situation.

"I see. How peculiar," said Lady Crofte, striving for an understanding tone, though her face betrayed her confusion and vicarious embarrassment. "Well, no matter, I am sure that we can all forgive your current state long enough for a brief introduction."

Should she inform the company that she and Mr. Ashworth had already met—twice? It was true that they still lacked a formal introduction.

She found the task of explaining the situation too daunting and settled for a polite smile at him. It was all quite ridiculous, and it was apparent that he, too, found no small humor in the thought of being introduced to someone he had been speaking with not thirty minutes before.

Lady Crofte continued. "Lord Ashworth, this is Miss Kate Matcham. She used to live at Coombe Park—I'm sure you know it—and is visiting Clara." She turned to Kate. "Lord Ashworth is a friend of Henry's, and his parents, Earl and Lady Purbeck are friends of Sir Richard's and mine. Lord Ashworth has come to discuss the Cosgroves' invitation for the picnic on Saturday."

Kate's smile had dimmed considerably on hearing the words "Lord Ashworth" and "Earl and Lady Purbeck." Her mind flashed back to the teasing conversation between Clara and Henry about Clara's love interest and "her earl-in-waiting."

Kate looked at Clara, who was looking back and forth between Lord Ashworth and Kate with a baffled and curious expression, as if she recognized that something had been passing between them that she did not understand.

Kate looked back at Lord Ashworth. He was bowing to her as part of their introduction. Remembering her duty amidst an inexplicable sinking feeling in her stomach, she quickly curtsied.

"A pleasure to meet you, Miss Matcham," he said with a wide smile.

"I feel sure there is an entertaining story behind those black spots." The corner of his mouth twitched. "I was telling the Croftes that my sister Anne has proposed that we set out for the Cosgroves as a group, and I thought I would come and suggest the idea to you all. What do you say?"

"I think it a splendid plan. Don't you?" interjected Clara, looking at Kate.

"It sounds very agreeable," Kate agreed hesitantly. She had noticed Clara's interest in her reaction and had no wish to give rise to any jealousy. "I think, though, that I shan't join in this time. Surely the household has need of the horses. I imagine the transportation of food for the picnic will require the use of a couple at least. I shall be quite happy to spend my time here."

Feeling that some further excuse was necessary, she added, "What's more, I have not yet paid my uncle a visit at Coombe Park, and I would not wish to be remiss."

She had no intention whatsoever of visiting her uncle, and the thought of doing so made her swallow uncomfortably. He had cast her father off upon his marriage to her mother, and there had been no contact between their families since Kate's family removed from Coombe Park years ago.

Lord Ashworth's brows drew together, and he looked at her as if trying to comprehend why she had declined the invitation with such feeble excuses. "I assure you we would be happy to supply you with a horse for the day, Miss Matcham."

"That is very kind of you, Mr.—" she corrected herself "—Lord Ashworth, but I would not wish to put anyone to any trouble, and I do owe a duty to my uncle."

"If you refuse to use one of the Croftes' horses, how do you plan to arrive at Coombe Park?" pointed out Lord Ashworth.

Kate hadn't considered that hole in her plan, and she wished she could kick him for exposing it, but she promptly responded, "I shall walk, of course."

"Fiddlesticks," cried Lady Crofte. "We have already been over this, my dear. My mare will be all too happy for a ride. And I'm sure, Miss Matcham, that your uncle will be perfectly happy to receive you any other day. I am persuaded you will enjoy the expedition immensely." She glanced at her son and then back at Kate. "Henry, you know, is very knowledgeable about the county and will be happy to act as a sort of guide."

Kate looked at Henry, who was regarding his mother as though she should perhaps be transported to Bedlam.

Lord Ashworth, on the other hand, looked at Henry with great interest and a smile trembling upon his lips. "Have you become an expert on Dorset since I saw you last, then? I seem to remember ending up in the Millwards' vegetable garden the last time you tried to guide us somewhere."

Henry shot him a churlish glance.

Knowing that further refusal would be uncivil, Kate admitted defeat and expressed her gratitude to Lady Crofte. Clara appeared more cheerful, so perhaps Kate's protestations hadn't been entirely without purpose. She promised herself that she would do her best to promote conversation between Clara and Lord Ashworth, and that she would spend her own time engaging with the other members of the expedition to allay any residual fears Clara might have.

6

William rode home to Ashworth Place with a deeply furrowed brow. Once home, he went directly to find his mother. Lady Purbeck was engaged in responding to correspondence in her small sitting room and turned at the sound of his entrance.

He chuckled at the expression on her face: eyebrows raised, an urgent question in her eyes.

"What? No greeting?" he said.

She smiled warmly at him, standing and putting out her arms. He took her hands and kissed her on the cheek.

"What a fetching cap, Mama." He held out his hands, still clasping hers, and surveyed her with a twinkle. "You look younger every day. You know Lady Prescott's daughter visiting from Ireland had the audacity to ask if you were my sister?"

"Stop flattering me, imp," she said in exasperation, though visibly pleased by his words, "and tell me what happened at the manor. Am I to felicitate my son?" Her eyebrows were raised in expectation.

His smile morphed into a thoughtful frown. He sat down in a chair across from hers. "I couldn't do it, Mama."

Her brows shot up, and she took her seat again. "Then what in the world have you been about these last two hours and more, my dear? I should think you had more compassion than to let your mother sit about, fretting over an event that didn't even take place."

Her words chastised him, but the kind light in her eye belied the tone.

William chewed his lip for a moment, saying distractedly, "Sir Richard, as it so happens, is away from home at the moment."

"Ah," said Lady Purbeck. "Well, no matter. There is no rush, is there? When does he return?"

"I didn't inquire."

She furrowed her brow and looked intently at him.

He lowered his gaze to his fingers which he interlocked and stared at pensively.

"I set out to Wyndcross of a mind to speak with him," Lord Ashworth said, "but it wasn't his absence per se that prevented that." He paused for a moment. "I experienced some...hesitation before arriving..." He trailed off, shaking his head.

"I see," said Lady Purbeck, reclining into her chair. "But what changed your mind? You seemed quite set on it this morning."

"I know." He paused then brought his chin to rest on his interlocked fingers. "On my way to Wyndcross, I ran into an acquaintance. Do you remember the Matchams, Mama?"

Her eyebrows knitted in thought. "As in John Matcham, the man who lives at Coombe Park?"

"Well, yes, it's the same family. But I'm referring to his brother. Charles, I believe."

"Oh," she said in recognition. "Yes, yes, I remember them." Her brow furrowed, and her head cocked to the side. "But didn't he die?"

William's lip twitched. "Yes, I believe so. Happily, it was not him that I happened upon but rather his daughter."

A wary look flitted across his mother's face, but it was gone as soon as it came, and her expression remained an inquiring one.

"Something about our encounter, Mama. I couldn't put it out of my mind. I know it seems ridiculous, and I did plan to proceed with offering for Miss Crofte. But when the time came, I couldn't." He was resting his elbows on his knees, looking at his hands again, and twiddling his thumbs.

His mother was silent for a few moments. "This woman you encountered—she is not, perhaps, simply interested in your title? Some ladies can be very engaging when it serves them."

"I believe I've learned to differentiate by now, Mama," he said. "Besides, she didn't even know who I was; didn't even know my name."

"Well, that is something, to be sure. But what is Jane Matcham's daughter doing here in Dorset?" she asked him. "I seem to remember that they moved after Charles' death."

He heaved a sigh. "She is visiting Clara Crofte," he said, tapping a finger on his pursed lips.

Comprehension dawned on the Countess' face. "I see," she said slowly. "That does make things awkward."

He shook his head and gave a low chuckle. "I think I must have been suffering from a case of nerves and simply jumped at the first excuse to abandon my plan. I shall likely regret my decision tomorrow and be obliged to return to Wyndcross to accomplish my original purpose once Sir Richard returns."

He looked up at his mother. She was looking at him with kindness, but it was apparent that the cogs were turning in her head.

"Perhaps so," she said, smiling and straightening herself to continue writing.

William stayed in his chair for another minute, eyes staring at nothing in particular, and the scratches of his mother's quill the only sound breaking the silence.

7

After the departure of Lord Ashworth, Lady Crofte directed her children and visitor to change for dinner. Kate was glad for an opportunity to think. She suspected that Clara's perception of her could change from welcome friend to potential competitor, and she needed to tread carefully, particularly given her own strange and unexpected affinity for Lord Ashworth.

Encountering him at Wyndcross had only served to strengthen the unaccountable attraction she felt toward him. It had been apparent that Lord Ashworth had also enjoyed their exchange—something which had perhaps given Clara the wrong idea.

Perhaps it had given Kate the wrong idea, too.

But that Clara could feel threatened by her in any way was laughable—almost as ridiculous as the idea of Lord Ashworth actually preferring her to Clara.

The encounter, though, had also highlighted two matters which brought Kate back to reality with an uncomfortable thud: first, Clara was in love with Lord Ashworth, and not for the world would Kate hurt her friend. Second, Lord Ashworth was the heir to an earldom.

Kate was reasonable enough to know that, however much it grated her to admit it, Sir Lewis's comment about her family connections held much truth. An earl's son couldn't, or at least wouldn't, marry into a family of tradesmen, be they ever so wealthy. She would be a fool to set her sights—or feelings—so presumptuously high.

The moment she realized that her mind had leapt to marriage at all, she muttered, "All these years of not caring the snap of your fingers for any gentleman, and suddenly visions of marrying a stranger, Kate?"

Lindley walked into the room. "What was that, Miss?"

"Oh," said Kate, a tinge of pink in her cheeks, "just that I'm so sorry for putting you to so much trouble with these ink stains. I promise you I tried to take care, and indeed it was not my fault."

"Well, if that's what's got you so distracted, don't go troubling your head over it. It's only what I had expected." She inspected a particularly large ink spot.

Kate turned in her chair to look at Lindley. "Expected me to spill ink all over myself? What a clod I must be," she laughed.

"Not a clod, Miss. Perhaps somewhat—" Lindley paused, searching for the right word "—prone to mishaps, shall we say?"

Kate sighed. "I suppose I am, aren't I?"

Lindley raised her brows as if Kate's response had been a vast understatement. "I shan't forget the day you tripped down the carriage steps on your way to the Elston Ball. It took me three days to get all the mud out of that beautiful champagne ball dress."

"Lindley!" Kate cried. "How uncivil of you to remind me of such a mortifying moment. And it wasn't my fault. Those dreadful shoe buckles caught on the smallest thing."

"Aye. I'm sure it had nothing to do with you, Miss," said Lindley consolingly.

Kate eyed her with suspicion. "Well, now I am thinking much too hard about how I walk for fear that I shall, as you put it, become prone to another mishap. I am sure to trip down the stairs now that you've been unhandsome enough to bring up such a memory."

She held up her dress with extra care as she left the room.

Scrubbing the ink off her face had taken longer than she had anticipated, and Kate was the last to enter the dining room. Henry and Clara were standing close to one another, conversing in low tones. Henry wore an expression of exasperation which transformed into a somewhat contrived smile on seeing Kate. Clara's head snapped around, and, perceiving Kate, she grabbed Henry's arm and pulled him along with her toward Kate.

"Ah, there! You are good as new. I had been wondering if those ink spots would wash off."

"That makes two of us then." Kate's hand made an involuntary brush at her cheek where a particularly resilient ink spot had been. "I was sure that you were all preparing to send me to the circus where I would inevitably become known as the Spotted Woman."

Henry gave a stiff laugh.

Clara's attitude toward Kate was free of any kind of reserve, but, all the same, Kate wished that she had the opportunity to converse privately with her so that she might allay any worry. On the other hand, Henry's stiffness was puzzling to her. What could she possibly have said or done to elicit such a reaction?

Henry was an agreeable person, prone to see the hilarity in any given situation which made his reaction so much the stranger. His love of fun made him good company and reminded Kate forcibly of the boy she had known as a child, forever getting into scrapes and playing practical jokes. He didn't seem the type to easily take offense, nor had she spent enough time around him to have given any.

THE DAY AFTER THE INCIDENT WITH THE INK, KATE AND CLARA walked the gardens together, cutting flowers for an arrangement Lady Crofte planned to take to one of the neighbors. The rose garden was in full bloom, and the scent was sweet and intoxicating as they strolled amongst the rainbow of red, pink, yellow, white, and multi-colored roses.

Kate sought a natural way to bring up the subject of gentlemen and marriage. Attempting to ease into the topic, she first spoke of London, knowing Clara would find plenty of interest in anything having to do with society and fashion. As it turned out, though, Clara brought up the subject before Kate even had the chance.

"Did you never find someone to marry in all your time in London, Kate?" she inquired.

Kate smiled. Two Seasons without accepting any offers of marriage clearly seemed like an eternity to Clara.

She paused before answering. In her first Season, she had received proposals from two very young men, obviously infatuated by her relative wisdom and confidence. She had rejected both, comforted in knowing that their mothers would thank her.

Simon Hartley's face swam before her for a moment. Before coming to Wyndcross and during her first days there, she had begun to think that perhaps a marriage to Simon wouldn't be such a bad life after all. She cared for him, he cared for her, and he came of good family.

But now she felt her stomach tie itself in knots at the prospect of marrying him.

Much as she felt affection for and loyalty to Simon, her personality craved laughter and adventure that was simply not to be had with him. He had a staid and steady disposition which was invaluable, but it was not in his nature to laugh or seek amusement in life. Everything he chose to do had a very particular and practical purpose. In many ways, he seemed the polar opposite of Henry Crofte—someone who lived for amusement. Kate preferred someone who had both qualities in moderation.

In any case, she recognized that Clara's question might well be an indirect method of discovering whether Kate had set her heart on Lord Ashworth.

"Well, I did find someone, in a way, though I haven't given him an answer yet." Guilt pinched at her, knowing her answer was a mixture of truth and prevarication. But she thought she saw some relief flash across Clara's face before being replaced with an expression of curious excitement.

"Oh, Kate," she exclaimed, grasping Kate's arm. "How very exciting! You know, it is good to make a gentleman wait sometimes. That is what Emily Baird says, and she has been offered for no less than five times."

Kate suppressed a shudder. Turning down five marriage proposals was not something she aspired to.

Receiving no response to her shocking revelation about Miss Baird, Clara continued. "But, that is beside the point. Do I know him? What is his name?"

Kate hesitated again but, feeling quite sure that Clara was precisely the type of animated woman Simon would avoid interaction with, she decided there could be no harm in it. "His name is Simon Hartley."

Clara put a pensive finger on her lips, her brows drawing together. "Hmm...it sounds familiar."

Kate swallowed uncomfortably.

Clara's eyes were squinted, as if she were trying to pinpoint why the name sounded familiar. "I believe Mama is acquainted with a Hartley family. Or is it Hadley?" She shrugged off the thought. "Shall you accept him then?"

"I'm not sure," Kate replied, finally feeling as though she were speaking whole truth. "He's a very good sort of man, and my affections aren't otherwise engaged." When another twinge of guilt arose at those words, Kate reminded herself that it was impossible to feel real affection for someone she knew as little as Lord Ashworth. "I simply don't know that I want to become his wife."

She looked at Clara whose expression had brightened perceptibly.

"Well, I shall feel bad if you reject his offer, but only for his sake," she said, linking her arm through Kate's.

Kate felt relief at the friendly gesture. Hoping she had done the right thing but determined to see it through regardless, she smiled at Clara, asking, "And what of you? Have you any lovers pining away for you in London?"

Clara laughed and assumed a mischievous grin. "Perhaps one or two. But I'm sure they will forget me soon enough. They so often do."

"Fickle London men," said Kate with pretended ferocity.

"Fickle indeed. Though," said Clara, looking pleased with herself, "I don't regard it, I'm sure. After all, Mama says she thinks that I shall receive a very promising offer soon."

Kate kept her head down. Was she referring to Lord Ashworth? Things must be quite serious if Lady Crofte anticipated an offer. Such confidence and glee were not, in Kate's experience, the frequent companions of uncertainty.

"Do you refer to Lord Ashworth?" asked Kate, wanting to be sure she wasn't making incorrect assumptions.

"Yes!" Clara clasped her hands together.

Kate felt her heart sink but managed a smile as Clara said, "Can you believe I shall be a countess?" There was a slight pause, and Clara added, "When his father dies, of course."

Kate's brows went up. She could hardly believe that Lord Ashworth would appreciate hearing his father's life disposed of with such elation by the woman he apparently intended to make his wife.

But he was more than old enough to know his own mind, surely. It was really no business of Kate's, and a match between the Crofte and the Ashworth families would indeed be a good match.

And yet somehow Kate still felt as though she had received a disappointment.

8

Henry gulped down the last bit of his gin, smacking the tankard down on the table. The top of his lip turned up in distaste as he swallowed. The air was thick and hot in the inn, the scent of alcohol wafting around from each table and mug.

"Wishing we had some of that fine burgundy instead of this shoddy Blue Ruin, eh?" said his friend Fitz with a knowing grin.

"Ah, if only." Henry's eyes glazed over as he pictured a wine cellar full of the spirits they'd just handled. He slumped back in his chair. "I'm more likely to spend the remainder of my days in debtor's prison than to ever have the chance to get bosky on burgundy of that caliber."

Fitz drank the last of his own tankard, his eyebrows raised. "Debts that bad?"

"Worse," said Henry. "Particularly since my luck took a turn for the worse at Madame Aubertin's." He felt sick even thinking on the sum he had lost.

Fitz had sworn the gaming hell was just the ticket for Henry's difficulties. And so it had seemed at first.

Henry shuddered. He couldn't bear to think what his mother would say if she found out—or worse, how she'd look at him.

Fitz shook his head. "Rotten luck, that's what it is."

"It's only gotten more rotten since," Henry said. "My mother has informed me that I am soon to be congratulated."

"Eh?" Fitz said, looking mystified.

"Married, Fitz. She's decided I'm to be married."

Fitz looked blankly at him for a moment and then began laughing hysterically. "You? Leg-shackled!"

Fitz gave into his mirth, wiping an eye only to then succumb to another bout of laughter. "Now that's rich!" Fitz said.

"Rich? Yes, Fitz! That's precisely the problem! She's to be rich as a nabob, and my mother is adamant that I make a push to marry her."

Fitz's laughter died down, and his frown returned. "Well, you've had a run of bad luck, my boy, but your pocket is a couple guineas the better for tonight's work, eh? And what a night!"

The side of Henry's mouth turned up in a smile. A night of disguised smuggling which ended with money in his pocket was precisely the type of adventure he never knew he'd been missing. "If I can keep this up, Marshalsea won't be able to get its hands on me."

Fitz chuckled. "Don't be silly, Crofte. You'd be daft to come back for more. It was a drunken lark, no more." He stood and clapped Henry on the back. "I'm for bed."

Henry nodded. "Go on without me, then. I'm not going home til I know my mother's fast asleep. I've had enough of her lectures to last me a lifetime."

Fitz tossed a coin on the table, and Henry watched as he left through the door.

Fitz had said he'd be addle-brained to make a repeat of the night. But Henry wasn't so sure. If it saved him from his mother's marital machinations, put money in his pocket, and kept him entertained, why not?

He looked around him at the pub. A large, surly man sat at a table at the far side of the room. Henry stood and walked over to him.

"Roberts, isn't it?" he said to the man, offering his hand.

The man looked up at him, and recognition dawned slowly on his ruddy face. He nodded, taking Henry's hand and grasping it with such strength that Henry wondered if he might bruise.

"You're one of the new ones," Roberts said in a half-question, half-statement.

"That's right." Henry sat down across from him, clenching and unclenching his throbbing hand. "How long have you been at it?"

"A year and more," Roberts said, sitting back.

Henry nodded, wondering how much money he could amass after a year of free-trading. "Is it worth it?"

Roberts mouth turned down as he considered. "Aye. It pays better than my other work." His brows went up and he nodded slowly. "The next shipment will give me more in two nights than I make in a year."

Henry sat up, leaning in toward Roberts. "What's different about this next shipment?"

"I don't rightly know," Roberts shrugged. "All I know's Emmerson isn't taking any chances with this one. And the payday will be far and above anything we've had."

"More than tonight's then?" Henry asked slowly, his heart picking up speed.

Roberts chuckled and indicated Henry's coat with his head. "You won't be able to fit the earnings in those pockets of yours. Nor in twenty pockets like them."

Henry's eyes bulged. He imagined how his mother would look if he were to tell her not to worry her head over their debts anymore. If he could take all that money and double it at the card table, such a conversation might well become a reality.

He could feel his skin prickling with excitement. This was his chance.

9

Clara's hopeful and happy spirits endured for the next few days. In such moods, Clara was at her most pleasant and engaging.

Kate awoke on the morning of the expedition with the Cosgroves prepared to have an enjoyable day riding and making new friends. She was pleased and grateful to see that her riding habit had been rid of all black spots, and she silently blessed Lindley for it. Fanny would have been exasperated to know that the brand-new riding habit she had gifted her niece had been forever ruined the first time it had been worn.

Kate looked at herself in the mirror. Though she didn't pretend to be much out of the ordinary, she was not unhappy with her appearance. She felt her eyes to be her one redeeming feature, and the subdued gray of her habit made their green seem all the brighter. Next to the striking blonde Clara, Kate was quite eclipsed, being much more average in all aspects but her height—Kate was still waiting for giants to become the rage.

She descended to the entrance hall at the same time as Henry.

"Good morning, Miss Matcham." He gave a stiff smile and a bow.

"Good morning," she replied with a warm smile. Why Henry was so tense again, she had no idea, but she hoped it wouldn't last. "As you see—" she held her skirt out to the sides and turned slowly "—I am entirely spotless, thanks to the efforts of my maid. So, I am afraid you have missed your window to send me to the circus."

Henry chortled. "Outsmarted us, you—no, wait! Hang on now. There's a spot there. Under your arm."

Kate lifted her right arm and, sure enough, a black spot peered back at her.

"So there is." Kate rubbed at it and laughed. "Well, there's nothing for it. I suppose I must embrace my new future."

Henry chuckled. "Clara has loads of riding habits. Not a bother at all to let you borrow one. She's probably standing in front of three or four right now, trying to choose. In fact, I'll lay you a wager that we don't see Clara for another half hour." He leaned against the wall, as if settling in for the wait.

Kate raised her brows and suppressed a laugh. "Surely she won't be that long?"

Henry's brows went up. "You're a true friend to think such a thing. Ain't a shred of promptness in Clara, though."

After a few minutes, they decided to walk out to the courtyard where Clara could meet them in her own time. They walked out to see Lord Ashworth and his sister approaching on horseback. A wagon full of blankets and baskets of food for the picnic stood waiting nearby.

Lord Ashworth was riding a handsome chestnut, and his sister sat atop a striking dapple gray. Lady Anne was an undeniable beauty, with porcelain skin, dark eyes, and curly, brown hair under a pale green bonnet with white ribbon. She smiled as they approached Kate, and Lord Ashworth dismounted.

"Good morning, Miss Matcham. Henry. I trust we find you well, Miss Matcham?" He wore his usual amiable smile.

"Yes, thank you, my lord." She thought back to their last encounter with only a slight warmth in her cheeks and revealed her empty hands. "You may rest easy knowing that I bear no ink today. I made the excessively painful decision to leave my writing utensils here." Her eyes twinkled, and his did the same in response.

"What a shame," he said. "I promised my sister an excursion quite out of the ordinary, in the presence of *une vraie artiste*. But now I see we are bound to have a humdrum expedition after all," he lamented. "Miss Matcham, allow me to introduce you to my sister, Lady Anne Ashworth."

Lady Anne smiled and inclined her head as Kate curtsied. "What a pleasure to meet you, Miss Matcham," said Lady Anne. Her voice was soft and kind, her demeanor calmer than her brother's.

"The pleasure is mine, I assure you," replied Kate.

Clara appeared at the doorway of the manor.

"Good morning, Lord Ashworth and Lady Anne," said Clara with an especially bright smile directed at the former.

Kate looked to Lord Ashworth, wondering if she would see any evidence of his regard for Clara, but he seemed to greet her with just as much polite amiability as he always showed.

"Shall we be on our way?" said Henry, mounting his horse.

The path from the Wyndcross courtyard out to the main road was wide enough for the five of them to ride comfortably in two rows, with the servants bringing up the rear. However, the shortcut to the Cosgroves was frequently narrow enough that only two could ride abreast. Lady Anne and Henry were engaged in conversation, leaving Clara, Kate, and Lord Ashworth to find an arrangement between them.

Anticipating the situation, Kate had already placed herself slightly behind Lord Ashworth and Clara, giving Clara a slight wink and a smile as she pulled her horse back.

Lord Ashworth looked back at Kate as if to protest, but Kate only smiled at him and then directed her eyes upward to watch the sun shining through the gaps in the tree branches above. She felt content, determined to enjoy the day to her utmost ability. The one thing missing from a potentially perfect day was her own mare. She gave her mount, Cinnamon, a pat on the neck, as if trying to atone for her train of thought.

Positioned behind the rest of the riding party, she had the opportunity to observe each of the other four.

Lord Ashworth and Clara made for a striking pair, with Clara's petite figure, golden hair, and blue eyes, and Lord Ashworth's athletic frame, dark brown hair, and brown eyes. They both had winning smiles which were apparent now as they conversed.

Kate observed Clara and found herself amused at what she saw. Lord Ashworth was the recipient of lash-veiled looks and exaggerated laughs. Clara was one who thrived in the spotlight, but Kate was surprised to see her acting with such affectation when her normal behavior was already engaging. Kate knew that some gentlemen were drawn to affectation but said a silent prayer of gratitude that she had never felt the desire nor developed the ability to flirt.

Clara was still captivating, though, and even if she didn't agree with Clara's approach, Kate admired her determination to pursue what she wanted with such purpose. Would that she could pursue her own goals with such confidence.

She shifted her gaze to Lord Ashworth's profile. He wore a kind expression as he spoke with Clara, but he didn't look to be a man in love. She felt a sense of relief. Could the marriage possibly be one of convenience on his end? Her eyes narrowed as she searched Lord Ashworth's face as if she might find the answer there.

He turned his head to look at her and, encountering her expression of intense focus, tilted his head, looking a question at her. She realized that she had been staring, and her cheeks grew warm: evidence of the subject of her thoughts. She smiled and then pretended to shift Cinnamon's bridle, aware that Lord Ashworth's gaze lingered for a moment before he turned to respond to Clara.

She was surprised at herself for acting so childish, unable to meet his gaze without blushing. It was not something that had occurred under the gaze of any other gentleman. It would be best to keep her distance from him.

She looked further on at Henry and Lady Anne. Lady Anne seemed amiable and kind, though somewhat quiet. Something about her made Kate wish to know her better. In her experience, it was uncommon to meet young women who were beautiful, confident, and reserved without seeming arrogant. Lady Anne somehow managed it.

Henry seemed to have shed the stiffness he had shown earlier upon greeting Kate as he regaled Lady Anne with his stories. Whatever the reason for his fluctuating behavior toward her, Kate hoped it would peter out as they spent more time in one another's company.

They arrived at the Cosgroves in a matter of ten minutes, finding the two sisters awaiting them in the courtyard. Kate's eyebrows shot up when she saw the younger of the two Cosgroves. Miss Cecilia Cosgrove looked more like an angel than any young woman of Kate's acquaintance. But even after a few short minutes, Kate was certain that she was more likely to get along with Isabel—she was much plainer than Cecilia, but she had a frank way about her that Kate liked immediately.

After introductions had been performed, the party headed in the direction of St. Catherine's Chapel. The road to the chapel passed by hills on one side, and long green fields on the other. Everything seemed to roll right into the ocean.

Fascinated by the beauty around her, Kate struggled to focus on the conversation. At one point, Isabel Cosgrove had to say her name three times before Kate realized she had been asked a question.

Blushing at her own incivility, she apologized. "What a terrible riding companion I am. Forgive me. It is only that I am so awestruck by the beauty that I find myself speechless."

"Speechless or deaf?" said Lord Ashworth.

Kate's head snapped up. Was he teasing or in earnest? She encountered a wink from him and laughed at herself.

"Both, it would appear. I beg your pardon, Miss Cosgrove."

"Oh, don't apologize." Isabel said with a kind smile. "It is wonderful to have someone so appreciative of the place we call home."

"I do envy you," Kate admitted. "None of you seem to be afflicted with a set of manners as poor as mine, but surely you have all become accustomed to the beauty, as I undoubtedly shall be in time."

"Oh, yes," declared Clara. "I'm sure I hardly regard it. But then, I have always much preferred the town to the country. After all, once one has seen one field, one has seen them all."

"I prefer the town, as well," said Miss Cecilia.

"But it is so nice to come home at the end of the Season, isn't it?" said Isabel.

"And which do you prefer, Miss Matcham?" asked Lord Ashworth. "Town or country?"

"Oh, the country," said Kate. "Quite unfashionable of me, I'm sure. I do enjoy London, but primarily for short visits. I'm afraid that I did not acquire the family trait of finding unending joy in balls and parties and late nights."

"You must have been miserable with Lady Hammond then," said Clara. "Mama says she is at all the parties."

"Oh no!" Kate said, anxious to disabuse her of such a notion. "I have been very content living with my aunt. She has been an angel to me, and I will never be able to repay her for everything. I just don't find my appetite for social events equal to hers."

Isabel smiled at her, nodding her understanding. "There is nothing so aggravating as desiring to be home but being at the mercy of one's friends or family. Shall you return to your aunt in London after your visit then?"

"I believe my aunt has plans to remove to Brighton where I anticipate I shall join her."

"But is she not going to marry that Wilmsey fellow?" said Clara. "Will you live with them once they are married? Or—" Clara's eyebrows wagged up and down "—shall you marry Mr. Hartley?"

Kate's jaw clenched, and she swallowed, glancing at Lord Ashworth. She had not anticipated that Clara would remember Simon. She felt irritated that his reaction had been of concern to her. He was watching her, but his expression was unreadable.

Kate felt an urgency to disabuse him of whatever ideas Clara's words might have given him, but she recognized that the impulse was ridiculous. She had promised herself to promote things between Clara and Lord Ashworth, not to ensure he had no misapprehensions about her own heart.

She was at a momentary loss for words, unsure how to explain her plans and reluctant to do so among people she hardly knew.

"Ah, there's the chapel!" interjected Lord Ashworth, looking up at the hill they rode alongside.

"How beautiful it looks in the sunshine," Lady Anne remarked in her gentle voice.

Kate looked gratefully at Lord Ashworth, and he smiled back as the group slowed their horses, coming upon the small gate which led up to the chapel on the hill.

Kate shaded her eyes as she looked on. The warm brown stone of the chapel was surrounded by green grass, bright blue skies, and, further off, a placid ocean of turquoise and navy which seemed to melt seamlessly into the sky.

Lord Ashworth cleared his throat.

She looked at him. "I apologize. Only it's so striking with all the colors. Please don't wait for me, though."

He laughed. "I'm afraid you've left me no other option."

She looked down. Cinnamon was grazing at her leisure in front of the gate, blocking Lord Ashworth's access. She tugged on the reins to pull the mare's head up and laughed. "I shall endeavor to focus for the rest of the day."

"Please don't," laughed Lord Ashworth. "Your enjoyment of the beauty is as delightful as the beauty itself."

She looked at him, wondering if he was trying to flirt with her, but all she saw was honest enjoyment.

"It is refreshing," he continued, "to see genuine appreciation for beauty after spending time in London where everyone disdains awe and strives to make each wonderful feat or marvel seem commonplace."

Up ahead, Kate saw Clara dismounting, her eyes on Kate and Lord Ashworth.

Kate cleared her throat and guided Cinnamon through the gate.

Though she would have liked to explore the chapel and surroundings, the party had already agreed that they would eat first. Each of the three families had brought dishes for the picnic, and the blankets were positioned so that the picnic party had a clear view of the chapel, the adjacent village of thatched-roof cottages, and the wide blue sea. Cows grazed peacefully along the hill and fields. How could anyone prefer London to such sights?

Arriving last to the picnic area, Kate and Lord Ashworth found themselves next to one another as the party began to seat themselves. Kate tried to think of a polite way of switching positions with someone else in the party, but there was no need. Clara came over and positioned herself between Kate and Lord Ashworth as she addressed a remark to Kate. Kate smiled and gracefully made room for her.

"Oh, Henry!" Clara said. "Do come sit over here." Clara indicated the open spot on the other side of Kate which Isabel Cosgrove was about to sit down in. "My arms are too short to reach the cheese, you see, and I know I can impose upon you whenever I want some, which you know I shall frequently." She gave a sweet smile which invited everyone's forbearance with her.

Kate's eyebrow went up. She was unaware that Clara had such an affinity for cheese or why she didn't simply switch places with Isabel. Isabel stopped in the act of lowering herself to the ground and said somewhat bemusedly, "Oh, by all means."

"Nonsense, Clara." Henry went to move the platter. "Move the cheese closer to yourself. Simple as that."

"What," Clara said with a censuring look, "and deprive Isabel and Cecilia of the cheese? For shame, Henry. Do come sit. I shan't bother you above three times, I promise."

Henry looked at Clara with narrowed eyes, and she smiled at him. His nostrils flared and his jaw set, but he sat down obediently next to Kate, forcing a civil smile. Kate wasn't sure whether his annoyance was directed at her or at Clara.

With three families who had known each other for years, the discussion naturally took a reminiscent turn. Kate rested her cheek on her hand and listened in appreciative silence as the group laughed and debated whose versions of recounted memories were correct.

She considered Lord Ashworth as he chuckled and chimed in from time to time. Her smile grew as she watched him throw his head back in enjoyment at one of Henry's exaggerated stories. It was impossible to dislike someone as genuine as he was.

Recognizing that such a train of thought was not conducive to her aims, she rose from the blanket and walked to the chapel.

She stood at its façade and inhaling the air which held a mixture of grass and salt. Running her eyes over the aged stones for a moment, she opened the chapel door to enter.

The small chapel was empty, and though light poured in through the arched window openings, her eyes took a moment to adjust to the relative darkness. The serenity inside was palpable, and she breathed in deeply, savoring the peace and beauty of the space.

Several cooing doves rested on various ledges throughout the chapel, and the midday light shining through the windows spilled in long arches onto the dirt floor. She walked along the walls of the chapel, brushing her fingertips on the stones and humming a hymn her father had loved as she looked up toward the vaulted ceilings.

There was no place like this chapel in London or Brighton or Birmingham, and even as she relished in the present, she felt a twinge of sadness for the time when she would leave Dorset to return to a bustling town.

She looked around the chapel again, noting the old pews stacked against the back wall. How long had it been since services had been held there? Her father had considered a vocation in the church, and she pictured him at the front of the chapel, giving a sermon to pews full of villagers.

A lone pew stood near the large arched window, and she sat down on it, lightly running her finger along the dusty, splintering wood.

She abruptly stopped her humming. Someone was standing in the doorway. With the light shining in from behind, it took a moment for her eyes to adjust.

Lord Ashworth leaned on the wall, one leg crossed artlessly over the other. He was wearing a serene smile and holding grapes which he periodically popped into his mouth. Kate could see the others behind him, rising from the picnic blanket.

"It seems I am destined to always encounter you humming in abandoned buildings, Miss Matcham," he said, disposing of an overripe grape through the nearest window and then standing straight.

"And it would seem I am destined to always be surprised by you in such places." Her voice held mixed exasperation and self-deprecating laughter. "When I frequent such places in the future, though, I shall take care not to hum."

He popped the last grape in his mouth. "That would be a shame, as that is the best part of the scene."

She looked at him with a considering eye, trying to discern the intent behind his words, but there was nothing in his expression to give her reason to read anything into what he had said.

Quite the contrary, in fact. He seemed to be in a funning humor. She couldn't decide if this was cause for regret or relief. If he had been flirting with her, she would have felt uncomfortable. But she admitted to slight disappointment when she realized that he was just being his usual kind and facetious self.

But it mattered little either way. She was supposed to have Clara's interests at heart, not her own.

"My mother would not agree with you, I'm afraid," she said, laughing away her thoughts. "She has been trying to rid me of the habit since I was a little girl."

A half-smile appeared on his face, and he walked over to the pew, sitting down far enough away from her that she was conscious of feeling let down.

"Well I, for one, am grateful for her lack of success," he said.

"Kate!" called Clara, her head peeking around the chapel door. "Whatever are you doing in here?" She peered around at the inside of the chapel. "What a quaint place. It looks positively cramped for a church service. Do come walk with us."

"Gladly," Kate said, eager to show Clara her willingness to leave Lord Ashworth's company. He stood politely as she rose.

She walked to the door where Clara stood waiting and took a backward glance at the chapel before exiting into the bright sunlight.

Henry stood next to Cecilia Cosgrove who was covering her laugh with a hand, and Isabel Cosgrove sat on the grass, reclined with her arms behind as she gazed out onto the sea.

Clara brushed past Kate, hand-in-arm with Lord Ashworth, her offer to walk with Kate apparently forgotten. Kate smiled and sighed.

Lady Anne approached. "Miss Matcham, would you care to join me for a stroll?"

"Please, call me Kate," she replied with a smile. "And yes, I would like that very much."

Lady Anne was, of the ladies, nearest to Kate in height. Though softer spoken than the other women in their party, she had a penetrating gaze, and Kate felt it rest on her as they began their stroll.

"I have been hoping for a chance to talk with you and to know you better." She pointed ahead of them. "Shall we walk down this small hill? I think you will enjoy the views."

"I have had the very same hope," Kate replied, "and I am never one to refuse a lovely view, so please lead the way."

Kate couldn't help but like Lady Anne. She spoke in soft tones, but they sounded more confident and energetic now that she and Kate were alone.

"Did I understand correctly," Lady Anne asked as they walked up the hill, "that your family is from Birmingham?"

"That is where my mother and stepfather currently reside. In truth, my family comes from here in Dorset. I grew up at Coombe Park until my father's death when the estate passed to my uncle." Kate felt a small knot in her stomach as she considered just how forthcoming to be with the rest of the story.

She stole a glance at Lady Anne who was listening attentively. Kate felt the desire for a friendship with her, and she knew a worthwhile friendship would not be hindered by honesty and frankness. She could glide through recounting her mother's remarriage without any mention of her stepfather's vocation, but part of her wished to make it known, if only to assure herself that Lady Anne would still wish for her as a friend. She didn't give the impression of one who would shun those not her equals.

Kate straightened her shoulders. "Not long after, my mother met and married my stepfather who owns a mill in Birmingham, and I went off to a seminary in Bath." Kate bit the inside of her bottom lip involuntarily, feeling mildly annoyed that she cared how Lady Anne reacted to the revelation.

"How foolish of me," Lady Anne said, "not to have connected you with the Matchams at Coombe Park. They do seem to be away from home most of the year. I understand they have a small estate in Somerset." She had not reacted at all to the information about Kate's stepfather.

"What I wouldn't give to trade my uncle places," Kate said on a sigh. "I miss the life that we had here." She bit her lip again. She barely knew Lady Anne.

Lady Anne squeezed Kate's arm sympathetically.

They came to a stop at the bottom of the small hill and looked out over the ocean. The coastline was visible from where they stood, a haze thickening around the water and hills the farther they looked.

There was a wistful note to Kate's voice as she gazed at the coast. "I think I will always feel most at home here."

Lady Anne linked her arm into Kate's, and Kate smiled appreciatively. It felt strangely natural to share such sentiments with Lady Anne, despite their short acquaintance.

"Well," said Lady Anne, "you must know that you are always welcome at Ashworth Place should you ever want for a reason to return to Dorset."

"Ah," said Kate, shaking her head. "You may live to regret that invitation when you find me at your door year after year."

"Nonsense," Lady Anne laughed. "I should be grateful for your companionship. William is a kind and thoughtful brother, but he cannot offer so many of the benefits to be found in friendship between women. I imagine you know what I mean."

She motioned with her head toward her brother who, along with the rest of the party, had walked further down the hill. He was attempting to throw a rock far enough to reach the water beyond. The water was far too distant, but he bowed with great pomp as his rock scared off the nearest group of grazing cows.

Kate laughed. "He seems to have a keen sense of humor."

Lady Anne smiled fondly at her brother's antics. "Indeed, he does. There is no doubt about that."

They stood there for a few moments, each enveloped in her own thoughts, before turning to walk back up the hill to the chapel and picnic area.

As they turned, Kate's foot caught on the hem of her dress, throwing her off her balance and onto the ground where her knee collided with a large rock. She called out as she fell, as did Lady Anne, drawing the attention of the others. Kate lay on the ground, attempting to push herself up into a sitting position but wincing in pain and grasping at her leg.

10

"Are you hurt, Miss Matcham?" Lord Ashworth said in an urgent, breathless voice as he knelt beside her.

"No, no," she dissembled. "I shall be well directly." She made another attempt to raise herself from the ground but failed, wincing.

"It is your ankle, is it not?" observed Lord Ashworth as the others gathered behind him.

"Yes," Kate said in a gasp. "I'm afraid I twisted it in my clumsiness. But perhaps in a few moments it will be able to sustain weight," she said with attempted optimism.

Lord Ashworth's expression was skeptical.

"Kate, are you alright?" Clara's voice was full of concern as she rushed and peered over Lord Ashworth's shoulder.

"Yes, yes, a clumsy fall is all. I am told that I am exceptionally prone to mishaps. Please continue enjoying the picnic. I couldn't forgive myself if I were to ruin the expedition." She braced herself to stand again, saying, "Clara, would you be able to help me up?"

She faltered, though, and before Clara could move to her, Lord Ashworth had grabbed Kate's arm and was steadying her to help her to her feet.

"Henry!" Clara sent her brother a look full of meaning. "Don't just stand there!"

Henry shot her a look of irritation, clearly displeased with being made to look foolish in front of so many people. But he walked over to Kate and supported her other elbow.

Kate thanked both gentlemen before turning back to Clara and the others. "Don't change your plans on my account, I beg you." Her ankle continued to throb, and only the tight set of her jaw betrayed her discomfort as she smiled convincingly.

"Hmm," said Clara doubtfully. "I'm sure that one of the servants may take you home in the wagon. You will be much more comfortable at home, and then we needn't change our plans for the rest of the day." Based on her expression, she thought it a capital idea.

Lord Ashworth was looking at Clara with a slight frown.

Anxious to show that she was not hurt by her friend's lack of concern, Kate quickly said, "Why, yes, I think you are exactly right, Clara. That would be just the thing."

"On second thought," Clara's face brightened, "Henry can accompany you in the wagon. To make sure you're quite comfortable," she added, as if some further explanation for his chaperonage was necessary. "I think it would be much more the thing."

Based on his expression of near horror, Henry did not seem to agree that it would be much more the thing. "Dash it, Clara. If you think I'm going to be bobbed about in a dirty, rickety wagon, you're daft! This coat is brand new!" He put out an arm to display the neat cloth, and finding a small speck, inspected it before flicking it off.

Clara looked prepared to persist, but Lord Ashworth intervened, offering to accompany Kate back to Wyndcross and then return to the picnic. Kate bit her lip, and Clara looked daggers at Henry.

Kate's expostulations and reassurances fell on deaf ears, and once Lady Anne threw in her lot with Lord Ashworth, she accepted defeat.

Henry, for one, seemed to think that Ashworth's accompaniment of Kate was a swell idea. "Seen him wear that coat at least a dozen times!"

Kate apologized once again to the group and thanked the others for a wonderful time before she and Lord Ashworth began walking further down the hill. Kate hopped a few steps with his assistance, but hopping on a hill was a perilous activity. She looked at the long trail ahead with misgiving. How would she ever make it without fainting—a pastime she abhorred—from the jolting pain of each hop? She lowered her foot, attempting to put weight on it, but she drew it back up immediately.

"My thoughts exactly," Lord Ashworth said, scooping her into his arms and continuing down the hill.

Kate opened her mouth to object but shut it lamely, knowing that the other option was to, in all probability, faint, forcing Lord Ashworth to heave her comatose form to the wagon. While that scenario was more desirable in that she would have been mercifully oblivious to the arm wrapped snugly around her waist or how she could feel his breath grazing her face, she was sensible enough to realize that it would likely have entailed the daunting prospect of her own head sagging limply on his arm, mouth unbecomingly agape. Such a vision was enough to make her grateful for his preemptive action.

But what must Clara be feeling to see such a sight? All of Kate's plans to encourage Clara and Lord Ashworth had not only failed but had gone miserably awry.

She realized that Lord Ashworth was watching her expression in interest as he carried her. When their eyes met, he said in an impressed voice, "What an expressive face you have! What troubles you? Is it the pain?"

"No," she said. Then realizing that she could hardly explain the true reason for her troubled expression, she corrected herself. "That is, yes. It is the pain."

"Very convincing," he said with a teasing nod of approval. He looked as if he would like to pursue the conversation further but said nothing.

When they reached the servants, Lord Ashworth instructed them to prepare a seat for Kate on the wagon they had used to transport the food.

"Yes, m'lord," said the servant, "but I'm afraid it won't be a very nice ride for Miss with her ankle bobbin' up and down with the wagon's every move."

"Yes, I believe you are right," said Lord Ashworth. "If you will transport my own horse and the horse of Miss Matcham, I shall accompany her in the wagon and endeavor to secure her ankle so as to disturb it the least possible amount."

"Lord Ashworth," Kate said in a final plea, "it is very generous of you but completely unnecessary, I assure you."

"You must learn to accept assistance, Miss Matcham," he said. "Or are you so very opposed to my company?"

Her cheeks reddened, and her eyes widened. "No, no! Please don't think that. It is very generous of you, only I—" she stuttered.

His mouth broke into a grin. "I am only teasing. But I'm afraid I will have to overrule you on this. If you have never twisted an ankle before, please know that I have, and I can tell you that a wagon ride home on dry dirt roads such as these will be agony as you have never before experienced."

She faltered in her refusal momentarily, jarred by the picture he presented. But the persistent thought of Clara again encouraged her to find another way.

"I am sure you are right. But there is no need for me to be transported home before the rest of the party. I shall wait here at the wagon and be quite comfortable."

Lord Ashworth smiled but sighed at her obstinacy. "Miss Matcham, your ankle needs attention, and not in a few hours' time. Unless you wish to have your ankle mistaken for that of an elephant," he said, looking down at her foot. "Good heavens! You are bleeding." He indicated her dress where a spot of blood had soaked through near her knee.

Kate glanced down. "It is really of no account," she said, brushing at the spot even as her knee throbbed under her careless touch.

He shook his head. "No no, my girl. A valiant attempt, but fruitless. I will escort you home and make sure your injuries are properly attended to. Then, and only then, will I return to the party."

Too surprised by being addressed as "my girl" to do any more than open her mouth wordlessly, Kate found herself placed with care into the wagon. With a deft motion, Lord Ashworth hopped in, helping her into the most comfortable position possible.

There were no seats, which meant that Kate was obliged to sit directly on the floorboards, her back supported against the side boards and her legs stretched out in front of her. An extra blanket was placed under her foot to absorb some of the anticipated bumps, and Lord Ashworth sat opposite her at the base of her feet.

As they started on their way, Kate closed her eyes and clenched her teeth to stifle the vocalizations of pain that rose to her lips as the carriage bobbled over stones and into dips on the uneven dirt road. The blanket was thin and absorbed only a fraction of the jolting, causing her foot to rise with the bumps and subsequently fall back down in a painful smack.

They had turned the corner onto the main road in Abbotsbury when Ashworth requested the wagon driver to stop.

"I am very sorry, Miss Matcham. I fear I must inconvenience you a little. Would you mind terribly if I spoke with one of my tenants for a moment?"

Kate followed Lord Ashworth's gaze to the side of the road where a young woman was standing. Her arms were occupied with a sleeping baby, tears falling down her cheeks.

"By all means," Kate rushed to say, secretly glad for a respite from the agony of the ride.

Lord Ashworth jumped down from the wagon and walked over to the young woman. When she noticed him approaching, she hurried to dry any accessible tears with her shoulders and made a valiant effort to smile.

A short, stout woman two doors down was beating a rug rhythmically on her doorstep, a cloud of dust forming with each hit. She looked at Lord Ashworth with a dubious expression.

"Mrs. Clarkson," Lord Ashworth said in a gentle voice, "Is something amiss?"

She sniffed. "You are too kind, my lord. Please don't bother your head, though."

Lord Ashworth looked as though he was unsure whether to inquire further. "I assure you it is no bother, Madam. I don't mean to press you, but I would like to assist in any way I can."

The rhythmic beating of the rug stopped.

Mrs. Clarkson's lip quivered, and she let out a small sob.

"Aye, my lord, and that will do, I think."

Lord Ashworth turned in surprise to see the woman who had been beating her rug walking toward him with an unmistakable glare. "I think you and your family have done quite enough."

"Oh please, Sally! Don't!" cried the distraught Mrs. Clarkson.

The woman Sally leaned her broom against the house, wrapping her arm around Mrs. Clarkson and saying in a motherly voice, "There, there, Louisa. Let me have the babe for a moment. Rest yourself." She took the baby and shot a darkling look at Lord Ashworth before pulling the blanket tighter around the baby.

Kate noticed that her stomach felt tight, as if she were listening to a conversation she had no right to hear. Beyond plugging her ears, though, she was powerless to avoid it.

Lord Ashworth was staring at Sally, visibly rattled by her behavior toward him. He seemed to shake himself back to the situation at hand, though, and turned back to Mrs. Clarkson.

"Madam, it would seem that I or my family have played some part in your distress, and this determines me even more to do something. What can I do?" He handed her his handkerchief, which she thanked him for and proceeded to wipe her eyes with.

"You are too kind, my lord," said Mrs. Clarkson, "but there isn't anything to be done." She paused and swallowed loudly as another gush of tears spilled over. "It's Jasper. He's been arrested, and they say he will hang." Her voice broke on the final word, and she covered her mouth with both hands.

"Good heavens," Lord Ashworth breathed. "For what?"

"They say he's a free-trader, my lord," Mrs. Clarkson said tearfully. "But he isn't! Not my Jasper! He's an honest man."

"And him with a brand-new babe and a wife to feed and care for," interjected Sally, incensed.

Lord Ashworth looked troubled. "No, indeed. Jasper is the last person I would suspect of doing anything contrary to the law. Did they present any evidence for the charges?"

"They say they found smuggled goods on the property. Fifty barrels full of French wine."

"Anytime I see a barrel in these parts," Sally said, "I shake my head and give 'em a wide berth. Lord knows what's hiding inside with all these free-traders about."

Lord Ashworth chewed his lip, his arms crossed. "Was it false evidence?"

Mrs. Clarkson shook her head. "There were indeed fifty of the barrels, but—" Mrs. Clarkson stopped herself and colored up.

Lord Ashworth frowned. "But what?"

Mrs. Clarkson bit her lower lip, her eyebrows drawn together in uncertainty.

Sally appeared to have calmed down and was looking at Lord Ashworth with a considering gaze. She kept her eyes on him but said to Mrs. Clarkson, "Go on, my love. Tell him."

Mrs. Clarkson seemed to find it hard to articulate what she had to say and would not meet Lord Ashworth's eyes. "It is just that...well, you see...I...."

Lord Ashworth intervened, taking one of her hands between his in a reassuring clasp.

"Please, do not feel a need to spare my feelings."

Mrs. Clarkson looked at him with a grimace and took a deep breath. "Jasper doesn't hold with the free-traders, my lord. But I believe there is a general understanding among the tenants here that we are to—" she hesitated "—look the other way, as it were, when our property is used for such purposes. That is, if we hope to remain tenants." She lowered her eyes.

Sally nodded in approval but also seemed wary of meeting Lord Ashworth's eyes.

He nodded, his jaw tight.

"Thank you for confiding in me. I will make things right. These things can take time, which is unfortunate, as your needs—" he nodded toward her baby "—are immediate in nature. In the meantime, please do not hesitate to call on me for any need at all. I will ensure that you are cared for in Jasper's absence."

He patted Mrs. Clarkson's hand before bowing to her and to Sally, who looked torn between approval and suspicion, and then he walked back to the wagon.

11

Kate's eyes stayed trained on Mrs. Clarkson as Lord Ashworth climbed back into the wagon with much less energy than he had done the first time. He ordered the driver to proceed then turned to Kate to make his apologies. His expression was sober, and it was apparent that his mind was elsewhere.

She was at a loss for what to say, feeling guilty for having been witness to a scene she was sure Lord Ashworth could never have wanted an audience for. She felt her stomach twist and turn at the thought of Mrs. Clarkson's plight.

The circumstances of Jasper Clarkson's arrest brought back a flood of unpleasant memories for Kate. But before she had time to come up with any response to Lord Ashworth's apologies, the wagon jolted forward, reminding Kate forcibly of her injury, and replacing all other thoughts with intense discomfort.

Just as she felt unable to bear any more and was on the verge of calling out to the driver to stop the wagon, her legs lifted off the wagon floor.

She opened her eyes.

Lord Ashworth placed the blanket and her feet on his own lap and then secured them with his arms to prevent them from moving, one arm underneath and one above. Though something inside her urged her to draw back from such an intimacy, she was too grateful for the relief from pain that his intervention had brought to do anything but smile weakly and utter a feeble thank you.

After a few moments, Kate glanced at him. He was staring at the wall of the wagon, his eyes glazed over, and his forehead creased. She was sure he must be reflecting on the encounter with Mrs. Clarkson. Whatever his reflections were, they did not appear to be pleasant. She was conscious of a wish to smooth out the crease in his brow and make him smile and laugh again.

He seemed to sense her gaze on him and looked up.

"I'm sorry," he shook his head, smiling ruefully. "I was lost in thought. I apologize for the exchange you witnessed. I am sure it could not have been comfortable for you."

"There is no need for an apology, my lord, though I am sure you were wishing me at Jericho."

He smiled but shook his head. "Quite impossible, ma'am, I assure you."

"And I assure you," she contradicted, "that it is quite possible. You need only ask my maid or my aunt; in short, those who know me best have wished me at Jericho any number of times."

He chuckled softly only to become grave again.

She clasped her hands in her lap. "I understand that the situation is quite serious," she said, her color slightly heightened. "Forgive my levity."

"It is a sobering situation," he said, biting a knuckle in distraction.

It was indeed sobering. The small baby Mrs. Clarkson had been holding was perilously near to growing up without her father. Kate's own youngest sister Julia had only been a baby when their father had died. Kate's nostrils flared and her eyes stung as she thought of another family experiencing such an injustice.

What would Lord Ashworth do? Would he stand up to the free-traders as her father had done? In a way, she envied him. He was in a position to act. Did he realize the good he could do? Perhaps she could help him see.

"I admit that I myself have very little patience with free trading." She spoke slowly, choosing each word with care. "My father's death was the indirect result of it."

Lord Ashworth again looked up at her, his expression unreadable.

It had been ages since she had spoken of his death. She took a steadying breath. "When he took issue with the local band of smugglers who had begun using our horses at will, he was shot for his trouble and died a few days later.

"I have spent my life," she continued, "wishing that I could have done something to prevent his death. Wondering why such an injustice happened to such a good person. He was trying to do right."

She exhaled. "I promised myself long ago that I would show the same integrity he showed at the end of his life if I ever had the chance." She looked at Lord Ashworth intently. "If you have that chance, my lord, please take it. You stand in a position to do much good for people like the Clarksons. Surely there will be others like them if nothing is done."

She swallowed the lump in her throat. "Perhaps things would have gone differently for my own family if someone with your influence had intervened."

Lord Ashworth drew in a long breath and let it out slowly, his eyes staring blankly at the pattern of Kate's dress which draped over his lap. He said nothing.

Had she overstepped a line or given offense? After all, who was she to tell him what to do or how to handle his responsibilities? Suddenly her passion seemed a gross encroachment and an undeniable impropriety. Her cheeks grew warm.

"Forgive me, my lord. It is a subject on which I feel strongly, and in my passion, I have forgotten myself. I'm sure the last thing you need is a lecture from a stranger. I am still learning to hold my tongue."

He smiled somewhat quizzically.

"What is it?" Kate asked.

He bit his upper lip before answering. "Nothing important. Your words simply brought Shakespeare to mind."

Kate's brows went up. "Shakespeare?"

One corner of his lips turned up. "'*I do desire we may be better strangers.*' I could almost hear you say it. I find it curious that you should call yourself a stranger to me."

She laughed shakily. "*As You Like It?*"

He nodded, visibly impressed.

"Well that is not what I meant," she said, "though I always appreciate a Shakespeare reference."

"Do you feel that we are strangers, then?" He looked contemplative, but to Kate this was a welcome change from his gravity.

"Well we are not strangers, per se," Kate conceded, "but we are very near it, are we not?"

He smiled and then looked at her through squinted eyes. "That is not an answer to my question. I didn't ask if we are actual strangers but whether or not you feel that we are."

She drew back, surprised by the question and unsure what to make of his asking it.

His quizzical smile remained, as if he knew that his question had hit home.

She thought about the set they had danced in London, their unexpected meeting at the abbey a few short days ago, and the limited time they had spent in one other's company since. Of course they were essentially strangers! But even as she went to answer, she stopped.

It would be to tell an untruth. She returned his gaze and for a moment searched for the answer to his question.

She had felt a baffling connection with him, even from their first meeting at the ball, before she had known his name or anything about him.

She had dismissed the feeling as silly and romantic, but it persisted despite her best efforts. Seeing a more serious and considerate side of him as she was now had strengthened the draw she felt.

When she finally answered him, her gaze had moved to the passing trees behind him, and her voice was calm and quiet, as if she was unsure whether she wanted him to hear the word.

"No."

Having uttered it, she almost wished the word back. It felt like a betrayal of Clara.

Lord Ashworth watched her for a moment. "How are your

injuries?" The tension broke with the question. His quizzical look had disappeared.

She realized that she had forgotten her ankle and knee altogether in the past few minutes. "Much better than before, thank you. I am sure it is nothing serious. So, you see I have quite needlessly ruined the day for you."

"Nonsense. I find myself in good company. Lancelot will be happy to return me to the picnic once I am sure that you are attended to."

His return to regular conversation soothed her inner agitation. She thanked him and fell silent again, wondering how long her clumsiness would put her out of commission.

"It is obvious that you are very much at home in the saddle, Miss Matcham. I presume you like to ride?"

"I do indeed," she replied. "More than I have found opportunity for in London, so the country suits me very well."

"I am glad to hear it." He looked around them at the undulating landscape. "There are plenty of fine rides along the coast in the county. I hope you will experience a few of them at least during your stay."

"I should be only too glad to do so." She tilted her head to the side, considering Cinnamon who was being led by a servant behind the wagon. "Though, I confess that I am sorely missing my own horse after today. Cinnamon—that is, this mare Lady Crofte has kindly allowed me to ride today—she's a sweet girl but quite without the spicy personality her name suggests."

Lord Ashworth chuckled. "Perhaps her name was chosen wishfully rather than descriptively. My own Lancelot, though a fine chap, suffers from a similar condition. He is an appalling coward, constantly shying at the smallest stick. He puts me entirely to shame, but he will respond to no other name."

"Well, take heart." Kate's eyes sparkled with merriment. "Courage can be learned. My own mare was named for her appearance rather than her personality." She stared off at a field which came into view as they turned a corner. "I actually feel a bit selfish being here without her. She loves a good gallop, which is simply not to be had in London. At least not without severe consequences, I have found."

"Well that sounds like a story if I ever heard one!" He folded his arms, ready to be entertained.

Kate shook her head adamantly, her eyes twinkling as she remembered the severe scolding she had received from Fanny.

"One day I shall hear the story, Miss Matcham," he said in a rallying tone. "You are quite attached to your mare, then."

She nodded slowly. "To say truth, I miss her quite as much as I miss my friends, though I'm sure it is not at all the thing for me to say so. Fanny is forever reminding me that Cleopatra is a beast, not a human. But I have had her since I was a girl. She was a gift from my father and so has more meaning than just any horse, I think."

The last sentence trailed off a bit as Kate realized how much she was revealing to him—someone whom she had pledged to view through a disinterested lens. She bit her lip, as if trying to stay her confidences. Her wont was to draw others out in conversation rather than speaking of herself. Both Lady Anne and Lord Ashworth, though, seemed to bring out a part of her that was more prone to share her own thoughts.

When they arrived at Wyndcross, Avery came out to meet the wagon, clearly wondering why it contained people rather than picnic supplies.

"Ah, Avery," Lord Ashworth greeted him. "Just the man we need. Miss Matcham has received an injury. We thought it wise to escort her home so that she can rest and receive any necessary treatment."

Avery's brows knit. "The mare is never hurt, Miss, is she?"

Kate had been gratified by Avery's concerned expression. However, it had clearly been not on her own account but on the account of the horse. She bit her lip to suppress a smile and looked at Lord Ashworth whose eyes twinkled in enjoyment as he glanced at her.

"As you can see," she indicated the horse being led by an approaching servant. "Cinnamon is unharmed. Thankfully my clumsiness brought injury only to myself."

"Well, Miss, I'm glad to hear that," Avery said, taking Cinnamon's reins and running his eye over the horse.

Lord Ashworth covered a laugh with a cough, and Kate pursed her lips to keep from smiling as their eyes met.

"Yes," Lord Ashworth said, "very fortunate that Miss Matcham was injured."

Kate nudged him.

Avery was still inspecting Cinnamon and seemed not to notice. He stood up, his eyes lingering on the horse, and said, "Only wait here while I fetch help to carry you inside, if you please, Miss."

"Allow me," Lord Ashworth said, "to assist you in transporting Miss Matcham inside. I am happy to do so."

Avery agreed, and using their arms, they made a makeshift chair for Kate. She made every effort to be as easy a charge as possible, but she cursed her clumsiness.

She was taken into the library where the two men placed her on the chaise-lounge. Avery rushed off to inform Lady Crofte of the situation, leaving Kate alone with Lord Ashworth. She thanked him for his escort, and, determined to subdue the desire she felt to spend more time in his company, begged him to return to the group at Saint Catherine's Chapel.

He looked at her for a moment. "I would like to stay to ensure that you are well-cared for, but my experience tells me, as yours does, I imagine, that Lady Crofte is an expert on all things invalid. You could hardly be left in more capable and empathetic hands. My only concern is that you may be crushed with concern. The best we may hope for is that her personal doctor is engaged elsewhere. I have no great opinion of him." He considered a moment and added, "I doubt if anyone could hold him in higher esteem than he holds himself." He flashed a charming smile at her. "I shall pay you a visit tomorrow to see how you go on, though."

He held her gaze for a moment with a warm smile and then, without waiting for a response, bowed and left her to herself. She blinked quickly and took in a steadying breath as she watched him leave the room, keenly aware of the way her treacherous heart had fluttered at his gaze.

Kate's promise to keep her distance from Lord Ashworth, to stop her burgeoning feelings in their tracks, to encourage things between Lord Ashworth and Clara; all had been utter disasters. A more miserable failure of her plans she could not have imagined. Of what use were her good intentions if what actually transpired had the opposite effect?

The only redeeming quality of the day was meeting and conversing with Lady Anne. Everything else left her feeling confused. Even Henry's behavior toward her was perturbing. She could find no reason for his strange demeanor. It seemed that Clara was going to some trouble to force association between Kate and Henry. Whether this was a result of Henry's constrained manner or the underlying cause of it, Kate couldn't be sure.

Lady Crofte entered, all kindness and concern for Kate's unfortunate injury. So full of stories of her own maladies and misfortunes was she that the doctor was only called for after a significant amount of time had passed. Kate breathed a sigh of relief when the doctor's request that a poultice be made took Lady Crofte out of the room, touting the merits of her maid's latest concoction.

Doctor Attwood was obviously well-matched as the caretaker of someone like Lady Crofte, indulgent and prone to exaggerate as he was. Though Kate was dismayed at first by his grave demeanor, she soon saw through the grim predictions and prognosis he provided. She was frustratingly reasonable and bafflingly oblivious to the martyr-like approach Doctor Attwood seemed to expect of his patients. She discovered quickly that the good doctor would not willingly allow her to undercut his professional opinion with her calm and composed rationality. He seemed to feel it incumbent upon himself to make her understand the gravity of her situation.

She had little patience for his style of care, though, and lost her will to endure any more of it, cutting short his grave ministrations. At his insistence on bleeding her, she drew the line in no uncertain terms.

Offended in the extreme, he seemed to realize that she was impervious to his counsel and ignorant of his fine training. He finally informed her very reluctantly that her ankle was swollen and bruised but not broken, and that it should mend with time and rest.

This sensible diagnosis almost put her back in charity with him. The good was undone, though, as he stalked out of the room, issuing an apocalyptic warning to those who would disregard medical wisdom and experience.

Kate laid her head back on the pillow and sighed, realizing that Lord Ashworth had spoken knowingly when he worried that she would be "crushed with concern."

12

Once they had parted ways with the rest of the group on the ride home, Henry and Clara slowed their horses to a leisurely walk, directing the servants to proceed ahead of them. Henry watched warily as Clara's social smile turned into something of a pout. His remarks about the expedition met with only short answers and unmistakable taciturnity.

Henry knew better than to ask Clara the reason behind her mood. His sense of self-preservation was far too great to pursue such an unselfish course, particularly after she had chastised him earlier for his lapse in chivalry toward Kate. He had no desire to be further rebuked and determined that, if Clara wished to speak on the subject again, he would not make it easier by bringing it up himself.

He maintained a steady monologue on any subject he could think of. If he could but occupy the time, Clara would have no chance to bring up the subject she was dwelling on.

But his hopes were futile. Clara broke in unapologetically on one of his stories, complaining again of his disobliging behavior that day.

He was well aware that Clara and his mother expected him to do everything in his power to encourage Lord Ashworth after her. They also expected him to do as much to secure his own interests with Kate.

Secure his family's interests, more like. Easy to bark such orders when it required nothing of them.

Henry's friendship with Ashworth was of long standing. That didn't mean, though, that it wasn't devilish awkward to suddenly express such an interest in his friend's affairs, to say nothing of asking Ash to dangle after his sister.

And this whole business with Miss Matcham was the deuce of a situation. Everyone who knew Henry Crofte knew he wasn't hanging out for a wife. He had a reputation to maintain. If he told any of his friends he was looking to get riveted, they'd have laughed til they cried, just as Fitz had done.

He was humble enough to admit that the part Clara had given him to play was largely his own fault. He had a duty to carry out where his debts were concerned. But that didn't mean he had to like it. Nor did it mean he couldn't look for options elsewhere. Options that weren't so dashed unpleasant.

He had received his mother's letter summoning him home late one morning as he nursed a nasty headache, the result of a long night of dipping rather too deep with his friends. It wasn't until he arrived back at Wyndcross that he learned what had prompted the summons: the visitor who had arrived the day prior. In her most stern voice, his mother had told him that he would do well to get in Miss Matcham's good graces if their family was to come about from their troubles.

He had considered telling his mother of his own plan. She wasn't prudish, after all. She had made it clear in the past, though, that she had no confidence in Henry's abilities to come about financially on his own. But if his own plan got the job done, well, no one could complain.

He had agreed to his mother's plan, knowing that he would never have to follow through with it, if only he could succeed in his own new strategy.

But the tide of blame Clara had been heaping upon him on their way back home from the expedition became too much for him. When he blurted out that he had an alternative plan that would require neither of them to sacrifice themselves upon the altar of marriage, she had looked at him with a mistrusting but hopeful expression and pestered him for more details. He had immediately regretted his words and done his best to make light of it, but Clara had persisted.

"If this plan of yours is successful," Clara said slowly, "would it truly solve our financial troubles?"

"Devil a bit!" Henry said. "It might solve most of our current troubles, but unless we can spend the blunt less freely—" he raced to continue when he saw Clara begin to expostulate "—myself included—then we'll be back right where we are."

He watched his sister and chewed his lip. She looked to be contemplating the merits of his plan. He doubted she would like it if she knew what it entailed. But she clearly had some reason for hoping for his plan to succeed.

"Not so keen on Mama's plans for you, are you?" he said.

Clara sighed. "I didn't mind. Truly!" She paused. "Until I met someone in London. I've tried to give up thinking of him. But I simply can't. Mama insists that I will be far more content as the Countess of Purbeck. Perhaps she is right." She tilted her head. "But perhaps she wouldn't mind me marrying Mr. Bradbury if we weren't in such dire need of money? What does this plan of yours entail, anyway?"

Henry chewed his lip. When he responded, he told her as little as possible, but Clara must have been smarter than he gave her credit for. She put two and two together quite easily.

"Smuggling?" Clara's voice held as much disgust as her face. "You can't be serious, Henry!"

"Well I am," he said defensively. "And don't play the pattern card of propriety to me. I know that your silks and laces ain't English."

Clara's curiosity seemed to overcome her for a moment. "Do you help smuggle fabrics?"

"Fabrics, tea, wine, all of it." Henry's half-smile appeared. "Not so opposed to it now, are you?" He well knew his sister's love of finery and *la mode*.

His mocking words seemed to remind her of the issue at hand, though.

"Well, yes," she said, "it is one thing to avail oneself of what is available—it is not my place to interrogate the linen-draper about how her fabrics are had, surely. But it is quite another affair to carry out the smuggling yourself. What will happen if you are discovered? Father couldn't bear the scandal on top of all the embarrassment we already face. It is very selfish of you."

His jaw clenched and unclenched. "Well it's a dashed sight better than this havey-cavey plan of yours and mother's. You can't really be serious about bamboozling two perfectly decent people into marrying us and then paying our debts. Even I know that ain't right, and I ain't precisely strait-laced!"

Clara's cheeks flushed. "Bamboozling? What a horrid thing to say! It is no such thing."

Henry cocked an eyebrow at her. "Are you telling me that Ash knows our family is under the hatches?"

The shade of red on Clara's cheeks deepened.

"Precisely," he said. "So, you mean to tell me that it's a love-match?" he pressed.

She held her head high. "I'm sure it would be no wonder if I were quite in love with him. Any number of ladies are."

Henry let out a bark of laughter. "In love with his title, I'd say. Admit it, Clara. It is no love-match at all but a simple marriage of convenience—the convenience being entirely on your end."

"It is quite rich to be receiving a lecture from you of all people," Clara said waspishly. "The reason both of us are reduced to such a necessity—and a necessity it is—is thanks to you and your horrid gaming."

Henry's cravat suddenly felt overly tight as he thought uncomfortably on the new debts he had recently acquired.

Clara looked him, continuing in a more understanding tone, "Never mind, Henry. We shall come about. But there is no need for you to take to smuggling. The law is never kind to such people. Did you not just hear Lord Ashworth telling Lady Anne about the Clarksons? They are Ashworth tenants, you know. Mr. Clarkson was found to be harboring smuggled goods and is supposed to be hanged. Marriage to Kate is far preferable to such an outcome."

Henry snorted. "Even if I were to get caught—which I would never —I wouldn't be hanged, sapskull! In any case, it's not that I dislike

Miss Matcham. She's a fine sort of girl, but I have no desire to become riveted, Clara. By jove, I'm in my prime!"

"Did Mama tell you what she will inherit?"

Henry shook his head, and Clara's expression lit up as it did when she was full of news.

"Twenty thousand pounds," she said, pausing between each word for dramatic effect.

Henry dropped the reins, and his horse lunged forward. After regaining control, he said, "It's all well and good to have twenty thousand pounds, and I wouldn't be so reluctant if she didn't seem like such a devilish decent person."

"What ever do you mean?" Clara said amid giggles.

Henry cocked his head to the side and squinted his eyes. "Well, I wouldn't feel half bad duping her if she was one of them arrogant chits, so full of herself and her fortune that she looks like she's always got some nasty scent plaguing her nose. But Miss Matcham doesn't seem to plume herself on her inheritance or let it affect how she treats anyone. And that's not the type of person to hoodwink into paying the family's debts, is it?"

Clara looked thoughtful. "I quite see what you mean."

Silence fell between them until Clara blurted out, "But don't you think you could come to love her? Then it wouldn't be so wrong, would it? Mightn't you try, Henry?" Seeing him open his mouth to expostulate, she hurried on, "You can keep on with your smuggling, though I can't like the idea, but please don't give up on Kate yet."

His agreement lacked enthusiasm, but Henry consented to keep the peace.

They continued on their way home, Henry still determined that his plan should win out.

13

"Shh!"

It was impossible to know who was shushing whom in the complete darkness of the stables. William reached backward, and the man behind him placed another barrel in his hands. William grunted as he hoisted it onto the growing pile inside the tack room. His arms hung limp at his sides as he awaited the next barrel, taking in a large breath, full of the scent of hay and sweat. In the darkness, his senses seemed to be heightened.

"What in the blazes is in these?" he wheezed as he took another barrel. "A ton of lead?"

The man behind him in the line chuckled breathlessly. He was short and stout and had a belly with that unmistakable shape unique to a frequent drinker. "The men are sayin' it's gold! Headed to Boney's army."

William's brows shot up. "How many more barrels are there?"

"Just a few, I reckon," the man panted.

William pushed his tricorne hat more snugly onto his head. "Won't the stable servants find it all when they come in the morning?"

The man shook his head as he reached for another barrel. He grunted as he handed it to William. "The servants 'ave been given orders that only the groom is to go in the tack room. On pain of dismissal, I 'eard. Til the shipment's gone, o' course."

William set the barrel down and rerolled one of his sleeves. The exertion of handling the barrels accentuated the veins in his forearms, and he could feel his shirt sticking to the sweat on his chest and back.

"Roberts'll be standing guard," the man continued. "'E's one of the Preventives who's in Emmerson's pocket. Reckon you knew that. But no one'll come or go without 'e knows it. Mr. Crofte o' the manor —" he indicated the house with a jerk of his head "—reckons we'll 'ave no trouble at all, though. 'E's not 'elping tonight on account of not wanting to raise any suspicions. But if ye ask me, 'e's just lazy like all the other high and mighty lords."

William looked toward the manor. With not a single light in the stable, the windows of Wyndcross glowed particularly bright.

"Last one," called out one of the men down the line.

William put his arms out to receive the barrel and placed it on the ground. He rubbed his hands together to free them of loose dirt. One of the men handed him a canvas, and William threw it over the tall stack of barrels, rearranging the corners to better cover the edges.

He leaned against the wall and brushed the sweat off his brow with his forearm.

"Yates, is it?" the short, stocky man asked.

"That's right," said William.

"My name's Briggs." He stuck out his hand, and Lord Ashworth shook it. "Roberts reckons you'll be plenty useful to us. Says you know the lay of the land hereabouts better than anyone."

William nodded. "I've made it my business to know every bit of the coastline from Osmington to Swanage."

"Glad to have ye, then," Briggs said. "Lord knows we'll need all the luck we can get."

He doffed his hat to William and then walked off.

Fifteen minutes later, William did a quick unsaddling and brushing of Lancelot before entering Ashworth Place through a side door. He hopped deftly up the staircase to his bedroom where his valet waited. Spires said nothing as he exchanged the wet cloth he held for the tricorne hat and muddied boots his master had been wearing.

William looked in the mirror as he wiped the dry sweat off his face. He caught eyes with Spires. "Don't look at me like that, Spires," he said, shaking his head. "It won't be like this forever. But I must do what's necessary for the estate." He seemed to seek reassurance for himself just as much as for his valet.

"I wouldn't presume to instruct you on your affairs, your lordship."

William chuckled as he pulled on his shoes and stood. "Not verbally, you wouldn't. But your face says it all."

"It's only that I worry for you, my lord."

William pulled at the ends of his sleeves, chewing his lip. "So do I, Spires. So do I."

14

Kate attempted to stand on her injured ankle and was scolded by Lindley for her pains. It was unstable and tender enough to prevent her from attempting it a second time. Lindley applied a poultice to the ankle, wrapping it gently and telling Kate in her sternest voice not to disturb the wrap for two hours.

Kate hid a smile, remembering all the times Lindley had tended to her injuries over the years. She was more like an aunt than a maid, in many ways.

Kate wanted anything but to be cooped up inside all day again, but she resigned herself to another day of reading indoors. She could almost smell the fresh air and feel the breeze on her face as she stared wistfully out the window. Feeling herself to be a burden, though, she didn't wish to add to the weight her current needs placed on her hosts. So, she sighed and settled into the settee.

It was just after noon, and she sat in the library with a book in hand and a look of disgust on her face. Lindley had given her three books that morning, each of which she had attempted to begin but had not been able to abide more than twenty pages of. Lindley was indispensable to her, but she could not help feeling that her maid's taste in books was lacking, tending far too heavily toward silly romances.

Closing the third book with a smack, she set it down on top of the others in frustration. She looked at the window but, knowing it was fruitless to wish herself outdoors, moved her eyes to the bookshelves that surrounded her. Surely there must be a book somewhere in the library that wouldn't bore or disgust her.

She spotted a title that intrigued her and mentally planned how she could arrive at the shelf in question using the available furniture as support. Carefully raising herself from the seat, she began hopping toward her destination, steadying herself on each piece of furniture she passed. She made it to the shelf without incident.

The book, however, was located on a shelf just out of her reach. Dismayed but not defeated, she hopped as high as she could and grabbed for the book. The book dislodged from its place, but another hop would be necessary to pull it from the shelf.

She gave one more hop, grabbing the book binding, and pulling it off the shelf. The few surrounding books came toppling off as well, smacking the arms she used to cover her head.

At that odd moment, the butler opened the door to announce Lady Anne and Lord Ashworth. Lowering her arms and looking at the door in consternation, she saw the siblings standing in the doorway, eyes wide at the scene before them. Once Lord Ashworth had taken stock of the situation, he rushed over to Kate and gave her his arm for support, helping her back to the settee.

"Did you manage to get the book you had hoped for?" he asked politely, his voice trembling with suppressed laughter as he guided her into her seat.

"William," scolded Lady Anne, wearing a scandalized expression. "You should be asking her whether she is hurt, not teasing her." She glared at her brother and then smiled at Kate. "Are you all right, Miss Matcham?"

Kate laughed. "Thank you, Lady Anne. The only thing injured is my pride."

Lord Ashworth's eyes twinkled.

Kate was conscious of a sense of relief as she glanced at him. He had come to check on her as he had said he would, and he seemed to be acting no differently than before their unexpected conversation in the wagon the day before. She felt annoyed as she noticed warmth steal into her cheeks at the memory.

"How is your ankle?" inquired Lady Anne.

"It is better today than it was yesterday, though still not strong enough for me to walk on. And quite as swollen as you predicted, my lord." She glanced at him with a self-deprecating smile.

Lady Anne sat down next to her and took Kate's hands in hers with an apologetic look. "I'm very sorry that it was my suggestion for a walk that led to your injury."

Kate brushed away her apology with an impatient hand. "Oh, don't be sorry. I'm persuaded that the view was quite worth it. And it is a wonderful excuse for receiving visitors."

"Have you been cooped up here since I left you yesterday, then?" asked Lord Ashworth.

Kate raised her eyebrows at his question, remembering that she had a grievance to air. "And this comes as a surprise to you? Knowing, as you do, Doctor Attwood?"

Lord Ashworth bit his bottom lip but failed to stifle a guilty smile.

"Indeed," she continued, "I have it on his very trustworthy authority that I can expect my—" she squinted her eyes, bringing back the memory of his visit "—willfulness and pridefulness I believe he called it, to bring me to my deathbed." She sighed and shook her head melodramatically. "My pride has always been a sore trial. I'm sure the blood-letting he prescribed was entirely merited."

A laugh broke from Lord Ashworth, and Lady Anne cried, "Blood-letting?"

"Surely he did not suggest such a thing for a twisted ankle," Lord Ashworth said, enjoying Kate's performance immensely.

Kate looked at him with wide, sincere eyes, "But, of course. He assured me that blood-letting is standard practice for a twisted ankle."

"Standard," he snorted. "There is nothing standard about the man or his practices." He looked at Kate, unable to keep from smiling. "Perhaps I did you a disservice in leaving before his visit."

"Perhaps?" Kate said, brows again raised, determined to continue teasing him. "It was a horridly selfish thing to do. I had the most appalling nightmares last night and live in constant fear of his return." She laughed. "In truth, I doubt he will after the rebuke he received from me. I only hope Lady Crofte doesn't hear of it from him."

Lord Ashworth shook his head. "It sounds as though I did *myself* a disservice in leaving before his visit. I would love to have heard this rebuke you mention. The man has needed a solid set-down for some time now, and I feel very put out to have missed it."

Lady Anne erupted in a laugh. "The two of you are incorrigible."

Kate broke into a large smile. "I don't deny it. But I hope you won't leave, despite that. Your entrance coincided with my attempt to find a fourth book to begin reading today." She glanced at the pile of discarded books. "I thought I quite enjoyed reading, but I suppose it is different when it is one's only choice, isn't it?"

"Quite so," agreed Lady Anne. "I am convinced that nothing is as sure to take the enjoyment out of an activity as the feeling of obligation."

"How true that is," Kate exclaimed, experiencing a small epiphany. "In fact, you have convinced me, I think, to revisit embroidery. It was something I detested in my years at seminary, but you have persuaded me that I might like it above all things. I am sure I shall if only it will save me the trouble of attempting another book."

Lord Ashworth nudged his sister urgently with an elbow, and a teasing pair of eyes twinkled at Kate. "Anne, do go and fetch some embroidery materials. Miss Matcham's artistic abilities cannot be overstated. I have personally witnessed the masterpieces she can create."

Lady Anne was smiling but looking confused. Kate glared at Lord Ashworth, but the glare was devoid of effect, since she struggled to school her mouth into a properly serious expression.

"What on earth are you talking about, Will?" said Lady Anne. She looked from her brother to Kate. "If you are teasing Miss Matcham, it is quite infamous of you and not at all what we came here to do."

Lord Ashworth was hugely enjoying Kate's attempts to stare him down and showed no evidence of having heard his sister. He donned a serious expression and shook his head at Kate, reaching into his coat pocket.

"No, no," he said, pulling out a quizzing glass and offering it to her.

"If you really want to give me a set down, you will have much greater success using this."

Managing to control her mouth's unruly desire to smile, Kate raised her head higher and continued glaring at him, determined not to encourage his antics nor give into her own inclination to laugh.

He tilted his head to the side and nodded approvingly, saying, "Yes, that is much better already, but only imagine how enhanced the effect would be with the aid of this." He turned his lips downward in an exaggerated expression of disdain, looked down his nose at her, and put the quizzing glass up to one of his eyes, which it magnified to appalling proportions.

"Will!" Lady Anne said, slapping his arm.

Kate burst into reluctant laughter.

"Well," Lord Ashworth said, cleaning off the glass on his coat hem before replacing it in his coat pocket, "we will have to work on that a little more another day. But today, Anne and I insist on escorting you out of doors." His cordial smile was replaced with an expression of feigned seriousness as he added, "Naturally, though, there is no obligation whatsoever. We wouldn't want to risk sapping the activity of enjoyment by making it an obligation."

"Ah, I see," Kate said, nodding her head in mock understanding. "Insistence but no obligation. It is a fine line, is it not?" She smiled but shook her head. "Unfortunately, neither insistence nor obligation are sufficient in this instance. You perhaps noticed from the avalanche of books toppling onto my head when you arrived that I am currently unable to complete even the simplest of tasks, including but by no means limited to, walking. I might attempt it for the alluring prospect of going outside, but I think I shall decline to make a further spectacle of myself by imitating a rabbit."

"Don't decline on my account," said Lord Ashworth. "The picture you paint is very enticing, is it not, Anne?"

"Do stop your teasing, William." She shot him a disapproving but not unkind glance. "Of course we would be happy to assist you outside, Kate. I think it would do you good to take air."

Kate hesitated. Her desire to be outdoors was strong. Her primary concern was how they intended to help her there. Knowing as she did that her feelings were not as immune to contact with Lord Ashworth as she could wish, she hesitated. She looked out the window. The sun was out, accentuating the bright green of the grass and the deeper hues of the boxwood hedges.

"I would very much like that, thank you," she said, deciding that she could at least temporarily steel her heart.

Lord Ashworth rose from his seat and bent down next to her, wrapping her arm around his neck and his arm around her waist. Lady Anne came to her other side, providing her arm so that Kate could rest her weight on it. They exited the glass library door, with Kate hopping between them.

Kate did her best to hold her own weight instead of resting it all on her friends, but she soon began to tire from the exertion of hopping while holding her ankle in a position that kept it from being knocked about.

"What do you say, Anne?" said Lord Ashworth. "I think the rabbit has hopped its last hop." He scooped Kate up into his arms and walked in the direction of the French garden.

Kate had felt quite proud of her steely heart prior to being swept off her feet and into Lord Ashworth's arms. However, the moment he picked her up was so unexpected that her lungs jumped into her throat.

Lord Ashworth was watching her expression with a mischievous smile on his face. He seemed to be enjoying her discomfiture. She hated that he could see how his actions affected her. She had always prided herself on her control and reason, so it was terribly provoking that he should see her acting like a girl just out of the schoolroom.

"Quite unnecessary," she said as he let her down, "though appreciated. You underestimate my hopping skills."

Lord Ashworth and Lady Anne kept her company in the garden for half an hour, talking and laughing. The contrast in personality between the siblings brought them into frequent yet good-natured conflict, Lady Anne chastising her brother for his provoking comments, and Lord Ashworth taking no small delight in scandalizing her and bringing Kate nearly to tears in laughter.

During a lull in the conversation, Kate leaned back on the bench and closed her eyes, inhaling the fresh air. It was every bit as refreshing as she had imagined it would be from the confines of the manor. She didn't know how long it would be until her next venture out of doors, and she inhaled again, wishing she could store the smells somehow.

She looked toward the manor and noticed the figure of Lady Crofte looking out one of the windows.

"Perhaps I should go in now," she said, shooting another glance at the window. "I believe Lindley was trying to persuade the cook to assemble a nuncheon, and she must be wondering where in the world I have gotten to."

The three young people re-entered the library, Lord Ashworth carrying Kate whose muscles were taut and her expression impassive but for the warmth in her cheeks. He had insisted on carrying her back inside.

Lady Crofte was in the library, and her face transformed with alarming rapidity from a smile to alarm when she saw Kate in the arms of Lord Ashworth.

Kate felt the need to explain, but the door opened to reveal a slightly disheveled Clara.

"Oh, I'm so sorry, Mama. Only I somehow came to fall aslee—" she stopped, seeing that her mother was not the only occupant of the room. A fading, pink handprint on her cheek and the slight drooping of her eyelids confirmed her words.

Lady Crofte's mouth smiled at her daughter, but her tone held reproof. "How careless of you, Clara, to leave the entertaining of guests to Miss Matcham—and in her injured state!"

Clara's cheeks reddened at her mother's words. "Oh, I do apologize, Kate! I had no notion that we had visitors."

Kate put out her hand, inviting Clara to grasp it. "Please don't apologize. It is my fault, Lady Crofte. I knew Clara was resting and didn't wish to disturb her. Lord Ashworth and Lady Anne came to see how I was going on, and I cajoled them into taking me outside. Very selfish of me!"

Lord Ashworth shot her a quizzical look, and Lady Anne said, "Not at all, Kate. It was our pleasure." She glanced at the mahogany clock.

"I'm afraid, though, that we have stayed longer than we should have and must take our leave."

Seizing the opportunity presented her, Lady Crofte encouraged Clara to see them out so that Kate could rest from the exertion of her expedition out of doors—a venture Lady Crofte took no pains to hide her disapproval of. Lady Anne shot Kate an apologetic glance.

"You look rather flushed, my dear," Lady Crofte said, walking toward the bell. "I shall call for Doctor Attwood. We would not want you to become feverish."

Kate sat up straight. "No!"

Lady Crofte's brow shot up in surprise at the outburst, and she paused with her hand on the bell.

Kate cleared her throat, adopting a softer tone and a smile. "That is, it is so kind of you, but I actually feel quite well. If my cheeks are flushed, I am sure it is only from being out in the sun with no bonnet. I will take some time to rest here—"

"—Perhaps a bit of reading?" suggested Lord Ashworth, wearing an expression of exaggerated innocence and handing her one of the books she had complained of earlier.

Lady Crofte had looked ready to do battle over the issue of a call to Doctor Attwood, but upon seeing the novel offered by Lord Ashworth, her thoughts were diverted. "Oh, indeed! I cannot recommend *Elvira* enough! I only finished it yesterday, but it is the most brilliant piece I have ever laid eyes on. I have no notion how I shall wait for the sequel."

Kate, too aghast at Lady Crofte's depiction of the novel to formulate a civil response, took the novel feebly from Lord Ashworth's hand.

He flashed a roguish smile at her before turning to Lady Crofte.

"Yes, Miss Matcham mentioned earlier how engaging she has found it. We found her loath to put it down when we arrived."

Lady Crofte looked at Kate with apparently reluctant admiration. She seemed eager to pursue the subject. Torn between the desire to box Lord Ashworth's ears and the fear of extinguishing the thrilled light which Lord Ashworth's comment had ignited in Lady Crofte's eyes, Kate found herself speechless.

Looking aghast at her brother's behavior, Lady Anne tugged on his arm and, through a forced smile, said, "Whatever her feelings on the novel, I am sure she is wishing us away so that she might rest. Thank you for a lovely visit, Kate."

She inclined her head and, with an inexorable grasp on her brother's arm, guided him toward the door, preventing him from anything more than a parting glance at Kate over his shoulder—a glance of mixed apology and mirth. Clara followed closely behind.

Once the door had closed behind them, Kate braced herself for a discussion of the novel she had so vehemently disliked after only a few painful pages. She was spared, however. Lady Crofte only inquired politely after Kate's injury.

"Such a shame to become injured so soon after your arrival," said Lady Crofte with a few clicks of her tongue and a head shake. "Here, my dear." She arranged a pillow behind Kate's back. "It was quite kind of Lord Ashworth and Lady Anne to come see how you do." She continued fluffing the pillow.

Kate thanked her with a grateful smile. "Indeed, you—and they—are too good to me."

"Yes," Lady Crofte replied, "they are quite proper and meticulous in observing social niceties. Lady Purbeck has always been a stickler about such things, no matter how beneath her a person may be."

Kate gripped her lips together to avoid smiling at the implied insult. She wasn't sure if Lady Crofte had meant it as a set down or if she was simply stating things in a matter of fact way, but something about Lady Crofte's manner gave Kate the impression that there was a particular reason for her continued presence in the room.

"I haven't had the pleasure of meeting Lady Purbeck," said Kate amiably, "but I am sure she is every bit as kind and good as her children."

"That she is," said Lady Crofte, speaking with authority on the matter. "She and I are quite well-acquainted, you know." She laughed suddenly. "After all, two mothers do not make a match between their children without being on very close terms indeed." She smiled at Kate until her eyes became bare slits.

Kate's eyebrows tugged upward. She had known that Clara

intended to marry Lord Ashworth. She had not been aware of an arrangement between the families, though. Her heart sank.

She dismissed her feelings and returned Lady Crofte's smile saying, "Indeed! And how fortunate they both will be."

"Yes, I fancy so. After all, it is a very smart match, to say nothing of how besotted the two are with one another." She laughed indulgently.

The door opened, and Clara walked in, eyes bright and fingers clasped together. She was so very engaging. Small wonder, then, that she should be the one to capture Lord Ashworth's fancy and future.

"What a scheme we have conceived, Kate! On Thursday we go to Weymouth."

Kate laughed. "What a scheme indeed. And who is 'we?'"

"All of us, of course," Clara said, as though the answer should be obvious. "Lord Ashworth has promised to take me up in his high-perch phaeton and let me handle his chestnuts!" She turned to her mother. "You see, Mama, it is quite a good plan because Henry and I can pick up the parcels for the dinner party in town instead of sending one of the servants." She waited for the gratitude which she clearly expected.

"Your concern for the exertion of the staff is quite moving," Lady Crofte said dryly. "They are indebted to you. Miss Matcham, however, is hardly in a condition fit for such an expedition. To be bouncing around in a high-perch phaeton would only exacerbate her injury."

Clara looked at Kate with sudden doubt in her eyes. It was unclear to Kate whether the expression was due to a fear that her plot would be ruined by Kate's injury or because she worried that Kate would have to forego it.

"But it is for Kate's particular pleasure that we decided upon such a scheme," Clara insisted. "She hasn't seen Weymouth—at least not recently. She needn't ride in the phaeton," she suggested. "There isn't room anyway. I thought we might take one of our carriages as well?"

Kate looked at Lady Crofte who seemed strangely hesitant. Her smile looked more like a grimace, and she looked to be thinking quickly about Clara's proposition. At Clara's suggestion of using the carriage, though, her eyes showed sudden interest.

"I suppose," Lady Crofte said, "that Henry might take her up in his curricle if Miss Matcham is enticed by the idea of an outing to Weymouth?" She raised her brows at Kate in a question.

Kate smiled. "I admit that I have been wanting to see Weymouth since we arrived. I shan't be able to walk around the town as I would normally do, though, and I don't wish to be a burden—"

This time, it was Lady Crofte who interrupted. "Nonsense, my dear. You may see a good deal of the town from the curricle, and I'm sure Henry will be quite willing to indulge you should you wish to step into a shop or two using his arm as support."

Kate looked at Clara, expecting to see her excitement rekindled now that her mother was supportive of the scheme. But Clara was biting her lip, brows drawn together in vexation.

"What is it, Clara?" Kate asked.

"Well, it is only that, between the curricle and the phaeton, there are only seats for four, which leaves Lady Anne with nowhere to sit." Her brows stayed knit in thought until rising suddenly. "We might take the landau instead. Then there will be plenty of seats and room for packages."

The enthusiasm Lady Crofte had shown at the prospect of Henry escorting Kate in his curricle dampened at the mention of the landau. She looked not at all pleased with the adjustment, but she nodded her agreement with an oddly shaped smile.

Having thus arranged things, Clara bounced out of the room, her mother following in her wake, giving her daughter instructions on what she should wear.

As the door closed, Kate let out a breath she hadn't realized she had been holding. Lady Crofte was an enigma to her—and an intimidating one. She couldn't help but feel on edge in the woman's presence.

15

By Thursday, Kate's ankle was feeling much less swollen and tender, and she was able to bear enough weight on it that she could limp without assistance for short periods of time.

Ever since informing Kate of the Weymouth scheme, Clara had been worrying aloud about the weather multiple times a day. Driving Lord Ashworth's high-perch phaeton in the rain would be quite out of the question, requiring them all to make the trek in a closed carriage, if they made it at all.

To Clara's pleasure, the day dawned with only a few wispy clouds in the sky. All signs pointed to an enjoyable day ahead. Kate, who knew Clara to be lukewarm about horses, saw in her excitement the anticipation of proximity with Lord Ashworth rather than any particular desire to learn how to drive a phaeton.

Kate's mind had been, against her will, somewhat preoccupied with the information she had received from Lady Crofte the day before. Her spirits were low, a state she was unaccustomed to, and various unwelcome emotions and thoughts strayed into her consciousness throughout the afternoon and evening before the planned trip into Weymouth.

It seemed that, despite her efforts, she had not managed to make herself immune to feelings of a romantic turn for Lord Ashworth.

She could reason with herself, repeating reminders that the heir to an earldom would naturally look to marry someone nearer his own social standing than the stepdaughter of a tradesman; she could convince herself, far more easily than she liked, that his behavior toward her was simply friendly; she could point out that she barely knew Lord Ashworth and had no intention of marrying for love prior to her arrival in Dorset; but none of those arguments and none of the reasoning could explain away how she felt upon hearing that Clara and Lord Ashworth were not only promised to one another but also in love.

Her stomach had felt sick at first, her chest strangely hollow. There was no logical reason for it, but there was also no denying it. Nor had the feeling left her. Instead it had morphed slowly into a heaviness, hopelessness, and even recklessness.

She had also felt embarrassment, her cheeks heating up as she thought back on the few interactions she had with Lord Ashworth. Surely it must have been quite obvious to him that she felt more than friendship for him. What must he think of her, making a fool of herself for someone who was in love with another—with her own friend?

Each time such thoughts and emotions crept back into her mind, she had forced herself to take a deep breath. If she let the thoughts run their course, she could convince herself that she had practically thrown herself at an unwilling and engaged gentleman. She knew in her more sensible moments, though, that this was a gross and silly exaggeration. She would not forego the trip into Weymouth for such a distortion of the truth.

The thought of facing him on the expedition to Weymouth made her cringe, though. She had tried before to convince herself that she would not allow more time in his presence to affect her. She had failed miserably. She had failed herself, and she had failed Clara, whose interests she had promised to have at heart.

But perhaps in this instance she truly could avoid Lord Ashworth. They would spend the day in separate vehicles, so her interaction with him would be very limited. It would be simple enough to avoid him almost entirely and to instead focus her attention on her other companions as well as on Weymouth itself. Her ankle would provide a welcome excuse for any unanticipated situation.

When Lady Anne and Lord Ashworth arrived at Wyndcross Manor in the high-perch phaeton, Clara's hands were clasped in front of her chest in anticipation. Henry had a slightly mulish look about him and had yet to utter a word to Kate or his sister.

Kate sat in the landau with feigned composure, knowing that this was one of the moments where interaction with Lord Ashworth was unavoidable. All the same, she attempted to delay the inevitable by pretending to be occupied with rearranging her bonnet.

Greetings were exchanged, and the sight of Lord Ashworth's new pair of matched chestnuts successfully pulled Henry out of his sour mood.

"By Jove, Ash! I'd heard rumors of these sweet-goers of yours, but I'm dashed if they didn't understate the case." He scanned both horses from muzzle to tail with obvious approval.

"Yes, and he has promised to teach me how to drive them," Clara exclaimed.

Henry's head snapped around, the look of approbation replaced by one of abject horror. Clara's smile only grew, and she nodded as if to confirm that her claim was true.

Henry looked to Lord Ashworth to refute his sister's words. Lord Ashworth only chuckled, leading Henry to shake his head vehemently.

"No, dash it, Ash! You can't let my chit of a sister drive those beauties. She hasn't the slightest clue how to handle the reins."

Clara's expostulation was cut off by Lord Ashworth. "Calm yourself, Henry. This isn't the first time I've taught someone how to handle the reins."

"Indeed, he taught me," chimed in Lady Anne. "He is quite a good teacher, you know."

"It isn't *his* skill I doubt." Henry shook his head again, slowly this time, but encountering Lord Ashworth's warning gaze, said, "But I suppose you know your affairs. Don't say I didn't warn you, though." He shook his finger at Lord Ashworth and climbed into the landau.

Kate, glad that no attention had been paid her yet, noticed Lady Anne looking down from the phaeton with hesitation. It would have been the sensible and chivalrous thing for Henry to have handed Lady Anne down and helped her down from the phaeton and into the other carriage, but he was already making himself comfortable in the landau, oblivious to any claims on his chivalry.

Kate's eyes shifted involuntarily to Lord Ashworth. What did he think of his friend's negligence of his sister? Lord Ashworth's twinkling eyes caught hers. She suppressed a smile and then reminded herself that he was as good as engaged. Her smile turned perfunctory, and she looked away.

Lord Ashworth stepped down to assist his sister down from the phaeton and into the landau. As he handed Anne up, he looked at Kate who found something on her gloves demanding her full and urgent attention.

"Oh dear," Clara said, drawing back as she took her seat in the phaeton. "I believe one of your servants must have left this—" the corners of her mouth turned down in disgust as she searched for the word "—sack on the seat." She indicated a dirty rucksack next to her.

Lord Ashworth hopped deftly up into the phaeton and took the offending object.

"Ah yes, it must be my groom's." He placed it snugly between his feet as Clara looked on with a dubious expression, as if the sack might find its way next to her again.

Lord Ashworth instructed the landau driver to pull ahead while he gave Clara a few words of instruction. She seemed to require much assistance, particularly in the manner of holding the reins, and as the landau pulled away, Kate's last image was of Lord Ashworth, his arms entangled with Clara's as he guided her hands in the correct technique.

She swallowed and looked away.

The drive was pleasant for those in the landau, the passengers being shaded almost fully by the half of the roof which was expanded for the ride. Though the landau began in front, the phaeton overtook them after only a few minutes. Kate caught a glimpse of Lord Ashworth grabbing the reins from Clara, a look of alarm on his face as they grazed by the landau with only inches to spare.

She smiled at the sight. Was Clara truly as inept as Henry had given them all to believe? If so, Lord Ashworth would have plenty of time to regret his decision. With the interaction between Lord Ashworth and Clara in full view, Kate's humor dissipated quickly.

Knowing that Lady Anne was of a more reserved disposition and Henry effectively oblivious to social niceties, Kate had worried that the responsibility of maintaining small talk would fall to her. To her surprise, though, Lady Anne performed the task, not only preventing any awkward silence but managing to keep Henry quite entertained. It was almost as if Lady Anne had sensed Kate's mood and left her to her thoughts.

Then she remembered Lady Crofte's words about how Lady Purbeck was such a stickler for social forms. Perhaps she was right. Perhaps Lady Anne and Lord Ashworth's behavior was simply instinctive and Kate had been reading too much into it.

As they approached the town, the traffic became heavier, and the dust from the phaeton kicked up in clouds ahead of the landau. Clara surrendered the reins to Lord Ashworth who looked relieved to be back in control.

Weymouth was almost unrecognizable from the town Kate remembered visiting as a child. The frequent visits of George III had resulted in a significant rise in visitors, shops, and buildings. Seagulls flew along the street facing the bay, sounding the familiar cackle she remembered from childhood. Though the street itself was barely recognizable to her, the coastline in the distance was the same as it had always been, chalky cliffs topped with green grass, dropping into a blue abyss.

The landau continued following the phaeton along the seafront, and Lady Anne identified points of interest which hadn't existed at the time of Kate's last visit. She regaled Kate with tales of all the famous people who had begun to frequent the town as a result of King George's visits. Henry had his own stories and embellishments to add to Lady Anne's tales, and the three of them passed a very agreeable morning riding in the town.

Kate found her stomach aching from laughter. She felt that she might well pass the entire expedition without any interaction with

Lord Ashworth, and only the slightest pang of disappointment marred the relief she felt in that knowledge.

The sudden stop of the carriage brought her laughter to a halt.

Henry descended from the landau, informing Lady Anne and Kate that he had some business to attend to on his mother's behalf before they returned home.

"Won't take above five minutes," he said.

The phaeton had stopped as well, and Lord Ashworth assisted Clara down to join Henry in the commissions they needed to fulfill.

At Henry's assurance of a quick errand, Lord Ashworth hopped back up into the phaeton.

"Ha!" he scoffed. "If they are back in a minute under twenty, I shall pull the landau home myself. Forgive me, Miss Matcham and Anne, but I have no intention of keeping my horses standing for twenty minutes."

He winked at them, and the phaeton moved forward.

Lady Anne and Kate sat patiently in the landau, Kate massaging her ankle gently. Harper, the Croftes' coachman, expressed his intention to follow Lord Ashworth's example if the ladies were agreeable. The landau lurched forward, and Kate clenched her jaw at the abrupt movement.

"It would seem," said Kate, "that Harper sets as little store by Henry's claim as your brother does. But I don't mind the chance to see more of the town if he is intent on keeping the horses moving."

The phaeton was still visible up ahead, but it soon turned onto a side street, leaving their view. In a matter of two minutes, the landau turned onto the same street, and Kate was surprised to see the high-perch phaeton sitting stationary up ahead on the side of the road.

A scruffy man stood at the horses' heads, holding the reins as Lord Ashworth pulled something from the sack which had so disgusted Clara. He threw what appeared to be a large cloak across his shoulders, took off his top hat, and placed a tricorne in its stead.

He hopped down from the phaeton, crossed the street, and entered an inn. It was not the sort of establishment Kate would have expected to see a gentleman frequenting, and she turned her head to see if Lady Anne had noticed her brother's queer behavior and destination.

Lady Anne, though, had her head down and was searching in her reticule for her handkerchief.

The door to the inn opened again, and two men walked out. Their feet shuffled, and they walked with a hint of instability, evidence of the drink they had consumed. Both were attired in dark clothing spattered generously with dirt. The edges of their faces were streaked with a dark substance, as if they had made only a half-hearted attempt to wipe it away.

Kate couldn't think what Lord Ashworth might have in common with such persons which would lead them to frequent the same inn.

As the landau approached the inn, it became clear that the two men intended to cross the street, despite the equipage bearing down on them. Whether Harper was unaware of them or simply confident that they would move, he seemed resolved on pursuing his course. Kate was sure that the men would take notice and move, but they did not.

"Stop!" she cried, and both the landau and the two men came to an abrupt halt. Lady Anne's head shot up. She stared, brows drawn together, as Harper made proper, though somewhat begrudging, apologies to the men. The two of them shouted slurred threats before continuing across the street.

"Good gracious," Lady Anne said to Kate as the landau resumed its course. "Those two men owe their well-being to you, though they seem not to be in state fit to recognize it."

"Who are they?" asked Kate, unable to contain her curiosity.

"Free traders," said Lady Anne in a dispassionate tone as Kate stiffened imperceptibly beside her.

"Did you not see the blacking on their faces?" Lady Anne dabbed her brow with her handkerchief. "One often sees them frequenting this particular inn the morning after a shipment, though they are more often found at The Crown in Osmington Mills."

"How ironic," said Kate, turning back to look at the inn.

"What is?"

"Smugglers choosing to patronize an inn called The Crown."

Lady Anne's brow wrinkled.

"Ironic," Kate explained, "because their livelihood is dependent upon defrauding the king and crown."

Lady Anne chuckled. "I hadn't even thought of that. I suppose it has been that way for as long as I can remember so that it never occurred to me."

Kate's nose and brow wrinkled. "Do they not fear being caught?"

Lady Anne tilted her head, not understanding.

"They don't seem overly concerned about being arrested despite their attire and despite the marks they wear being such obvious indications that they are smugglers."

Lady Anne shook her head. "Not here. Free-trading is largely accepted. And even among those who dislike it, no one is fool enough to go up against Emmerson and his people. They have ears and eyes in places you would least expect, and they can be quite ruthless to any tale-bearers. Even the excisemen hold Emmerson in awe. I believe many of them turn a blind eye to his affairs."

Kate's throat constricted. "Emmerson?" Her voice came out hoarse. She cleared her throat.

"Yes, Charles Emmerson. He is the man whom everyone believes to be behind the rise of smuggling in Dorset. He and his family."

Kate stared ahead with blank eyes. "I am familiar with him," she said in a colorless voice.

Though no one had ever been convicted for the shooting of her father, the man responsible had been arrested—the young Charles Emmerson.

Witnesses had been brought to testify against him, but once the trial began, not a single one remained willing to testify. Each one had been intimidated by Emmerson's cronies, and Emmerson had been released due to a lack of sufficient evidence.

For years, Kate had reflected on the person Charles Emmerson, and for a long time, she had felt great hatred toward him, a stranger. He had not only altered the course of her life, he had taken away her greatest friend. As a young girl, she had wished Emmerson harm, but as the years passed, those fiery emotions had given way to a simpler pain, dull and deep-seated.

Her great dislike of free trade was a natural product of her father's death, but never had she imagined that the very person responsible would not only be roaming free but also directing the entire trade along the coast.

She thought of Jasper Clarkson, his wife, and his baby, and she felt sick. In general, she was a proponent of giving people the benefit of the doubt, but she found it hard to understand why Lord Ashworth would be frequenting the well-known haunt of smugglers—in secret and partially disguised, no less. If there was a reason for it, she couldn't think what it might be.

But everyone in the county was apparently either apathetic toward or hand-in-glove with the free traders. Perhaps Lady Anne wouldn't bat an eye to know of her brother's behavior.

"Is something wrong, Kate?" Lady Anne asked. "You don't look well. Is it your ankle?"

Kate forced a smile. "Forgive me, I'm not feeling quite myself. Perhaps it is my injury."

Lady Anne looked at her with concern and then shook her head, brow furrowed. "I should have listened to William."

Kate, who had been dazedly gazing ahead of the landau, turned her head. "What do you mean?"

"He was insistent that you shouldn't come, but Clara and I overruled him. Very selfishly, I'm afraid."

Hearing that Lord Ashworth had wished for her absence on the expedition could hardly have been expected to assuage the emotions Kate was experiencing, but she was spared the necessity of a response due to the sight of Henry and Clara up ahead. Both stood with various packages and boxes and were engaged in conversation with two gentlemen Lady Anne identified to Kate. Henry stood with Mr. Robert Chapman, Clara with Mr. Patrick Bradbury.

Before the landau stopped, Mr. Bradbury relieved Clara of her burden. He was rewarded for his troubles by as warm a regard as Kate had ever seen. Her eyebrows went up at the sight.

"There you are, Harper," yelled Henry with a touch of annoyance. "Been waiting an eon for you."

"Don't believe him, Harper," said Mr. Chapman, pretending familiarity with the coachman. "He hasn't been out here but two minutes."

Harper began to make his apologies to his master.

"Never mind that," Henry dismissed his coachman's apologies with the impatient wave of a hand. "Where's Ash, Clara?"

Clara turned from Mr. Bradbury, her cheeks tinged pink with pleasure.

Henry was obliged to repeat his question.

"I'm sure I have no notion where he might have gone," she said dismissively, turning back to Mr. Bradbury.

"Has he not returned?" asked Lady Anne, surprise in her voice. "He rode just ahead of us."

Henry shook his head. "Should have guessed he'd be up to some havey-cavey business, leaving us to kick our heels." He seemed to be in a particularly irritable mood.

Kate shifted in her seat. She was the only one who knew Lord Ashworth's whereabouts, and though she had spent the past ten minutes fighting suspicion and questions, she suddenly knew an inclination to defend him.

"I believe he stopped at a shop down the street," she said in as offhand a voice as she could manage. Why was she vouching for him? She had no idea whether he was worthy of her defense.

The phaeton came into view in the distance in that same moment. Whatever Lord Ashworth's business had been, it had been quickly transacted. He was once again wearing his top hat, and the cloak was nowhere in sight.

Kate glanced at the dirt-covered sack in front of his legs as he slowed his horses.

"Very pretty behavior, Ash!" said Henry. "Leaving us to await your pleasure, while you sneak off on your own."

Kate watched Lord Ashworth's reaction closely for any hint of guilt, but he only laughed at Henry's accusation as he descended from the phaeton. Either he was dead to any sense of guilt, or his reasons for entering the inn were innocent and she had wronged him.

Kate watched as Clara said something in a low voice to Mr. Bradbury who still stood beside her, holding her things. She turned to Kate.

"Kate, would you like a turn in the phaeton?" she said.

"It would be better," Lord Ashworth replied with a slight frown, "if you or Anne rode with me."

Kate herself had been about to demur. She did not wish to spend the journey alone with Lord Ashworth given the many conflicting emotions she was feeling. But, on hearing his words, she looked at him with a mix of surprise and hurt.

He returned her gaze with a questioning look, but she had regained command of herself and made a point of avoiding his eyes.

"I say, Henry," interjected Mr. Bradbury, following a discreet nudge from Clara. "Would it be a great bore if I were to ride in your carriage as far as Hookham? I came into town with Chapman here, but he has a number of errands still to accomplish, and I am anxious to return home."

"No bore, my good man," said Henry cordially as he climbed up into the carriage, seating himself opposite Lady Anne and Kate. "Be happy to." Mr. Bradbury hesitated, shooting a look of uncertainty at Clara as he made to move toward the carriage.

Clara needed no prodding. "Lady Anne," she said in a voice which drew immediate sympathy for its pathetic tone, "would you mind terribly if I rode in the landau instead? I have a touch of the headache. I believe it is the result of being bounced around in the phaeton." She touched her temple with a delicate hand.

Lady Anne readily assented, expressing concern over Clara's discomfort as Mr. Bradbury handed her down from the carriage.

Kate began to understand Clara's offer to have Kate ride in the phaeton in her place as an attempt to make the journey in the company of Mr. Bradbury. She felt perplexed by the knowledge. Why would Clara make such an effort to be in his company rather than in the company of the man she loved and was promised to marry?

It was quite evident during the journey home, though, that Clara looked at Mr. Bradbury with something more than common friendship. Kate had never seen her look at Lord Ashworth the way she looked at Mr. Bradbury. She had seen Clara look pleased and flattered, piqued and bothered, but her interaction with Mr. Bradbury was something quite different. Her smiles for him held a warmth which Kate realized was quite absent from her interactions with Lord Ashworth.

She felt bewildered by the contradiction between what she was seeing and what she had been told by Lady Crofte. There had to be some explanation.

Mr. Bradbury was eventually let down at Hookham, and the rest of the party continued on until Lord Ashworth and Lady Anne parted ways with the others, bidding Kate and the Croftes a temporary goodbye until the dinner party in two days.

By the time the three had arrived back at Wyndcross Manor, some of Henry's reserve and ill-humor had returned. He hopped down from the landau as soon as he was able and walked directly to the manor, leaving Clara and Harper to help Kate down from the landau and to instruct the servants on where to deposit the packages.

Kate thanked them both, expressing a hope, once Harper had left with the carriage, that Clara had passed an enjoyable morning.

"Oh yes, didn't you?" she exclaimed as she helped Kate inside. Not waiting for an answer, she continued, "I haven't enjoyed myself so much in quite some time."

"Yes," Kate replied, "it was quite kind of Lord Ashworth to let you handle his chestnuts. Lady Anne says he is very protective of them."

Clara looked as though she had completely forgotten that part of the day, but quickly concurred. "Oh, yes, very kind. I've always wished to drive a high-perch phaeton! How did I look handling the reins?"

Kate laughed. "You looked famous, of course! Is your head feeling any better?"

Clara looked nonplussed for a moment. "Oh, yes. Much better. I'm sure Lord Ashworth's phaeton is very dashing, but it knocks one about in such a way."

She changed the subject, prattling on about the purchases she had made for herself and for her mother. The conversation soon moved to the approaching dinner party, Clara expressing her excitement for the upcoming evening. Kate was unsure how to feel at the prospect, but she listened with appreciation to Clara's delight.

"And you will be able to meet the Kirkpatricks, the Cottrells, the Bradburys—so many of our dear friends."

Kate had been retying her boot lace which was too tight for

comfort, but she stopped for a moment on hearing the names, looking up.

"Are those the same Bradburys as the Mr. Bradbury who joined us in town?"

Clara looked at Kate with a touch of wariness. "Yes," she said.

Realizing that she had touched a nerve, Kate tried to sound casual as she said, "How lovely! I look forward to it. He was very agreeable, and it is always such a comfort to see a familiar face in a crowd of new people."

16

Kate entered the breakfast parlor the following morning with only a slight favoring of her ankle. Her boot was beginning to go on with greater ease, as the swelling had almost completely disappeared.

Lady Crofte was already partaking of her breakfast. It was unusual to see her at the breakfast table—she normally took it abed. But this day and the one following were bound to be full of tasks to be accomplished before the guests arrived for the party.

She and Kate exchanged greetings, and Lady Crofte inquired civilly about the time Kate and the others had spent in Weymouth the day before. Kate recounted some aspects she thought Lady Crofte would find interesting or entertaining, as Lady Crofte sipped her chocolate.

"...after which," Kate recounted, "we dropped Mr. Bradbury at Hookham and returned to Wyndcross. It was all very lovely, and everyone was very kind to adapt to my limitations."

Lady Crofte, who had been listening to Kate with an expression of polite interest, paused for a moment in the act of buttering her roll.

"Mr. Bradbury, you say?" She reached for the preserves. "I was not aware that he was one of the party."

Lady Crofte's words and tone were devoid of any blame, but Kate had the sense that she had made a misstep in mentioning Mr. Bradbury at all.

"Oh, he was not," she imbued her voice with as much casual indifference as she could muster, adding more sugar to her already-sweet chocolate for an excuse not to meet Lady Crofte's gaze. "We happened upon both him and another gentleman—Mr. Chapman, I believe—in town, and he requested that we take him as far as Hookham rather than waiting for Mr. Chapman to finish his commissions."

"I see." Lady Crofte was silent for a moment before donning a smile which had the effect of making Kate feel quite tense. "Mr. Bradbury is thought to have quite amusing conversation, as I understand. Did he manage to divert you and Lady Anne during the ride home?"

Kate had felt somewhat diverted during the journey home, but that it was intentional on Mr. Bradbury's part was doubtful. The mutual attraction between Clara and Mr. Bradbury had been obvious. The looks passing between the two were entirely out of place for people professing only friendship. Their verbal interaction, on the other hand, had been innocuously and painstakingly polite.

Kate cleared her throat and placed a serviette in her lap, smoothing it over several times as she spoke. Lady Crofte was clearly more interested in Kate's recounting since Mr. Bradbury's presence had been made known.

"In fact," said Kate in as light a voice as she could muster, "Lady Anne sat up beside her brother for the ride home. Clara was not feeling entirely well after the ride to Weymouth in the phaeton. I must say that I sympathize with her after having ridden in Fanny's phaeton. Fashionable they may be, but comfortable they most assuredly are not. Mr. Bradbury was a very pleasant and attentive companion to us in the landau, though."

Lady Crofte widened her smile so that creases formed at the corners of her eyes. Kate couldn't remember a time when she had seen a smile look so devoid of the emotions it normally conveyed.

The door opened, and one of the footmen walked in, bringing a letter to Kate and bowing before leaving the room again. The letter was from Kate's mother. She and her mother did not in general correspond with the degree of frequency which might be expected between a mother and her oldest child, so Kate was somewhat surprised to see the letter.

She had last written to her mother before leaving London to come to Wyndcross. It had only been a quick response to inform her that she would be spending the better part of the summer at Wyndcross Manor in Dorset with the Croftes and that she had received her mother's letter regarding the inheritance issue. She had been at a loss as to how she should convey to her mother that she had no intention of accepting any potential inheritance, so she had put off the task.

She felt Lady Crofte's eyes resting on her.

"It is a letter from my mother," Kate said, looking up with a smile. She was glad for a reason to change the subject.

"Ah," said Lady Crofte, this time wearing a more genuine smile. "I hope she is well."

Kate opened the letter. It was short, and there was no mention of her mother's health.

Dearest Kate,

I write only to inform you that Alfred Dimmock has been located...

Kate's hand shot up to her mouth in surprise.

...living in the West Indies and is, despite what we had been given to think, in quite robust health, attested to clearly by his six children, three of whom are boys.

The number six was underlined twice. Kate smiled wryly behind her hand, imagining her mother's chagrin upon finding that any chance of her or her children inheriting her husband's fortune was now out of the question.

"Is everything well, Miss Matcham?" Lady Crofte's voice was infused with curiosity.

"Oh yes, yes. It is just such a relief," Kate exhaled.

She reread the words. The knowledge that she wouldn't have to explain to her mother and stepfather why she was refusing a fortune immediately removed a weight from her shoulders. That the decision was made for her was no small relief—after all, it was one thing to think on refusing a fortune. To give it up in practice was another thing entirely.

"I'm so glad," Lady Crofte said kindly. "And what, my dear, is such a relief?"

"It will seem quite silly to you, I'm sure, but it is indeed a relief to me. My stepfather has a brother with whom he has not spoken in many years. He was believed to no longer be living but has just been found alive and well in the West Indies."

"Your concern for the man's well-being is moving, my dear," said Lady Crofte in an amused and indulgent voice.

Kate laughed. "Oh, I have never met him. My relief is due to the fact that the question of my stepfather's inheritance has been decided. It was uncertain for a time, and it is always a relief to know one way or the other, isn't it?"

The amused expression Lady Crofte had worn at the beginning of Kate's response had, by the end of it, been replaced by one devoid of anything which might be mistaken for amusement.

Why did Lady Crofte stare at her so? But Kate had long given up understanding the woman, so she sipped her chocolate as she read the final lines of her mother's letter.

She excused herself from the table not long after, making her way outside to consider her situation anew, the letter in hand. Though her mother's letter had contained welcome news, Kate's initial feelings of relief began to give way to a renewed sense of urgency.

She walked the grounds, taking in a deep breath of the air that held such an invigorating mixture of seaside and country smells. She wished she could stay in Dorset for the remainder of her days. Perhaps she could seek a position in a household in the area as a governess or some such thing. But the thought of experiencing the county as a member of society was quite different than experiencing it as an employed servant.

What about Simon? Could she pursue the option of a marriage of convenience which he had offered? He had told her to let him know if she had a change of heart or mind.

She reflected on the state of her heart and sighed. It was, stubborn as ever—even in the face of his strange and suspicious conduct—still very much attached to Lord Ashworth. She felt a deep and loyal friendship for Simon, but what she felt for Lord Ashworth seemed to somehow run just as deep, yet wide enough to cover both friendship and love.

What had at first seemed to be a silly infatuation had transformed. The affinity and affection she held for him were beyond doubt, and as the amount of time she spent in Lord Ashworth's presence increased, the affinity and attraction deepened. The more she resisted, the stronger it tugged.

If she could have transferred those affections to Simon Hartley, she would have done so in a heartbeat. It would have made life so much easier. But, as if to spite her, those feelings seemed to have dug their heels into the ground. Her heart simply could not be given to Simon Hartley.

Simon had not only mentioned her heart, though. According to him, a change of mind would be enough.

What of her mind, then? Could she bring herself to marry someone she respected and cared for but whom she did not love?

She pictured a life at the side of Simon. She admired him and appreciated so much about him. But to be unable to share laughter or love with her husband? It made her ache.

Before coming to Dorset, she was almost convinced that such a life would suit her well enough. But now that she had tasted what it felt like to catch eyes with someone, to share secret amusement, to feel her heartbeat quicken at the mere sight of someone; she didn't know how to sacrifice it, even if it meant being alone.

Bleak though a marriage devoid of such things might be, the alternative she faced was bleaker still, if it was even a feasible option. Would it not be better to marry than to fail in an attempt at making her own way in the world, only to end up obligated once again to her stepfather?

The thought of marrying to avoid such a possibility did not seem so terrible to her. But she would not be marrying in thought. She would be marrying a real person with feelings and aspirations, and her conscience recoiled. How could she use someone as a selfish escape? Especially someone as good and decent as Simon Hartley. He deserved so much better than that. But what did she herself deserve?

17

Henry dangled his legs over the side of his armchair as he read *The Morning Post*. Clara was perusing the latest edition of *La Belle Assemblée* while Kate sat with a book in her lap and a glazed over expression. Every so often a scoffing noise erupted from Henry, and he would recount the object of his derision to an attentive Clara and an inattentive Kate.

A knock sounded on the door, and a footman entered, holding a silver tray with a card sitting atop.

"For you, Mr. Crofte. A gentleman here to see you."

Henry sat up, taking the card and reading it with a wrinkled brow. "Sir Lewis Gording?" he said with no recognition.

Kate's head shot up, an arrested expression replacing her abstracted one.

"If you please, sir," expounded the footman, "he mentioned that he knows your father and is a little acquainted with you. He recommended me to remind you of a night at White's and," he cleared his throat and glanced at the ladies, "an unfortunate run-in with the Watch."

Recognition dawned on Henry's face, and he let out a crow of laughter, directing the footman to show the man into the library.

MARTHA KEYES

Henry entered the library to find Sir Lewis flipping through the pages of a book which he shut with a thud when the door opened.

"Sir Lewis," Henry said with a large grin as they shook hands.

"Crofte," said Sir Lewis with a half-smile. "Glad to find you at home. Forgive the unexpected visit—I was in the area and remembered that your father's estate was nearby. I understand he's away from home?"

Henry nodded. "He's set to arrive later today, but he's been away for a fortnight. Can't say I blame him. It's a deuced bore here."

Sir Lewis only smiled slightly. "Do you not have any visitors to keep you entertained?"

"No." He bethought himself a moment and then corrected himself. "Well, I suppose we do, but I don't consider Kate a guest. She's been here some time."

"Ah, yes," Sir Lewis said. "Is that Miss Matcham you speak of? Her aunt mentioned her visit to me. We are acquainted."

"Yes, that's right," said Henry in something near a sigh.

Sir Lewis considered Henry. "I confess," he said, "that I have been hoping for an opportunity to further my acquaintance with Miss Matcham. How fortunate that she should be here."

Henry snorted, plopping down in a wingback chair. "Fortunate? I should rather think not."

A smile broke over Sir Lewis's face. "Shall I take her off your hands?"

Henry sat up straight, looking at Sir Lewis with a painfully hopeful stare. "I say, I'd be devilish glad if you would!" As if to incentivize Sir Lewis further, he added, "You know, she's to inherit a whopper of a fortune."

Sir Lewis's half-smile reappeared. "Is that so?" He reflected a moment. "Ah, yes, I believe I did hear something along those lines."

Henry suggested that they might arrange it so that he could speak alone with Miss Matcham. Sir Lewis had no objection at all to the plan, and the two of them left the library on the best of terms, Henry feeling that the stars had finally smiled upon him.

IN THE MORNING ROOM, KATE HAD BEEN UNABLE TO STRING together a coherent response to Clara's constant chatter about the fashions she was reviewing. Thankfully, Clara seemed not to require any response. Nor did she look up to see the haunted and anxious expression worn by her friend. When the door opened, Kate jumped slightly.

Henry walked in, followed by Sir Lewis, and Kate froze in her chair as Henry performed an introduction between Sir Lewis and his sister.

Turning toward Kate, Henry glanced at Sir Lewis with a devious grin. "You two need no introduction, do you?" Henry shot an enigmatic brow raise at Kate. "What do you say we venture outside for a short walk? I need to talk to you, Clara." He pulled Clara up from her seat, leaving Kate to the care of Sir Lewis.

Without precisely being able to say how it happened, Henry and Clara far outpaced them in the gardens, leaving Kate very much alone with Sir Lewis and required to lean on him much more than she liked.

Once the Crofte siblings had disappeared from view, Sir Lewis turned toward Kate.

Kate looked up ahead at the corner Clara and Henry had just turned and said, "Oh dear, I believe we have lost them! Shall we increase our pace a bit?"

She made a move to continue forward but was detained by Sir Lewis's hand grasping her arm. She looked at him, fear and anger warring in her eyes. The protection she had felt speaking with him at the Levenworth ball was palpably absent in the solitude of the garden and its high hedges.

"My dear Kate," he said in a voice that raised the hair on her neck. "I must speak with you alone."

"I can't think," she said, striving for a light tone as she removed his hand from her arm, "what you could possibly have to say to me in private."

"Can you not?" He took both her hands in his grip, pulling her towards him. "Allow me to enlighten you."

Stunned, she pushed off him using her elbows, but her hands remained tightly in his grasp.

"Spare me," she said with an angry glint in her eyes. "I've no desire or intention to become your mistress. Some other lady will have to claim that very questionable pleasure."

"Mistress?" He dropped her hands and stared at her with an unreadable expression for a moment. His mouth curled into the arrogant smile which was so unique to him. "I desire us to wed."

It was Kate's turn to stare. Had she really misunderstood his intentions toward her? Had she done him a disservice in believing his character to be so black?

She thought back to the Levenworth ball, to the way Sir Lewis had looked at her, to his words. Had he not told her that she couldn't choose what terms she accepted a man on? That she would have all she could want under his protection? She had been sure at the time that, had they not been in public, he would have attempted to coerce her.

She looked into his eyes and saw, to her surprise, suspense. But it was not the suspense bred of the uncertainty and excruciating hope worn by lovers. It was a fearful suspense.

What could have changed his attitude toward her from the possessive and aggressive callousness of their last encounter to the anxious intensity of today?

She smiled wryly as it all began to make sense. "Who told you?"

"Told me what?" Sir Lewis said, a wary expression flashing across his face.

"About the inheritance." Her fear began to dissipate as a sense of control coursed through her.

He paused before speaking.

The pause was all the proof she needed that he did indeed know. She toyed with the idea of refusing him without telling him that there was no such inheritance to be had; to send him away having failed at his goal, believing that thousands of pounds had slipped through his fingers. She longed to tell him what she thought of him, to tear his character to shreds without giving him the satisfaction of knowing that he was not losing what he wanted.

But in the seclusion of the garden, she knew that to do it would be to court danger. She didn't know how far he would go to pursue the large fortune he believed her to be inheriting, and she didn't intend to put him to the test.

"I think I can guess how you heard," she said. "I only hope you didn't come all this way based on an ill-founded piece of gossip."

His eyes narrowed, his grip on her hands tightening uncomfortably. For a moment she caught a glimpse of the demon she might unleash if she let him believe he was losing an heiress.

"I'm afraid," she said, tugging a hand free, "you've been misinformed. I am still, as I always have been, a woman with no prospects or fortune."

He shifted his weight from one leg to the other and stared at her with the confident sneer she so despised. "You lie," he said.

She raised her brows, and a smile played at her lips. "Your accusation is offensive, but I suppose it is understandable given the disappointment I am handing you." She looked him in his cold eyes. "I am not lying to you, Sir Lewis. I have no fortune and no prospect of inheriting one. I myself discovered the state of things only this morning. It was only ever a far-fetched chance."

He swallowed but looked at her through squinted eyes as if he still doubted that she was telling the truth.

She sighed impatiently. "Do you always disbelieve someone when they claim to be fortuneless?" She couldn't help herself, and added as an afterthought, "I admit myself slightly bewildered that you could have expected success in this mission. I believe I have frequently made plain my distaste for your company."

"If what you say is true," he said, "why, then, have I had the information from multiple parties, of which one was your own aunt?"

Kate smiled drolly at his unwillingness to believe her.

"My aunt, bless her kind heart, was too ecstatic on discovering that the inheritance was a possibility to reign in her emotions and, very much against my wishes, let the news slip to Charlotte Thorpe. Knowing Charlotte Thorpe as you do, I imagine you can guess how news traveled from there. But that really is immaterial. Of all the people you might hear such news from, should my own word not carry the most weight?"

He stared at her, chewing his lip.

"Rest assured," she said, unable to resist driving the point home, "that, even were I to inherit a fortune, your suit would not have been successful."

His brow began to blacken, and she hurried to add in a cheerful voice, "But no matter. Now you have the truth, and there is no harm done. How fortunate for you that I did not accept your proposal, is it not?" She shot him a knowing smile.

Amused at his reaction to her revelation and giddy with the feeling that she had finally put Sir Lewis in his place, she recognized her opportunity to make an escape. She gripped her lips together in a last glance at him, claimed to hear Clara calling out to her, and discreetly made her way, limping slightly, out of the garden.

Her smile faded once she left his view. The knowledge that an inheritance had changed her prospects with Sir Lewis from mistress to wife was unsurprising yet maddening. It was not that she wished to be his wife. But it underscored to her the gulf that stood between her and anyone she *should* wish to marry.

It was nothing personal nor anything within her control. People seemed to like her quite well. She had never wanted for partners in conversation. And yet that was poor consolation. What good was a pleasing disposition if it was not accompanied by a tolerable marriage settlement or a strong family name? Disposition seemed to matter the least where marriage was concerned. Money or a good family name could overcome all manner of ills, and a combination of the two more still.

Simon, though, would marry her despite her undesirable family connections and her lack of fortune. Wasn't that preferable to the life of a spinster?

18

Henry pulled Clara along by the arm out of garden path lined with freshly trimmed boxwood hedges. She was as bullheaded as their mother sometimes.

"But she didn't seem to want to be left alone with him, Henry." She tugged against his grip. "And I can't say I blame her. Something about him is so sinister."

Henry guffawed as he opened the front door, pulling her into the entry hall. "The ideas you ladies get from your novels!"

"Henry."

His mother stood at the top of the stairway. He swallowed uncomfortably and let Clara's arm drop. If his mother knew he had tried to pawn Miss Matcham off to Sir Lewis, there would be hell to pay.

He looked up at her with the innocent expression he'd worked to perfect anytime he felt a lecture coming on.

"Clara, this concerns you as well," Lady Crofte said, descending the stairs. "Please join me in the parlor."

Henry looked at Clara, but she only shrugged and followed her mother down the hallway.

Lady Crofte stood at the door, closing it behind Henry and Clara and then clasping her hands.

"We have been harboring a deceiver in our midst." She looked back and forth between him and Clara.

Henry swallowed again. How in the world had the woman discovered his exploits? He leaned back on the wall behind him, crossing one leg over the other and hoping that the relaxed posture would somehow calm his nerves.

"Mercifully," Lady Crofte continued, "I discovered the deception this morning, and we can take action to avoid what might have been disastrous consequences."

If the woman thought that preventing him from fulfilling his commitment to Emmerson would avoid disastrous consequences, she was in for a nasty surprise. Unless his mother wished to find that he had been brutally murdered, Henry had no choice but to finish what he had started.

"Henry," she said.

He chewed the inside of his lip and twirled his quizzing between his fingers. His throat felt peculiarly dry.

"On no account must you fall in love with Miss Matcham. On no account must you raise any hopes in her treacherous heart."

The quizzing glass dropped to the rug beneath him, and he rushed to pick it up. "Come again?"

"Miss Matcham is not, as we were so falsely given to understand, the heir to her stepfather's fortune." Lady Crofte looked at Henry and then at Clara.

Gad, she was always composed. Only her flared nostrils betrayed her anger.

"She has no inheritance to speak of," Lady Crofte continued. "None whatsoever." She paused. "I had great hopes for her visit here. With a match you and her, Henry, and one between Clara and Lord Ashworth, our family was to rise above the adversity which surrounds us. Those unions would take us to new heights." She looked pointedly at Henry. "Henry will now have to look elsewhere for redemption. Our hope lies with you, Clara"

Henry thought of his plan and how close that redemption was. He could almost taste it. It was a great relief that he wouldn't have to tell his mother that he didn't wish to marry Kate. He couldn't help but feel some sympathy for Kate, though—he wouldn't wish upon anyone the position of being the object of his mother's wrath.

Whatever weight was removed from his shoulders on hearing his mother's words, a look at Clara told him that it had settled squarely on her.

"What if neither union is necessary?"

He regretted the words immediately. There was good reason he never risked his skin for others. The gaze directed at him by his mother was enough to make a braver man than Henry cower. He glanced at Clara. She was looking at him with an expression he had trouble identifying for a moment, so unfamiliar was it: admiration.

"I only mean," he said, encouraged by Clara's expression, "that I am devilish close to solving our financial difficulties. So, you see, there's no need for Clara or me to marry money." He shrugged.

One of his mother's thin brows were raised. He felt the need to drive home his point. "What's more, I don't think Ash has any plans to marry Clara."

"What do you mean?" Clara asked. "Why do you say that?"

He saw both sets of female eyes boring into his soul and became defensive. But he wasn't blind, even if they were. "It's plain as a pikestaff that he's head over heels for Kate."

Clara's eyes went wide and round. Lady Crofte's thin nostrils flared.

There was an uncomfortable silence. Feeling he had hit a mark with his words, Henry walked over to the decanter of brandy on the side table and poured a glass.

"Impossible," Clara said.

"What," Henry said, "that a chap should prefer someone to you? A little humble pie will do you good, Clara." He tossed off his brandy.

Lady Crofte exhaled calmly. "Surely, if that is the impression you've had, it is only because Lord Ashworth mistakenly believes the same thing we did: that Miss Matcham will soon be possessed of a large inheritance. That error is easily rectified."

"Not by me it ain't!" Henry said, shaking his head. He had no desire to meddle in his friend's affairs nor to be a talebearer.

Clara stared at him. "Even if he is in love with her, which I very much doubt—" she sent Henry a skeptical glance— "Kate's as good as engaged to that Simon Hartley man."

Lady Crofte paused in the act of straightening a portrait hanging on the wall. "Hartley?"

"Yes," said Clara. "And they've been corresponding, for I saw her letter to him. It was destined for Weymouth."

Henry snorted. Clara didn't seem to mind talebearing.

"So what?" Henry interjected. "Just because Kate's not free for the taking don't mean Ash will fall into your lap, Clara. Besides, surely she'd rather have an earl than some fellow no one has ever heard of."

Hadn't Clara said she wished to marry Bradbury? Why, then, was she acting so dashed foolish about the whole Ash business? He would never understand women.

Lady Crofte put up a hand, commanding his silence. She looked to be having some sort of epiphany.

"How fortunate," she whispered as if to herself. She straightened her shoulders and looked at Clara. "I am acquainted with the Hartleys. I believe the gentleman you refer to, Clara, is a nephew. He comes to care for Agatha from time to time." She seemed to be talking herself through things, taking slow steps as she spoke. "It is unusual to send an invitation so late, but Agatha won't regard it. We will send her an invitation for the dinner party, addressed to her, her son, and her nephew. If Miss Matcham has an understanding with the nephew, it would be unkind in us not to invite him."

Henry snorted and tried to turn it into a cough. His mother always managed to make her scheming seem like the decent thing to do.

"And, Clara," Lady Crofte added. "It would only be right to drop a hint of the understanding between Miss Matcham and Mr. Hartley in Lord Ashworth's ear. I imagine you can manage that easily enough."

Henry shook his head. Women and their wiles.

19

Kate's mind was occupied well into the following day with the same unenviable thoughts which had plagued her so much since coming to Wyndcross. At one point, she began a letter to Simon, pausing with her quill to the paper, stuck at the greeting. She vacillated between a desire to put off a decision and the urgency she felt to have her future arranged. She had received a letter from him the day before, but he had made no mention of the conversation they'd had prior to his departure for Weymouth.

Had he changed his mind about marriage with her?

She looked down at the paper. There was a small pool where the ink had gathered at the tip of the quill, waiting for her. She crumpled the paper in frustration and threw it to the floor, toying with a desire to smash it with her boot.

Lindley opened the door.

"Miss," Lindley said, "I am told you are wanted in the stables."

Kate's forehead wrinkled. "Wanted in the stables? What for?"

"I couldn't rightly say, Miss."

Kate frowned. "I shan't attempt a ride until tomorrow, I think. Besides, I haven't time to ride before the dinner party." It was very unlike Lindley to suggest anything that would hurry her mistress's toilette prior to an event such as the one taking place at Wyndcross that evening.

"Good heavens, Miss!" Lindley laughed. "As if I should suggest a ride when we have barely any time at all before the party."

Kate's lips trembled as she suppressed a smile. "Shall I take offense at the suggestion that we need all of four hours for my toilette?"

Lindley's eyes narrowed, and her lips tightened. "I shan't rise to your bait, Miss."

Very much at a loss to understand why Lindley would send her to the stables with no explanation whatsoever, Kate made her way outside at a slow and steady pace, knowing that any carelessness could lead to the longer recovery she was all too eager to avoid.

She met Avery on her way to the stables, leading Henry's horse to the courtyard at a brisk pace.

"Ah, Miss Matcham." He gave her an enigmatic look but did not stop. "On your way to the stables, I reckon? She's waiting for you."

Kate thanked him in an uncertain voice as he passed her by. She had been certain that Clara was occupied in assisting Lady Crofte with preparations for the dinner. Had there been a misunderstanding leading Avery to prepare Rosebud for Kate?

As she entered the stables, she saw neither Clara nor Rosebud. Two other horses stood between the rows of stalls. She stopped in her tracks. It was her own Cleopatra. She rushed forward with as much careful quickness as she could.

"What is this?" she exclaimed, going to Cleopatra's head. "Where in the world did you come from, girl?"

She looked around the stables and could see no one. She had half a mind to go find Avery and ask him what—or who—in the world had brought her own mare to Wyndcross. But he was engaged in his duties, so she would have to await his return to find out if he could offer any information about the horse's sudden and very welcome arrival.

A shaky laugh erupted from her, and she wrapped her arm under Cleopatra's neck, pulling the mare toward her in an embrace and stroking her face with her other hand. Half of the horse's mane was tangled, a strange circumstance until Kate noticed the brush laying on the floor nearby. Avery must have been in the middle of brushing her when he was called to take Henry's horse out.

She picked up the brush and began brushing the tangled half of the mane. Cleopatra tossed her head, and Kate smiled.

"I know. I have neglected you shamefully. But I am nearly rid of this nasty limp, and I shan't let anything stop me from taking you on a ride tomorrow."

She heard a sound coming from the other side of the barn and peeped over Cleopatra's neck.

Lord Ashworth exited the tack room, the corners of his mouth tugging upward into a playful grin. "I don't think 'nasty' is the proper description of your limp," he said. "Endearing, perhaps."

Kate let out a sigh, wishing she could understand this man who frequented smuggling inns one day and charmed her the next. Only for a moment did she consider confronting him with her knowledge of his whereabouts in Weymouth. It was none of her business, and part of her was afraid to know the answer.

"Endearing?" she said doubtfully. "I wish I could say the same of your eavesdropping habit. It seems that if I am ever in need of your presence, I have only to do something mortifying, and you are transported here on the instant."

"I hope for many more mortifying moments, then," he said. "I'm afraid you must acquit me of eavesdropping this time, though. I happened to be in the tack room, no more. But I must ask you one thing."

"Which is?" Kate returned to the task of brushing the mare's mane.

"Do you always speak to your horse as you do to humans, or is it only when you have gone a long stretch of time away from one another?" His face was the picture of innocent curiosity.

She turned toward him, dropping the brush to her side and tilting her head. "Do other people not talk to their horses?"

He chuckled. "Not in the same manner as they do to other humans. Or if they do, they must do it in secret, outside the presence of eavesdroppers."

"How fortunate for them," she said with a provoking arch to her brows.

She brushed Cleopatra's mane, head cocked to the side in thought. "Perhaps I am indeed alone in speaking to my horse," she admitted, "but I have always considered Cleopatra to be my most loyal friend, and it is only natural that one should talk to one's friends, is it not?"

He considered her words. "Yes, I think I agree with you. However, I believe that, under normal circumstances among friends, it is more of a dialogue than a monologue. Having said that, I personally find your habits of humming and speaking to your horse to be refreshing. On par with your artistic talents, even."

His eyes teased her in the way that was so particularly his own.

She held her head high. "I am a woman of many talents, my lord."

A genuine laugh shook him. "Not least of which is that singular capability to say what I least expect."

She couldn't help but grin watching him laugh in her company. She found extraordinary pleasure in conversation with him. While it was clear that he enjoyed provoking her, he was also undeniably able to make her laugh, something she dearly loved to do.

She shook her head, smiling and looking back down at Cleopatra's mane which was nearly detangled. The knowledge that she would likely never see Lord Ashworth again once she returned to Fanny brought a lump to her throat and tempered her smile.

If she were to encounter him in the future, it would likely be hand-in-hand with Clara. If, on the other hand, she pursued employment instead of marriage, life would take her into an entirely different circle, and Lord Ashworth would only be one of many people she would be unlikely to encounter.

She was used to being apart from those she cared for, but she had never felt such bleakness as she did considering her future after leaving Wyndcross.

"I believe you have successfully brushed that particular part of the mane," Lord Ashworth said, a laugh in his voice.

She looked down. In her abstraction, she had been brushing the same part of the mane over and over again. She smiled wryly at herself and pulled her hand back from the mane, watching her mare swat her tail at a fly.

"Allow me," he said, reaching for the brush in her hand.

Their fingers touched briefly in the exchange, and Kate felt her heart beat erratically. It was a strange sensation. Had he felt it, too?

She looked up at him.

He was looking at her with searching eyes. Her heart beat so loudly she was sure he could hear it. She wondered for the hundredth time what he was thinking and whether he could read her thoughts just by looking at her. His eyes moved to her lips, and she swallowed.

He frowned suddenly, looking away toward Cleopatra and brushing her mane.

Kate felt her cheeks burn. Surely, he had been able to perceive her thoughts and emotions with such a penetrating gaze. Her blush took on a more scarlet hue as she considered the possibility that his frown was a result of perceiving her regard for him.

But why had he looked at her so intently?

"Well, Miss Matcham, she is a beautiful mare," he said, setting the brush on the stall. It did not escape her notice that he avoided returning the brush to her where they might risk direct contact again.

He paused for a moment before giving the mare a final stroke and adding with a half-smile, "Welcome to Wyndcross, Cleopatra." He turned to look at Kate. "How did I do? Am I supposed to listen for a response?"

Kate smiled weakly. "You are a quick study, my lord."

Lord Ashworth moved over to the other horse, crouching down to check a spot on one of the horse's front legs.

The action reminded Kate that she was still in the dark as to how her horse had arrived at Wyndcross so suddenly. She stroked Cleopatra's jaw, shaking her head.

"I haven't the slightest notion," she said absently, "how she comes to be here. I am extremely grateful, but it is very perplexing. I can only assume that Fanny sent her from London, though Fanny is normally too—" she paused as if rethinking the word she had been about to say "—well, let us say that she is normally too scatterbrained to think of such things. But I admit to feeling surprised that she would send no accompanying note. Perhaps there is one inside."

Lord Ashworth looked up at her from his hunched position and opened his mouth only to then close it. He smiled wryly before standing up.

"What is it?" Kate said.

Lord Ashworth smiled and shook his head. "Nothing at all." He set a foot in the stirrup and heaved himself over his horse. "Unfortunately, I must take my leave of you. I have some business to attend to before the dinner party begins." He directed his horse toward Kate, leaning to pet Cleopatra a final time and saying, "Take good care of your mistress, my girl, or you will have to answer to me." And with those words, he left the stables.

What exactly would he do were Cleopatra to ignore his endearing but ridiculous order?

She took in a breath. It would be most prudent to ignore his words, to ignore that moment of intensity between them.

It was easy to forget the divers barriers between them when she was in his presence, but her mind was all too ready to bring them to the forefront of her thoughts at the first opportunity.

It was possible that Clara had feelings for both Mr. Bradbury and Lord Ashworth. Perhaps she felt herself torn between the two gentlemen. It certainly didn't seem that way, particularly given Clara's painfully obvious regard for Mr. Bradbury and, by contrast, her more theatrical behavior in the presence of Lord Ashworth.

Lord Ashworth's feelings on the matter were just as much of a mystery to Kate. But whatever their feelings, an agreement existed between them, and it would be wrong of Kate to do anything to sabotage that, even were she capable of it—something she heavily doubted.

She had too often caught herself reliving conversations and situations in an attempt to understand just what Lord Ashworth thought and felt about her. It was as silly as it was fruitless to spend time thinking of such things.

For Lord Ashworth to look so far below himself as to pursue a woman in Kate's position would be seen as a dereliction of duty by many. And even entertaining the possibility that he would do so was nothing short of ridiculous and presumptuous on her part.

Her energy was much better spent deciding on a practical course for her future.

The excitement she had felt upon seeing Cleopatra was dampened significantly. She would likely have to sell the horse should she choose to support herself by employment.

A half-smile appeared on her face as she considered what a shame Lord Ashworth would think it if she could no longer speak to Cleopatra.

What would Simon think of her unusual habits? He was one of her closest friends, but he wasn't aware of her heedless humming, her conversation with animals, or the extent of her clumsiness. And even if he were aware, he would likely find it all nonsensical, childish, or unfathomable rather than amusing or endearing.

She had much to think on, and she spent the entirety of her toilette vacillating between her two options.

From the way Lindley furrowed her brows and made muted but disgruntled noises during her toilette, Kate knew she wasn't looking her best. She was not vain enough, however, to assume that her appearance would be a matter of importance to the host of strangers she would be meeting, and so she sighed softly at her reflection in the mirror and turned to leave her room.

20

"On your face, your lordship?" The valet stood in front of William, shoe blacking in one hand, a cloth in the other, and a blank stare on his face.

William's mouth twitched. "Yes, Spires. On my face." He waited a moment, but Spires seemed glued to the spot. He chuckled, reaching for the blacking and cloth, and turned toward the mirror.

He stared intently at his reflection for a moment, took in a quick breath, and dipped the cloth in the blacking. He wiped the cloth broadly across his forehead, down the bridge of his nose, and under his eyes which were narrowed in concentration. The smell of brandy and lemon—two of the many ingredients in Spires' blacking recipe—assailed his nose.

He ran the cloth through the blacking again and shot a quick glance at the reflection of Spires who seemed both horrified and on the verge of tears.

"Really, Spires," he said with amusement. "Surely you see the necessity. Brass buttons, white cravats, and gleaming Hessians hardly lend themselves to smuggling. Besides, I happen to know that you have a dozen of these blacking cases below stairs. A low supply cannot possibly be the cause of your misery."

"Will you also require that, my lord?" Spires looked down at the chair nearby. A large and ratty cloak lay over the chair back.

William chuckled. "I'm afraid so. I know the thought of my poor shoulders concealed under such an object must offend you."

"Deeply, my lord." He eyed the cloak again with misgiving. "It pains me to see you thus. To witness you involved in something so far beneath you."

William said nothing, continuing to rub the blacking on his cheeks. When his face was covered to his satisfaction, he put a hand out for the cloak.

Spires gingerly draped the cloak over his master's form, his mouth turned down in disgust, his hands held out from his body as if the article might be covered with plague.

When he saw the pair of boots his master requested him to bring over, Spires let out something between a whine and a groan.

William smiled appreciatively. He picked up a tattered and muddied boot and inspected it with admiration. "They are a sight, are they not? I think they bring the ensemble together nicely. Complete to a shade, as they say."

Spires closed his eyes in acute distress.

William let out a loud laugh. "Go, Spires. I've provoked you to the point of making you unwell. Go, then. I will finish up."

Spires looked torn between the urgent need to distance himself from the repugnant clothing he found himself surrounded by and the desire to fulfill his duties as a valet. A dismissive nod from Lord Ashworth tipped the scale, though, and he bowed and left the room with a look of gratitude.

William smiled wryly and shook his head as the door closed behind his valet. He placed a tricorne hat firmly on his head, turning toward the mirror, staring at his reflection with a critical eye.

There was a soft knock on the door, and Spires reappeared, recoiling slightly at the sight before him.

A lopsided grin appeared on his master's face. "I thought I told you to go!"

Spires took a deep breath, closing his eyes as if in a divine plea for restraint. "I only come to inform you that Lady Purbeck and Lady Anne await you below stairs."

William's brows shot up, and he grabbed for the pocket watch lying on the nearby table. "Good heavens, I had no idea the hour was so advanced. I shall need your help dressing after all. Tell my mother and sister that they will have to go without me."

"Very good, your lordship. I shall return in a moment," said Spires, bowing and closing the door behind him.

William snatched up the damp towel and began hurriedly wiping the blacking off his face.

21

Sir Richard and Lady Crofte were already welcoming guests in the drawing room when Kate entered. Sir Richard gave her a warm smile upon seeing her enter. Lady Crofte's smile, however, looked more like a grimace.

Clara looked characteristically charming in a dress of white crepe. She was engaged in conversation with a middle-aged couple who stood next to Mr. Bradbury—his parents, no doubt.

Kate smiled at Clara, noting her rosier-than-usual cheeks and how she looked to Mr. Bradbury as she responded to a comment, as if for affirmation.

The guests came in steadily, and Kate did her best to balance amiability and proper reserve as she met and conversed with them. It was with relief that she noticed Lady Anne walk through the door, accompanied by, Kate assumed, her mother and father. It did not escape Kate's notice that Lord Ashworth did not make one of their party. She ignored the vexatious feeling of disappointment she felt and went to greet Lady Anne.

Lady Anne noticed Kate right away and extended a hand toward her, smiling and linking her arm into Kate's. "You are walking without a limp."

Kate laughed. "I have given my ankle no say in the matter this evening. How horrid it would be to be remembered as the woman with the limp. I will pay for it all tomorrow, no doubt."

They were interrupted by the sound of Lady Anne's mother summoning her to exchange greetings with Lady Crofte. Kate made as if to move away, but Lady Anne kept their arms cuffed together.

Lady Anne greeted the Croftes with her customary kindness before turning to her mother and father.

"Father, Mama, I don't believe you've been introduced to Miss Matcham yet."

Kate looked at the woman who was the mother of Lord Ashworth. Like her children, she was tall. The way she held herself and the kind lines of her face reminded Kate more of Lady Anne than of Lord Ashworth, though. Her eyes, remarkably like those of her son, scanned Kate. It was not an unkind exercise, but rather one of curiosity.

Lord Purbeck glanced at her disinterestedly before resuming his slow surveyal of the crowd.

The Countess smiled at Kate and opened her mouth to speak but was interrupted by Lady Crofte.

"Ah yes, Miss Matcham is a guest of ours here at Wyndcross. But perhaps you remember her! She is the daughter of Jane Matcham. Or I should perhaps say Jane Dimmock, for she has remarried." She leaned in toward Lady Purbeck and said in undertones loud enough that Kate and the others were able to hear her, "You may not have seen her in some years. I'm afraid she has strayed from the company we keep."

Lady Purbeck's eyebrows lifted, and Lady Anne blinked slowly. Lord Purbeck considered Kate with a touch of contempt.

Kate's cheeks burned, but she returned Lord Purbeck's gaze.

Lady Crofte looked around at Lady Anne and the Purbecks. "But what is this?" she asked, scanning the crowd. "Is Lord Ashworth not joining us this evening?"

"I wish I could give you an answer," said Lady Purbeck. "I believe he planned to come, but we were obliged to leave without him."

Kate smiled to counteract the sensation of her heart sinking.

Lady Crofte frowned slightly and remarked how much they would miss him. She was tapped on the shoulder by Clara and obliged to excuse herself to greet another guest.

Lady Purbeck turned back to Kate, taking Kate's hands within her own. "Miss Matcham, it is such a pleasure to meet you."

How kind her eyes were. She felt relieved that Lady Crofte's remarks hadn't given Lady Purbeck a distaste for Kate's presence.

"Anne speaks so highly of you," Lady Purbeck said. "I have been anxious to make your acquaintance."

Kate's cheeks blushed in modest embarrassment. "As you know, my lady, your daughter is one of those wonderful people who, the kinder she is to someone, the better she thinks of them. And she has been crushingly kind to me. So, I'm afraid you must take what you have heard of me with a grain of salt. A very large grain."

Wrinkles appeared at the corner of Lady Purbeck's eyes as she smiled at Kate's words. Lord Purbeck blinked and walked away from the group. His wife gave only the slightest evidence of noticing his departure, her eyes moving briefly in his direction before returning to Kate.

"Anne is my little angel," she said, tucking one of Anne's stray hairs behind her ear. "But William has also been very complimentary, my dear, and he is not quite so generous with his praise in general. We are always so happy to welcome amiable company into the neighborhood, or back into the neighborhood, in your case."

No sooner had she finished speaking than Lord Ashworth appeared at her side, slightly breathless. He kissed his mother's and sister's cheeks and made his apologies. He smiled at Kate and made his bow to her.

Her heart seemed to skip at the sight of him. It was better not to look at him. She curtsied without meeting his eye.

"My dear," said Lady Purbeck, smiling at her son with affection. "We hear nothing from you all day, only for you to arrive quite out of breath and wearing what I can only assume is Spires' special boot blacking on your face."

She lifted a hand to his brow to wipe away the small streak of black, but his hand shot up to his hairline before hers. His fingers searched, and once they had found their mark, he pulled them away. The fingers were streaked with black.

Kate froze. She stared at the spot of black, fading into his hairline. She would likely not have noticed it, had it not been pointed out by Lady Purbeck. Now it was all she could see.

"Ah, yes," Lord Ashworth said with a laugh. "How clumsy of me. Spires left out the blacking, and I set a hand in it, unheeding. I must have touched my face after. I thought I had cleaned it all."

His mother wiped away what remained of the mark with her handkerchief. The loving gesture and the indulgent expression she wore made Lord Ashworth look like a little boy. It was an endearing exchange tainted by the circumstances under which it occurred.

Unless Lady Purbeck was an incredibly skilled actress, she was clearly unaware of the significance of shoe blacking on her son's face.

During their conversation in the wagon, Lord Ashworth had seemed sympathetic, both to her and to Jasper Clarkson. Was it possible that it had all been an act? That he was actually complicit? And the connection she had felt with him only hours ago in the stables —had she fallen in love with a skillful deceiver?

Lord Ashworth turned to her, and his smile wavered upon seeing her face. To her horror, Kate felt her eyes begin to sting and then water. She blinked rapidly.

He put out his hand to her, his expression of concern pronounced, but she excused herself from the group on the pretense that she had something in her eye.

Kate had no particular destination in mind, only a determination to put distance between herself and Lord Ashworth. Such an emotional reaction to his suspected duplicity came as a surprise to her. It was, of course, possible that his story was true. But viewed in connection with the circumstances at Weymouth, it seemed too great a coincidence.

"Miss Matcham."

She blinked rapidly to dry her eyes and turned toward the voice.

It was Simon. Arm in arm with a woman unfamiliar to Kate.

"Simon," Kate exclaimed. "What a surprise! I had no notion you would be here."

He inclined his head. "Aunt Agatha and Lady Crofte are friends.

Miss Matcham, I'd like to introduce you to Miss Susan Graham. She has been somewhat of a companion to Aunt Agatha."

He looked down at the young woman on his arm, and Miss Graham smiled shyly at him before looking to Kate.

Kate's jaw slackened, leaving her mouth open slightly. They were in love.

Dinner was announced, and Kate stood dazedly until she was approached by Mr. Bradbury, offering his arm. She smiled weakly at him as she placed her arm in his.

Clara went in on the arm of Lord Ashworth, as Lady Crofte looked on with a satisfied smile. Clara shot a backward glance at Mr. Bradbury and Kate, her smile flickering for a moment at the sight of them.

Kate found herself seated at the low end of the table with Mr. Bradbury on her right and Simon on her left. Simon's head was turned toward Miss Graham on his other side.

She looked to the head of the table where Lord and Lady Purbeck were seated nearest Lady Crofte and Sir Richard. They seemed a great distance away.

Lord Ashworth had his head down, speaking to the hunched octogenarian at his side who responded in a startlingly loud voice. Clara was to Lord Ashworth's other side and seemed unable to resist frequent glances at Mr. Bradbury.

Kate had begun the evening in a humor that was a confusing mix between anger and despondency, but she knew she had a duty to carry on conversation. The niggling thoughts about what Simon's newfound love meant for her she determinedly pushed aside for a time when she could put her mind to the problem. She smiled and talked, but her stomach felt tense.

Mr. Bradbury seemed to be in a distracted and somber mood. Having temporarily set aside her own concerns, she decided she would apply herself to whatever made him look so grave. Before long, she had successfully drawn him out and made him laugh. By dessert, she felt that they had come to a good understanding of one another.

Judging from the way his eyes frequently traveled to where Clara and Lord Ashworth sat, Clara occupied no insignificant place in his thoughts. From various casual comments Mr. Bradbury made, Kate seriously suspected that, absent pressure from other sources, he and Clara would have made a match of it.

Kate looked at Clara. She was talking to Lord Ashworth as his hands moved back and forth, cutting a carrot. From the way Clara's eyes constantly flitted to Kate, Kate knew she was the subject of their discussion.

Lord Ashworth's wrists rested on the table as his hands went still, the carrot left half-cut. He looked at Kate and then Simon and finally back to Kate.

Why was he looking at her in that way, as if seeing her in a new light? Her eyes shifted underneath his gaze, and her sleeves felt too tight. She turned toward Simon for something to occupy her, trying not to wonder what Lord Ashworth had just learned from Clara.

She leaned over to Simon. "Am I to wish you happy, then, friend?" The words were whispered. She didn't wish Miss Graham to overhear.

He looked over at Miss Graham. She was occupied in conversation with the gentleman to her right. Simon leaned back toward Kate, matching her low tones. "I wished to speak to you on that subject. I would prefer to do it in private, but I don't know that we will have opportunity." He looked around and seemed satisfied that no one would overhear.

"First and foremost, I wish to say that, if you have had a change of heart or mind about—" he again glanced around the table warily "—what we last discussed...." He looked at Kate, and she nodded her understanding. "I hope you know that I am a man of my word." He straightened himself in his chair.

Kate swallowed and put a hand over his with a grateful squeeze. She smiled at him and sighed.

"But?" she said. She schooled her expression into a teasing one. She couldn't let him see the dismay she was feeling.

"But," he said slowly. "Miss Graham and I have formed an attachment."

Kate's hand came up to cover her smile. She was genuinely happy for Simon. He deserved to love and be loved.

"Simon," she said. Her eyes stared into his forcefully. "If you hesitate even a moment in offering for Miss Graham for my sake, I shall never speak to you again." She let a smile break the gravity of her gaze. "Allow me to felicitate you."

Simon shook his head. "I have not yet asked her. Nor have I received any formal indication from her that she will accept me."

"The way she looks at you," Kate said, "is the most positive indication I can think of."

It was the same way Clara and Mr. Bradbury looked at one another.

It was decidedly not the way Clara looked at Lord Ashworth or the way that Lord Ashworth looked at her. But it would be best not to put much stock in that observation. It was possible that they simply knew one another too well and too long to exhibit the obvious signs typical of more immature love.

And if that were true, surely Clara was aware that Lord Ashworth was involved in the free-trade. It was entirely possible that it would be seen as a benefit to her, given her love of all things French.

While she could understand the dire circumstances which sometimes led people to free-trading, she could never agree with the means used. Many who had taken to the trade as an act of rebellion against the tyranny of their government seemed to have created a new tyranny of their own; others sought only to further cushion their wealth.

All the while, innocents like Jasper Clarkson and Kate's own father suffered the consequences.

She had been so sure that Lord Ashworth had been disturbed by Jasper's situation. How she could have so misinterpreted and misjudged him, she was at a loss to know. And when she remembered telling him of her father's death, something she had kept to herself for so long, she felt a flash of anger toward him.

Their eyes met once more at dinner, his looking a question at her; her own full of the confusion and betrayal she felt. Her eyes refused to hold his gaze.

When the men joined the women in the drawing room, Lady Crofte convinced Clara to play and sing at the pianoforte. Clara didn't seem to be in the mood for playing and singing, but she capitulated. Kate had come to see that Lady Crofte's requests were more like commands.

Kate stood at the back corner of the room, admiring Clara and enjoying the expression of unalloyed admiration which Mr. Bradbury wore as he watched her play and sing.

She became aware of Lord Ashworth standing at her side. He held a teacup and followed her gaze.

"Ah yes," he said, stirring his tea. "It's bellows to mend with Bradbury."

Her smile faded, and his own followed suit as he noticed her change in demeanor. He lowered the cup from his mouth, his expression bewildered.

"Miss Matcham," he said in a low voice, "have I done something to upset you?"

She looked at him for a moment. He seemed genuinely perplexed. Had she wronged him in her assumptions?

With the genuine concern she saw on his face, she needed a reminder of why she felt hurt and betrayal. Her eyes moved to his hairline. Or had it truly been just a bit of shoe blacking?

No, his strange and suspicious behavior in Weymouth, his choice of inn. It was too much coincidence.

She shook her head and looked away. If she were to speak, she would say something she would regret or, heaven forbid, succumb to her emotions.

He persisted, "How have I come to be in your bad graces? You must know that not for the world would I offend you."

Kate felt eyes on them and noticed Lord Purbeck staring at them from the other side of the room. His eyes held no humor, and his jaw was clenched.

"Please," she said with a weak attempt to smile for the eyes watching, "no purpose can be served...." A lump formed in her throat. "Excuse me," she said, moving away from him toward the tea tray. She poured herself a cup of tea, willing her hands to stop shaking so treacherously.

She couldn't remember the last time her emotions had threatened to overcome her in public. Much less twice in the same evening. She owed it to her hosts to remain at the party until the guests left, but she spent what was left of the evening flitting from one person to another to ensure that she had no chance to interact with Lord Ashworth.

Her feelings toward him had become bewilderingly complex, and she had no desire to converse with him in front of other people without time for reflection. Only then could she decide what her comportment should be toward him.

She seemed not to be the only one whose enjoyment of the evening had suffered. As Clara rose from the pianoforte, she was approached by Mr. Bradbury. Clara raised her chin defiantly and passed by him without a word. Mr. Bradbury stood still, his cheeks reddening.

Kate watched Clara who, reaching the tea table, looked briefly over her shoulder at the man she had just slighted. Whatever Clara had wished to see, the sight of Mr. Bradbury's back to her caused to raise her chin high a little higher and make her way over to Lord Ashworth.

BY THE TIME KATE REACHED HER BEDROOM, EXHAUSTION MADE HER eyes dry and her eyelids heavy. Thoughts rushed around in her head despite the haze of fatigue enveloping her.

"I don't like what this place is doing to you, Miss," Lindley said with a darkling look as she helped Kate out of her dress.

Kate sighed. "And you so certain that leaving London would be just what I needed."

Lindley lifted her head. "That was before I knew what type of place this was, Miss. I don't hesitate to tell you that I don't like it at all. And I don't believe Lady Hammond would approve if she knew the half of it."

"Good gracious, Lindley," said Kate, turning to her maid in disbelief. "Whatever could she disapprove of?"

Lindley seemed to balk, looking at her mistress with a searching gaze before returning to the task at hand. "Never you mind, Miss. It isn't my place, and I beg your pardon for forgetting myself."

Kate's eyes narrowed. "No, no, Lindley. That won't do. You will tell me, if you please, what you meant."

Lindley paused with Kate's night cap in her hands. Kate looked at her expectantly, and Lindley rubbed the strings between her fingers absently, finally breaking the silence to say, "There is quite a bit of talk below stairs, Miss, and though you know I don't hold with servant gossip or listening at doors, I've seen my fair share of strange goings-on as well."

Kate's expectant expression had morphed into one of barely concealed impatience when Lindley mentioned talk below stairs, but upon hearing that her maid had witnessed things herself, she swallowed the rebuke she had been about to give.

She didn't want to encourage Lindley in gossip about the family who had received her into their home, but Lindley was not the type to listen to or relay frivolous tales from the servants.

"Go on," she said in a cautious voice.

Lindley looked hesitant. "Perhaps what they say is true, Miss, and ignorance is bliss."

"Perhaps. But I'm afraid we will not know in this case. You will explain."

Lindley sighed and pursed her lips, "Just that there are goings on in this house that aren't what I'd call respectable, Miss. Not to mention the matter of you being brought here under false pretenses." She hung up Kate's dress.

Kate's brows knitted. "What false pretenses?"

Lindley looked at her with an amused smile. "Well, Miss, it would seem that her ladyship and Miss Crofte were under the impression that, in inviting you to Wyndcross, they were welcoming quite the heiress. Evidently they hoped to make a match of it between you and Mr. Crofte." Lindley's shoulders shook with laughter until she saw Kate's face.

Kate's eyes were wide and round, glazed over. Her mind, already full to the brim with conflicting thoughts, reeled at Lindley's words. Images from recent memories flashed through her mind. Things which had confused her began to make sense, and things she thought she had understood suddenly took on a different hue and meaning.

She had been flattered by Lady Crofte's initial benevolence toward her. Lady Crofte had been very attentive during her stay, and though Kate had always suspected that her hostess' kind demeanor was somewhat tenuous, she had tried to disabuse her mind of such unhandsome suspicions.

However, the past few days had gone further to prove than to disprove such suspicions, as Lady Crofte's demeanor shifted from attentive to something nearer contempt.

Kate had been at a loss to discover the cause, and, consistent with her practice of believing the best of everyone, had attributed it to her hostess being in a bad humor. But coupled with both Lady Crofte's and Clara's past attempts to throw Henry and Kate in company together, and Henry's own stiffness toward her—no doubt rebellion and resentment at being forced to court her—it made sense of so much that had perplexed Kate.

When had Lady Crofte's kindness begun to wane?

Kate remembered the breakfast parlor where she had received her mother's letter.

"Miss!"

Kate looked at Lindley. Her maid wore a concerned expression.

Kate turned the conversation to less fraught avenues before dismissing her maid for the night. She lay down on her bed, staring at the ceiling, arms extended to each side, her palms up.

Now that she had a moment to herself, she couldn't even decide where to begin. What was most pressing? Trying to understand the Croftes' motives? Sorting through her thoughts and feelings in regard to Lord Ashworth? Deciding her future now that both an inheritance and marriage to Simon had disappeared from the equation?

More than she had realized, Simon had been her safety net. Knowing that he would gladly marry her, that he would care for her, had been a constant which had kept her from succumbing to despondency over her situation. Her options were now employment or continuing to hang upon her stepfather's sleeve.

The sacrifice of some of her own dignity seemed inevitable no matter which route she chose.

22

When Kate awoke the next morning, her eyes opened to the ceiling above. It was the same view her eyes had closed to, and her arms were still outstretched. Her mind jumped instantly to the point where it had left off when sleep had mercifully overtaken her just a few short hours before.

Her feelings toward Lord Ashworth should have the least bearing upon her decisions, but they refused to be ushered from the forefront of her mind. Even in the moments where she successfully pushed Lord Ashworth to the side to address other concerns, she found herself at an utter loss.

While the information she had gleaned from Lindley had initially brought enlightenment, upon further inspection, Kate found herself with just as many questions as answers.

Nothing made sense—Lord Ashworth's behavior, Clara's situation with Lord Ashworth and Mr. Bradbury, even Kate's own options regarding her future. The thought that she had been brought to Wyndcross only for her reputed inheritance made her feel sick inside. Sick at the feeling of being valued for a fortune; sick with a heavy feeling of obligation to the Croftes for her having presumed upon them as an unknowing imposter; sick with a feeling of loneliness.

It was in valiantly masking this dismal state of mind that Kate met Lady Anne for a morning ride. She had considered sending a note to Ashworth Place to cancel the plans, but she needed fresh air to clear her head.

Familiar enough with Kate to know what type of ride she would most enjoy, Lady Anne guided them toward the coast where they followed a small path. It passed by a large cove and down to the pebbled beach where white cliffs loomed above. With each step the horses' hooves poked hoof-shaped pockets in the pebbles below.

Kate looked out at the waves rolling onto shore, some approaching them closely enough that sea spray tickled their faces. As each wave receded, it dragged pebbles back out to the ocean in an irresistible and rhythmic motion. It was calming.

"Are you well, Kate?" Lady Anne's voice intruded into her thoughts.

She smiled reassuringly at Lady Anne. "Yes, only caught in a daze of admiration, yet again." Did Lady Anne, too, believe her to be an heiress to a large fortune? If she did, Kate hadn't noticed anything in her demeanor to suggest it.

"Oh, don't apologize," said Lady Anne. "I know you are an admirer of nature, and I am happy if our path gives you something to admire."

Though the beauty of the scene had not been the subject of her thoughts, Kate smiled and stretched her neck to look up at the tall cliffs above. Two gulls circled above in the sky.

"It is very majestic, isn't it?" Kate said.

"It is. I fear I have come to take it for granted." Lady Anne gazed wistfully out at the ocean. "I shall miss it terribly when we leave."

Kate frowned. "Why must you leave?"

Lady Anne looked down at the pebbly beach below. "Our stay was never meant to be permanent. Ashworth Place is William's residence, and he has been working for years to put to rights the myriad problems which have resulted from generation after generation of financial incompetence and lavish living. My mother and I joined him because he likes the company and my father because he prefers Ashworth Place to his own seat in Bere Regis. But we will naturally remove there when William marries."

Kate was momentarily silent. Did Clara know that Lord

Ashworth's family was in financial trouble? How far was Lord Ashworth willing to go to bring the estate back to solvency?

Kate pushed her thoughts aside. "Then you will be leaving soon?"

Lady Anne cocked her head to the side. "I hope not, unless you know something I don't." She directed a teasing look at Kate.

It was Kate's turn to look confused, and her cheeks blushed. "Oh no! Only—" she hesitated. "I was under the impression that a match was impending. It was clumsy of me."

"No, no," Lady Anne reassured her. "Do tell me what you meant. I'm very curious."

Kate's confusion grew. Was it possible that Lady Anne was unaware of the arrangement between her brother and Clara? Lady Crofte had spoken of it as though it were common knowledge, at least between the families.

"I had gathered," Kate spoke slowly, "that there was an understanding between your families."

"Between what families?"

"Your family and the Crofte family." Kate said the words slowly.

Lady Anne scrunched her nose. "What? Between William and Clara?"

"Yes." Kate took her lips between her teeth, feeling foolish.

Lady Anne looked contemplative for a moment before asking, "May I ask how you arrived at such a conclusion?"

Kate bit her lip, and Lady Anne rushed on, "It is just that I know William quite well, and I am tolerably certain that no understanding exists between him and Clara."

Kate hesitated, still biting her lip. Had she perhaps misunderstood Lady Crofte?

No, Lady Crofte had been quite plain with her. Unmistakably so.

"I don't mean to press you," said Lady Anne, reaching over to grasp Kate's hand reassuringly. "I understand your hesitation. But I am sure you can appreciate that whoever is communicating such untruths must be set right. Otherwise, it could create a very awkward situation for both my brother and Clara."

There was no denying the force of her argument. Surely Lord Ashworth did not deserve to be forced into marriage simply because his and Clara's names were being paired together unjustly. But would she be doing Clara a disservice by divulging anything more to Lady Anne?

Kate was certain that Clara and Mr. Bradbury were in love. It seemed unthinkable that Clara would wish to marry anyone besides the person her heart belonged to—particularly since her love was returned. But that was still a decision for Clara to make. Any interference from Kate might very well be unwelcome.

If there was truly an understanding between Lord Ashworth and Clara, though, surely it would not be damaged by Lady Anne being made aware.

"You are quite right, of course," Kate replied. "I was told that Clara and your brother were promised to one another by Lady Crofte. She seemed to believe that the understanding between your families was of long standing."

Lady Anne nodded and sighed. "I might have guessed as much. Lady Crofte has hoped for a union between our families for as long as I can remember."

Kate felt relief bubble inside her. Lord Ashworth was not promised to be married. Not to Clara. Not to anyone, apparently. Her mouth twisted to the side. "But why would Lady Crofte talk so surely of such a thing if it is not true?"

Lady Anne watched Kate's bewilderment with a half-smile. "I think I know the reason." But before Kate could inquire about her meaning, Lady Anne continued. "I believe William knows of Lady Crofte's wishes and has considered the option. But nothing more. He has been far too engaged in the business of the estate for the past few years to have devoted much time to courting."

"That is very admirable," Kate said, unsure how else to respond.

"Yes, there are many luxuries attached to a title, but there are also many duties and obligations. My grandfather and great-grandfather seemed not to have cared for anything but the luxuries. William, however, understands his duty to maintain the estate and, preferably, to leave it better than he found it. He is very conscious of the weight of that duty."

How far might he go to relieve that weight? Certainly, such

pressing financial difficulties coupled with a strong sense of duty could drive someone to engage in smuggling.

"I admire your brother's sense of duty to his family." Kate was unsure what else to say. She thought of her sisters and mother; their hopes for her to make a good match. "I wish I could be as dutiful to my own."

"I am sure you are every bit as dutiful."

"I am not," Kate said simply. "My family hopes for me to make a good match. I have not been able to bring myself to do it, though. I have been too selfish to marry out of duty."

Lady Anne looked at her hands on the reins. "If I may, Kate, I would not encourage you to sacrifice your own happiness merely for the social possibilities it might afford your family." She paused, taking the reins in hand and looking to Kate. "I trust this will stay between us, but my own mother and father married out of duty. Their marriage has been a painful one. It is not a fate my mother or myself or my brother would wish upon anyone."

Kate digested what Lady Anne said. But she found herself facing the same dilemma she had faced before coming to Wyndcross. Which was the more miserable option between marrying out of necessity or facing a life of penury and unrelenting work? Lady Anne might be right, but she gave her advice from the position of security which had been afforded by the very same type of marriage she was counseling against.

In any case, a marriage of convenience was no longer within Kate's reach.

23

When Kate arrived back at Wyndcross, she found Clara sitting in the morning room with a sampler in her hand, attempting to unravel a roll of thread. As she entered the room, Clara threw down the roll in frustration and looked up. Her expression changed from one of frustration to something between a smile and a grimace.

"Oh dear," said Kate with a laugh in her voice. "This is a scene I am all too familiar with." She walked over to Clara and sat down on the floor next to her chair, picking up the thread and beginning to sort through the chaotic entanglement. The conversation naturally turned to the dinner party, which Clara declared to have been terribly insipid.

"And Mama can never bear to end a party," she complained, "without obliging me to play the pianoforte, which she knows I dislike above all things."

Kate's fingers tugged at a particularly tight knot. "You may dislike it, but I can tell you that others did not." She paused a moment, stealing a glance at Clara. "Mr. Bradbury in particular did not seem able to tear his eyes away. Indeed, I believe his father was obliged to speak his name several times before he was attended to." Kate winked.

Clara tossed her head. "Pooh! What do I care for the opinion of Mr. Bradbury?"

Kate's fingers slowed their movement. She hesitated before saying, "I thought you both cared a great deal for one other's opinions."

Clara snorted her disdain, but Kate wondered if it was the makings of tears which she spotted in Clara's eyes. "I'm sure I have no time to spend worrying about the Mr. Bradburys of the world when I will be a countess."

Kate was silent. She could only hope that Clara was in a fit of pique to speak so ill of Mr. Bradbury. But for what reason? They had appeared to be on such good terms just a few days ago, indeed, even at the beginning of the dinner party.

Shortly after her conversation with Clara, a letter was brought from Fanny. Fanny had no patience for letter writing and had made it a practice to dictate her letters to Kate instead of writing them herself, but this one she had clearly written herself. Her script had an impatient flow to it.

DEAREST KATE,

I HAVE BEEN QUITE REMISS IN REPLYING TO YOU, BUT RECEIVING LORD *Ashworth's letter reminded me that I hadn't yet responded to you. Injured your ankle? Of all the things! I hope you are quite mended by the time you receive this, but please take better care. I worry so for you.*

We arrived in Brighton two days ago, and things here are very much as you would expect. I have so much to tell you that has happened since you left. Can you believe that Lady Carville has been quite throwing her youngest daughter —the one with the hideous freckles—at all the bachelors in Brighton? Though no one will take her, poor thing!

I was not aware that you were acquainted with Lord and Lady Purbeck, Kate. You might have mentioned it, as I would naturally wish for you to convey my best wishes to the Countess who is a friend of mine. In any case, how very thoughtful of Lord Ashworth to send for Cleopatra! His letter was quite civil, and he insisted that it was no trouble at all. I own that I wish I had sent her to you myself, but the truth is that I am quite selfish, as you know, and never even thought of it. I know you'll forgive me, though, because you are always doing so.

I have much else to tell you, but you know I can't abide writing letters, so I will treasure up all the tidbits and tales as an incentive for you to come to Brighton as soon as you may. And now I must ready myself for the Regent's ball tonight. Walmsley is escorting me. And since I can already hear you asking, yes, I have accepted him. We will likely marry after Michaelmas. When will you return to us? Brighton is so dull without you!

LOVE,
Fanny

KATE'S HEART RACED AS SHE READ AND REREAD THE THIRD paragraph, certain that she had misread the words on the page. *"And how thoughtful of Lord Ashworth to send for Cleopatra?"* Surely there was some misunderstanding.

Her mind returned to the day before when she had found Cleopatra in the stables. Lord Ashworth's unexplained presence there with his own horse hadn't made her wonder at the time, but given Fanny's letter, it made more sense. If he was indeed responsible for her horse's sudden arrival, though, why had he not said something? And why in the world would he have gone out of his way to send for her horse?

The mess of feelings she had been attempting to sort through tangled even further at this new knowledge. She couldn't reconcile the various things she knew of Lord Ashworth, and it frustrated her to no end.

Lady Anne's insistence that no understanding existed between her brother and Clara had fanned the persistent but flickering hope which had refused to be extinguished. The resentment Kate felt toward Lord Ashworth for being involved in smuggling was, she admitted reluctantly, further evidence of the depth of her feelings for him.

Knowing now that he had been kind and thoughtful enough to transport her horse to Wyndcross added to both her confusion and her appreciation for him. How could someone be so thoughtful and yet so duplicitous?

Her conversation with Clara had brought her spirits down again, and along with them any inclination to dwell on a future that included Lord Ashworth in anything but the role of Clara's husband. The irony of finally coming to feel the desire to marry someone she could not have was not lost on her.

If she could not have Lord Ashworth, what did it matter whom she married or where she ended up?

She wished she had never come to Wyndcross. Before, she had accepted her future, if not with happiness, at least with equanimity. Her visit to Wyndcross had provided her with a glimpse of what she had desired but had thought could not exist.

Feeling an unbearable restlessness nag her, she descended the stairs to dinner, blessing the early dining hours they kept in the country—they would allow her to excuse herself from the dinner table complaining, not untruthfully, of a headache.

She made her way to the stables with the knowledge that there was enough light left for a short ride, feeling only a twinge of guilt at the knowledge that the Croftes would assume her to be in bed. But only a ride would clear her head in the way she needed.

24

Kate tucked a piece of hair back into her bonnet. The ride had been gusty, and great care had been needed to steer clear of the cliff edges that the dirt riding path hugged so closely—cliffs which dropped precipitously down onto jagged rocks and choppy sea water.

Cleopatra's wet coat glistened a final time as the sun dipped behind the hills. Its final rays peeked through the barn door. The diminishing light left the surrounding countryside a dull blue after a glowing sunset. Kate needed to act quickly before the light was completely gone.

As had been the case when she had entered the stables earlier that evening, there was no sound of anyone else, and only a single light within.

It was an unusual circumstance, but it was very likely that the Croftes had given some of the servants a night off after the previous evening's dinner party. In any event, she didn't mind unsaddling and brushing Cleopatra herself, so she lit one of the candles near Cleopatra's stall, knowing she would need its light before long.

She lifted the saddle off the horse's warm back, the smell of wet horse hair permeating the air. Cleopatra's mane was unusually tangled after their gusty ride along the coast, but there was no time to attend to it. She spoke softly to Cleopatra as she brushed her sweat-covered coat, praising her for the good ride they had enjoyed.

Though she felt no closer to deciding on her future than before her ride, Kate felt much calmer and more collected. She had no marriage prospects. Employment was the only option to achieve the independence she craved.

The next hurdle would be to obtain a reference. Fanny would never agree to do it; she would never agree to Kate's plans.

She hefted the saddle over her shoulder, slipped the bridle over her arm, and made her way carefully toward the tack room. The absence of the usual sconces left very little light in the barn. As she approached the room, precious few beams from the candle reached her destination.

Crossing the threshold of the tack room, her boot hit something round and wooden, sending her and her load crashing to the dirty floor. She let out a frustrated cry. The saddle lay before her, but her eyes searched the dark in vain for the bridle.

She hunted her surroundings with her hands but had no success. Cursing her luck, she picked herself off the ground and returned to Cleopatra's stall for the candle she had lit.

When she returned, the gleam of the small candle cast moody shadows along the rows of tack. Kate looked down near her feet where the missing bridle lay and bent down to pick it up. Immediately to its right lay the culprit responsible for her fall—a wooden object which looked to have been covered up by a canvas which her clumsiness had displaced.

She let the light fall on the object that had tripped her. It was a wooden tub, out of place in a room full of saddles, bridles, and bits. Her brow wrinkled in confusion, but she bent down to replace the canvas. She lifted the corner off the ground, and the light of the candle reached underneath.

Her eyes grew wide and her jaw tensed.

Beneath the canvas were rows, stacked four feet high, of wooden barrels.

The villager Sally's words reverberated in her head: *"Lord knows what's hiding inside with all these free-traders about."*

The sound of footsteps on dirt met her ears. She turned, holding out the candle in her hand to illuminate whoever had joined her in the stables.

The man squinted as the light hit him. He wore a uniform.

Oy!" he said between a whisper and shout. He carried a tankard in one hand, and liquid dripped from it, landing in the puddle which had formed on the floor when he had jolted in surprise.

Kate breathed a sigh of relief and lowered the candle which shook in her jittery hand. "Thank heaven! You're an officer. I thought you were perhaps a free-trader."

The man paused in the act of walking toward her, a hand on the pistol he wore on at his side. "That's right. I'm an officer—Preventive Officer Roberts, ma'am. And who might you be?"

It suddenly occurred to her that he might suspect her of a connection to the barrels she stood before. "Catharine Matcham, sir. I am a guest here at Wyndcross. I stumbled upon these barrels as I was trying to return my horse's saddle."

"Well don't you worry your mind over the barrels. This is no place for a young lady. It isn't safe."

What was he doing there, anyway? "Not safe, sir?"

He put a hand down to the pistol at his side. "That's right. I'm here on orders. Investigating."

"Investigating whom? The Croftes? Surely not!"

But she was not sure. Not at all. *"There are goings on in this house that aren't what I'd call respectable."* That's what Lindley had said. Kate had never inquired into what she had meant. She had been too caught up in her own troubles.

"Don't worry your head, ma'am," said Officer Roberts. "I have things well in hand. But I must insist, for your own safety, that you leave."

HENRY LAID HIS HAND OF CARDS ON THE TABLE AND TOOK A SIP from his glass, looking at Lord Ashworth with triumph. "Ha!" he said.

The corner of Lord Ashworth's mouth twitched, and he laid down his hand.

Henry's triumph turned to disbelief, and he smacked the table. "The devil's own luck!" he exclaimed.

The door opened, and Clara rushed in. She stopped abruptly at the sight of Lord Ashworth.

"Clara," Henry said. "What the devil?"

"I must speak with you instantly, Henry," she said, glancing at Lord Ashworth.

Henry turned away from her and began picking up the cards. "It will have to wait, Clara. We're about to begin a new hand, and I have a feeling my luck is finally going to turn." He shuffled the cards. "You shan't fleece me tonight, Ash." He took a long swallow of the drink in front of him and then began shuffling the cards.

Lord Ashworth looked at Clara consideringly before turning his eyes to his own hand.

Clara looked exasperated. "Henry, I really must speak with you. It cannot wait, even if your luck is supposedly about to turn—a claim which I highly doubt, seeing as you've never been able to do anything but lose at cards!" she said waspishly.

Before Henry could retort, Lord Ashworth intervened.

"Henry, let us resume this game another evening." He looked at his pocket watch. "I gave my mother my word that I would make an appearance at this unfortunate evening party where she insists on hosting all the most cantankerous geriatrics in the vicinity." He rose as he spoke, glancing at Clara.

"Nonsense, Ash. One last hand." Henry's words had begun to slur slightly, and as he reached to tug on Lord Ashworth's coat to prevent his departure, he nearly tipped over his chair.

"Oh, for heaven's sake, Henry," cried Clara, losing the last vestige of patience. "I must speak with you instantly, or we will very likely be ruined by your stupid smuggling!"

Henry whipped his head around, sloshing some of the brandy in his glass onto his pantaloons.

Lord Ashworth paused in his efforts to put his coat back on, while Clara bit her lip and drew back as if to shield herself from the repercussions of her words.

Her words effectively jolted Henry from his inebriated state, and he looked at her aghast.

"Clara, you...." he sputtered, unable to find the words to express his feelings.

"If you need to be private," Lord Ashworth said, "but say the word, and I will go. But I should perhaps make it clear that I am well acquainted with the particulars of what is being hidden in your stables."

"The devil you are!" Henry exclaimed, bolting upright.

Lord Ashworth's mouth turned up in a half-smile.

Henry looked bewildered. "Knew your father was part of it all, but I'm dashed if I thought you were, too!"

Lord Ashworth scoffed. "While you were undoubtedly sound asleep, I was heaving those accursed barrels into the tack room."

"Dash it, Ash!" Henry cried. "I was ordered not to be there. That's not to say I was sorry about it. Those barrels are devilish heavy this time."

"Have you looked inside?" Lord Ashworth's intense gaze rested on Henry. He didn't blink as he waited for the answer.

Henry sat back with his glass in hand, kicking his heels up on the table as he considered for a moment. "Not this shipment, I haven't. But what a fellow I should appear if I was forever asking to see inside of every barrel."

"None of this matters!" Clara shouted in exasperation. "There is a Preventive Officer in the stables at this very moment."

Henry sat bolt upright but then relaxed. "Ahh, that'll be Officer Roberts."

"And," Clara continued, "Kate is in there as well!" She tossed her head. "So much for the headache she claimed."

Lord Ashworth snatched his hat off the table. "I must bid you goodnight," he said as he pulled the door open. He turned back toward Clara and Henry. "I will go to the stables. Leave Miss Matcham to me."

The door shut with a smack.

Henry turned toward Clara. "What a completely beetle-headed thing to do!" He slammed a fist on the table, sending stray cards trembling onto the floor. "Especially if you're hoping to snag Ash for a husband. What if he informed on us?"

"Well he obviously won't." Clara glowered at him.

"And a luckier chance there never was," Henry said, shaking his head and making his way toward the door.

"Rich of you to scold me," Clara cried, "when you are the one who has allowed smuggled goods to be stored in our stables."

"It's only for a couple of nights." Henry reached for the door.

"If the officer has found it, it makes no difference how long it has been here!"

Henry laughed. "Found it? He helped put it there! Roberts is with us."

Clara drew back. "Really?"

Henry nodded impatiently.

Clara tapped her foot, arms folded. "And what of Kate? How do you know she won't inform on you?"

"She wouldn't." Henry shook his head dismissively. "She couldn't."

"Oh, wouldn't she? Have you forgotten? The Matchams have always been opposed to smuggling. Emmerson and his men killed her father, for heaven's sake! If anyone were to inform on you, it would be Kate Matcham."

Henry chewed his lip, his forehead wrinkled. He shook his head. "It's too late to do anything but forge ahead. You don't know these men, Clara. They're stark, raving mad! If I don't fulfill my end...." He shuddered.

"What do we do about Kate, then?" she said, a frantic note in her voice.

Henry chewed his lip again. "We must make sure that she has no chance to do any mischief tomorrow." He looked at Clara with a grim expression. "If you wish to have your precious Mr. Bradbury, we can't afford to foul things up. As long as we can get through tomorrow night, we have no reason to worry." He sounded as though he was trying to reassure himself as much as Clara.

She hardly looked comforted by his words. "Lord Ashworth said he would handle things."

Henry rubbed his chin. "Normally I'd trust my life to Ash. But if there's anything I've learned, it's that you can't trust a man in love. And I can't take any chances. Not this time. Not even on Ash. My life is at stake."

Clara's cheeks burned red. "A man in love?"

Henry dropped his head resignedly. "Oh, Clara, surely you aren't still miffed about that? You want Bradbury, don't you?"

Clara nodded, a tear falling down her cheek. When she spoke, it was something between a sob and a shout. "But Kate seems determined that I shan't have either of them!"

25

Kate walked toward the manor, staring at the dimly lit ground before her. She felt equal parts relieved and anxious after her interaction with Officer Roberts. The excisemen were aware of the smuggling operation—this was what she had wanted. But the Croftes were implicated in it all. That was much less desirable and much more awkward.

"Miss Matcham? Thank heaven."

Kate looked up in time to see Lord Ashworth's hands reaching toward her to prevent a collision. He was short of breath.

"Are you quite well?" he asked, bracing her elbows with his hands and looking at her with concern.

She looked up at him, at a loss for words. Was there no one she could unburden her mind to?

His eyes raced back and forth between hers. "Clara said you had gone to bed with a headache. But then she saw you ride into the stables. I came to find you."

She felt sick with confusion. Who was this man? She couldn't make any sense of him. He looked at her with such genuine concern. Every interaction with him had felt genuine.

But Weymouth, the blacking on his face—those seeds of doubt had taken root. If Lord Ashworth was involved in smuggling, unburdening herself to him would be the act of a fool.

"It's not safe to be alone in the dark," he said, and there was an inflection of anger in his voice.

Officer Roberts's words came to mind. He had said something similar.

"I won't press you to confide in me," he said, "but I hope you know that you can rely on my discretion. You can trust me."

Trust him? She looked into his eyes, searching for any hint of guile. She found none.

This frustrated her more than it pleased her. How could he speak to her of further confidences when he seemed not to value what she had confided in him about her father? Was it possible to be so dead to one's own conscience that one could speak such things while acting in direct contradiction to them?

She met his eyes, and what she saw pained her. He looked almost frantic for her to say something. It was difficult to imagine him as anything else but what she saw before her: the concerned and caring gentleman her heart had stubbornly chosen. Her heart had never led her astray before. Why would it do so now?

The burden of her discovery weighed on her mind heavily, and she wavered again in her resolution to keep her own counsel. If she did speak with him of her suspicions, perhaps she could learn whether he was truly involved by observing his reaction. She felt paralyzed with indecision, and the pause grew long.

"I should not be keeping you," Lord Ashworth said, breaking the unwieldy silence. There was a note of frustration in his voice. "Allow me to walk you to the door."

Kate gave a small, grateful smile but maintained her silence as they walked toward the manor alongside one other. Lord Ashworth filled the silence with mundane small talk which required no response from Kate. The gesture was not lost on her, and she felt grateful that he had not pressed her to speak, even though he had clearly desired her to.

"—as you can imagine," he said with a chuckle, "it has been no small endeavor to apologize to all the people Henry's and my friendship has affected."

"Lord Ashworth." She interrupted him.

He slowed to a stop. "Yes?"

She took in a slow breath. "Do you remember when I spoke to you of my father's death?"

"I remember it well." His reply was soft, as if he knew that the subject deserved a subdued tone.

She paused. Was it guilt?

Could he say such a thing with near-reverence if he were secretly engaged in the very same activities with the very same people that caused her father's death? She couldn't find it in herself to believe it of him. "I believe I mentioned the promise I made to myself after his passing." Her voice was level, but her eyes stung.

They paused in their walk, and she turned to face him. His gaze was direct, intense.

"I remember," he said, nodding. "You promised yourself that you wouldn't let it be for naught, what he had done; that you would act if you should ever find yourself in a similar situation."

She nodded, anxiously rubbing the fabric of her dress between her fingers.

"I find myself in a situation where I must act on that promise."

He waited, his gaze never faltering.

"I have reason to suspect that the Croftes are some of those people I swore to stand up to." She bit the inside of her lip as she watched for his reaction. If he looked at all uncomfortable, she would have her answer.

Lord Ashworth was silent for a moment. "You have seen the barrels in the stables."

It wasn't a question.

"You know?" Kate drew back from him.

"I am aware of the situation, as are the Preventive Officers."

Kate let out a large breath. Relief made her feel lightheaded. "Yes, I was met by one of the officers in the stables."

"Roberts?"

She nodded. "You know him?"

Lord Ashworth nodded.

"He claims he has everything under control," Kate said.

"Let us leave it to Roberts, then."

Kate let out a puff of air, shaking her head as she reflected on the interaction. "There was something strange about him." She thought of the tankard he held in his hand when she had met him. What kind of serious investigation involved a tankard?

When Lord Ashworth spoke, it was slowly. He seemed to be choosing his words with care. "I have every confidence in the law officers to handle this. Thank you for confiding in me—you've done right to do so." He glanced at the manor. "I mustn't keep you out here in the dark. But I beg you to keep this to yourself. Don't do anything. It is too dangerous."

Kate's eyebrows snapped together. "You would have me break my promise to myself."

"No," he said. "I would have you leave the matter in my hands. In the hands of the law. To entangle yourself in such an affair can only do you harm."

She knew a moment's doubt. Could he have another, less altruistic motivation for asking her not to get involved? "If something is the right thing to do, is danger to oneself really a reason to avoid it?" She looked up at him, her eyes challenging him.

"Your integrity does you credit," he said. "Would that more of us were like you. Please at least promise that you will advise me before taking any action."

She shook her head. "I can't make such a promise. I admit that I am not well-versed in the particulars of smuggling, but I understand enough to know that time is of the essence. I can't say that I trust Officer Roberts. I have heard tales of excisemen turned free-traders."

Lord Ashworth thought for a moment. "What do you propose to do? Inform on the Croftes and then sit down to dine with them, treating yourself to some sweetmeats as they are arrested and removed from Wyndcross Manor by the authorities?"

Kate bit her lip. She simply couldn't continue trespassing on the Croftes' hospitality while potentially orchestrating their ruin.

Lord Ashworth continued, "We can hardly discuss particulars at this hour of night and in this courtyard. Allow me to call on you tomorrow." Seeing her open her mouth to protest, he rushed on, "I promise I will not attempt to dissuade you from whatever plan you have in mind, provided it is reasonable. But I think it essential that this plan be well-thought out, and two heads are better than one, they say."

She considered for a moment, acknowledging the good sense in his words and wondering what her father would do in her place. She felt unsure and alone and suddenly exhausted by it all.

There was no denying that sharing the burden of deciding upon a course of action was an inviting thought. And though she felt a small doubt niggle at her, her heart told her to lay the load at the feet of Lord Ashworth.

She nodded and sighed.

A look of relief settled onto his face, and he grimaced in understanding.

They continued their walk, arriving at the door without speaking another word. Lord Ashworth turned toward Kate once again, scanning her face. She returned his gaze, feeling simultaneous relief and uncertainty about placing things in his hands.

He reached a hand to her face, brushing his thumb lightly over her brow as if to smooth the creases away. "Don't fret."

Her breath caught in her chest.

He put a finger under her chin, softly pulling her head back to face him and looked her in the eye.

"Trust in me, Kate." He brought her hand up and lightly kissed it, then opened the door for her before turning back toward the stables.

Kate swallowed, her heart thumping. She fought the urge to look at Lord Ashworth's retreating figure. As she closed the door behind her, she felt a desire, entirely foreign and nearly overpowering, to let out a high-pitched squeal. A separate sensation warned her she might lose her dinner.

She rested a hand on her abdomen to quell the sensations. The emotions she felt swirling around inside felt strange, though not unpleasant.

Her stomach knotted. Had she made a terrible mistake to confide in him? She found it impossible to reconcile the picture of a deceitful smuggler with the considerate and helpful man her experience had taught her Lord Ashworth was.

If her reading of Lord Ashworth's character was as wrong as some of the evidence seemed to indicate, though, then his request that she wait to act could quite easily be interpreted as self-preservation—to protect his own interests until the smuggled goods could be moved.

If this was the case, she stood on dangerous ground. A fatalistic voice inside asked her, though, what exactly she had to lose.

26

The night brought little rest to Kate's battling mind and heart. Her eyes didn't close to grant her the peace she needed until her room had begun to lighten with the sunrise. Lindley, bless her heart, must have known she needed more than her usual rest, since she didn't pull back the curtains until an advanced hour of the morning.

Though she was grateful for the thoughtfulness of her maid, Kate awoke with a pit in her stomach. Time was not something she had in abundance if she were to act on her knowledge. Or could she truly place everything in Officer Roberts's and Lord Ashworth's hands?

She remembered Lord Ashworth's promise to call on her and wondered with slight panic if she had missed him. Questioning Lindley on the subject, her fears were confirmed.

"Yes, Miss, I understand that his lordship came around quite early this morning—I don't know that I shall ever accustom myself to these country hours," she added with a disapproving shake of her head. "He insisted that you not be disturbed, though, and took himself off in a hurry."

Kate sighed. "Very well. Thank you, Lindley."

Once she was dressed, Kate descended the stairs. At the bottom,

Clara swung around on hearing Kate's footsteps, a look of relief on her face.

"There you are!" The relief was mixed was something which seemed nearer to anger than anything Kate had seen Clara exhibit in the past.

"Yes, I apologize," Kate said. "Lindley let me sleep far longer than I had planned."

"You've been asleep this entire time?" Clara asked. "And you such an early riser."

Kate smiled, knowing she couldn't explain the reason she had struggled to fall asleep. "I know. I barely recognize myself."

"Well I am glad you've had a good rest. So much the better, for I have quite a day planned for us."

Kate's eyebrows went up.

Clara reached for Kate's arm, tucking it in the crook of her own and shepherding her towards the morning room.

Clara had instructed for various periodicals to be brought into the room so that she and Kate might peruse them together in hopes of finding a dress design.

"Mama insists I look very smart when the engagement is announced."

Kate had fought with the impulse to clarify—what engagement was Clara planning for?

She was just as caught off guard by Clara's sudden desire to schedule out an entire day. Something was clearly different about Clara. Her laughs had a forced quality to them, and she seemed to be jittery. Had something happened between Clara and Mr. Bradbury?

The door opened.

"Miss Matcham," said the footman Davies. "Lord Ashworth is here to see you. I have left him in the library, ma'am."

Kate hadn't considered what Clara might think of her, a guest in the house—and a female one at that—receiving a gentleman—and Lord Ashworth at that—at Wyndcross. The activity they were engaged in only heightened the awkwardness of the visit.

She glanced at Clara. Her brows were raised and nostrils flared in an expression reminiscent of her mother.

"Thank you, Davies," said Kate, setting the magazine on the table next to the sofa and standing to leave the room.

Clara stood suddenly. "Yes, Davies, thank you. Please have Lord Ashworth shown in here." She smiled. "Quite silly to leave him kicking his heels in the library when we can receive him here."

Davies' eyes shifted toward Kate in uncertainty, but he said, "Very good, ma'am," bowed, and closed the door behind him.

Kate hadn't the faintest idea how she and Lord Ashworth would manage to discuss a plan when Clara was in the room.

Once the door was closed, Clara turned her head to Kate. "A secret tryst with Lord Ashworth?" She clucked her tongue and shook her head in mock disapproval, but her eyes held an unforgiving light despite her smile.

Kate chuckled to dispel the tinge of annoyance she felt at Clara's words and at the way her presence complicated things. "I admit I am no expert on the matter, but it hardly seems fair to call it a secret tryst when a gentleman is announced in broad daylight by Davies."

"You looked very cozy with Simon at dinner. And now Lord Ashworth? My my, who could be next?" She tapped the side of her chin with a finger, wearing a roguish half-smile that didn't extend to her eyes. "Based on last night, perhaps we should expect that Mr. Bradbury will be announced. At this rate you will have all the men in the county calling upon you. I never took you for a flirt, Kate."

Kate flushed. She hadn't thought Clara to be petty or spiteful.

"Lord Ashworth," Davies announced.

Kate blinked quickly to dissolve the tears pooling in her eyes.

Lord Ashworth, holding his hat in his hands, stopped short just beyond the doorway. He had clearly not been expecting to see Clara in the room.

Clara offered him a seat, and as she moved a pillow to make room for him, Lord Ashworth caught eyes with Kate and grimaced. His grimace, though, turned to concern as he looked at Kate. He looked a question at her, but Kate only shook her head and forced a smile.

The visit was short. Clara prattled on about various topics, not seeming to need much input from her companions beyond a "yes," a "no," or a laugh. The opportunity for private conversation was not to be had, and after ten minutes, Lord Ashworth began to take his leave. Almost as an afterthought, he asked Clara if she happened to have a quill, ink, and paper.

"I promised Miss Matcham I would provide her with the name and address of the woman who assisted in furnishing my London house. I understand Lady Hammond intends to refurnish a number of rooms in Berkeley Square and is searching for someone reliable."

Kate's eyebrows raised, this being the first time she had heard a word on the subject. On encountering Lord Ashworth's speaking glance, though, she composed her face and said, "Ah yes, thank you. Fanny will be so grateful." She paused a moment, entering into the spirit of the fib, and added, "As will I. I can tell you that, while Louis XIV may well have known how to decorate in opulence, his attention to comfort seems to have been sadly lacking. I speak from personal experience with the chairs in Fanny's dining room."

Lord Ashworth smiled appreciatively at Kate's improvisation as he gratefully accepted the quill and paper from Clara.

When Clara seemed inclined to peer over Lord Ashworth's shoulder, Kate said, "Clara, surely you agree. Do you remember the chairs at the Levenham's ball? They suffered from quite the same problem, and, while they may well do for a short sitting, they leave one quite...quite —" she searched for the appropriate word "—numb after a long evening."

Clara smiled distractedly and turned her head to Lord Ashworth. "Good gracious," she exclaimed with a forced laugh and smile, "what a long address this person has!"

Lord Ashworth chuckled and wrote a final word on the paper. "It is not the address that is long but rather her name." He held it out to read from it. "Giselberta Ottovordemgentschenfelde."

Both Clara's and Kate's eyebrows shot up, and Kate bit her lip.

"Good heavens!" she said.

Lord Ashworth's eyebrows knit as he looked at the piece of paper doubtfully. "If I'm remembering it right, that is, which I never seem to." He shook his head.

"I'm afraid," said Kate, clearing her throat to gain control of her impulse to laugh, "that Fanny may take exception to her for no better reason than her name."

He shrugged his shoulders. "I've tried to convince her to adopt a different name—Frieda Schmidt, for example—but, like the small number of Germans I'm acquainted with, she is very proud of her name and completely unapologetic to oafs like me who can't for the life of them remember how to pronounce or spell it.

"In any case, I can vouch for Giselberta's passionate opposition to chairs in the style of Louis XIV. She has very strong opinions, especially when it comes to the French."

He handed the paper to Kate with a wink and took his leave.

Kate didn't know whether to feel reassured by the wink or concerned that Lord Ashworth was taking the situation too lightly. Her stomach clenched as she thought of all the time that had been wasted since her discovery the night before. She hoped that the paper in her hand would have some indication of Lord Ashworth's plan and not, as she fear, the name and address of Giselberta. She didn't dare look while Clara was in the room.

It was welcome, if somewhat surprising, when Clara insisted that they go for a ride. Kate had suggested rides on numerous occasions, but Clara had always insisted on a different activity.

Kate assented, knowing that she would at least have the opportunity to look at Lord Ashworth's note as she dressed for the ride. They agreed to meet in the courtyard in ten minutes.

Once she closed the door to her room, Kate rested her back against it and unfolded the paper with shaking hands.

Everything is arranged. You may rest easy. Yours, Ash

Kate stared at the words in disbelief.

Angry tears sprang to her eyes. He was refusing her a part in things when she had so clearly explained how important it was to her. And how could she know that he did indeed have a plan of his own? Or that he would be successful in carrying it out?

But he had given her no choice in the matter. Trusting him seemed her only option.

She crumpled the paper in her hands, and, in a very unladylike gesture, threw it toward the window in frustration. It was only when she was leaving the room that the idea struck her to suggest that she and Clara ride into Weymouth. Surely, she could find some way to relay a message to the authorities there. If Lord Ashworth insisted on keeping her in the dark, she must find her own way to keep her promise to herself.

She doubled back and wrote a quick note on the discarded piece of paper from a letter she had been writing to Fanny.

Tonight. Smuggling operation. Crofte stables.

Her heart beat rapidly as she hesitated about whether to exclude the last two words. But there was neither time nor paper available to redo it. She folded the note and placed it in the pocket of her habit.

When she proposed a ride into Weymouth, however, Clara put her foot down. There was a particular place Isabel Cosgrove had told her about that she was intent on seeing. With such insistence on Clara's part, Kate found it impossible to argue without raising suspicion. She patted the pocket holding the note to reassure herself it was still there. Could she direct Lindley to send it into Weymouth for her? But Clara looped her hand through Kate's arm.

"We should leave immediately," she said, "if we don't wish to miss dinner."

27

Happy though she was for any excuse to ride, Kate felt an odd misgiving as she watched Clara. Something was unarguably wrong with Clara, and Kate couldn't help but think that it must have something to do with Mr. Bradbury, especially given Clara's strange and barbed comments before Lord Ashworth's entrance. Her conversation was pleasant enough, both she and her horse seemed to be on edge.

After a spirited string of conversation, Clara suddenly entered into a fit of abstraction, staring between her horse's ears.

"Clara?" Kate said in a gentle voice.

Clara's head snapped up. "What is it?" she said, her wide eyes glancing rapidly ahead and to each side of them.

"Nothing at all," Kate laughed, though her brows were knit. "I was only wondering if you were well?"

"Of course," Clara rushed to say, adding an unconvincing attempt at a chuckle.

Kate tried to meet her eyes, but Clara would not meet her eyes. "If you are quite sure," she said doubtfully.

The silence resumed, both women deep in thought.

What was Lord Ashworth doing? Had everything really been

arranged as he had promised? She gripped her lips between her teeth, her stomach feeling unsettled. It felt like an eon since her heart and mind had felt settled about anything.

But whether Lord Ashworth was the kind and loyal gentleman her heart believed him to be or the devious smuggler her head feared him to be, her feelings would, in the end, still be collateral damage.

Accepting that fact gave her the bit of strength she needed to ask Clara the home question she had been wondering about for, as it seemed to Kate, ages and ages; the question which might allow her to help Clara unravel the entangled mess she seemed to be in. If Kate herself couldn't have what she wanted, at least she could try to ensure Clara's happiness.

"Clara, do you love Lord Ashworth?" She felt the stiffness in her own neck as she awaited the response.

Clara was taken off her guard. "No!" Her cheeks flushed. "That is, what a strange question."

Kate laughed aloud from relief at Clara's words. "Is it such a strange question?"

"Well, yes. After all, what does love have to do with anything?"

"A great deal for many people, I should think," said Kate softly, thinking of Mr. and Mrs. Clarkson, her own mother and father, and so many others.

"To be sure. People not so—" Clara searched for the word, eventually settling on one "—fortunate as you and I seem to put great stock in their feelings when it comes to choosing a spouse."

"Does it not seem to you that such people are perhaps more fortunate in that way? Would you not like to marry for love?"

Clara stared ahead. "Mama says that love is a poor substitute for loyalty."

Kate considered Lady Crofte's words. "Perhaps in many cases that is so, but the two needn't be mutually exclusive."

Clara was silent.

Kate went on, "I know of someone who both loves and is loyal to you."

Clara's head shot up, and there was no mistaking the glint of hope in her eyes.

"Mr. Bradbury, of course," Kate said with a quirk of her brow.

Clara's hopeful look intensified for a moment before being replaced by a small scowl and a shake of the head. "I'm sure I don't know why you should say such an absurd thing."

Kate smiled at her indulgently. "Because he told me so, of course."

Clara's head whipped around. "He did?"

If those bright eyes weren't enough to tell Kate everything she needed to know about Clara's feelings for Mr. Bradbury, the painfully hopeful tone in which she asked her question would have more than done it.

"He said so in no uncertain terms," Kate said significantly. "But even if he hadn't done so, it would take a greater fool than even myself to remain oblivious to his feelings."

Clara flushed with pleasure.

For a few minutes, they rode forward on the best of terms as Clara recounted the story of how she met Mr. Bradbury. It wasn't long, though, before Clara's manner shifted once again to a more restless and strained one. Shuffling in her saddle almost incessantly, she couldn't seem to keep from looking around them in a manner Kate could only describe as paranoid.

Suddenly Clara stopped her horse altogether.

Kate slowed Cleopatra, turning to ask Clara what the matter was.

"It is so silly of me," said Clara, looking around them and then down to her boot, "but my boot lace has come loose, and it is causing the boot to rub my ankle in the most uncomfortable way."

"Well, that won't do. Allow me." Kate steered Cleopatra back toward Clara, dismounting and applying herself to the boot in question. "There is nothing quite so awful as being obliged to continue forward in discomfort when a quick stop could set all to rights. There," she said, finishing the knot with a tug and looking up at Clara.

But Clara was not looking at her. She was looking behind Kate, her eyes wide, an expression of dread on her face.

"Oh dear! Please forgive me, Kate!" she begged in an urgent voice. "It was the only way!"

Baffled, Kate said, "What do you mean?" She turned her head to follow Clara's gaze and was met with the alarming view of two rapidly approaching strangers. The nearer and taller of the two, rugged and menacing, wore an unyielding and sneering expression on a face covered in blacking.

It was Officer Roberts. Gone was his uniform from the night before.

Kate drew back, but his long stride brought him to her quickly, causing Cleopatra to shy and scramble away. One of Roberts's burly arms wrapped around her as his other hand covered her head with a sack.

Tiny holes of light like pinpricks shone through the sack, but otherwise her vision was of no use to her. Her hands were brought roughly behind her back where they were tied together with a rope knotted so tightly that she couldn't hold back a yelp of pain.

"Oh, please be gentle," Clara's distraught voice pleaded, muffled to Kate's ears through the thick and scratchy sack covering her head. "She is my friend."

"Just following orders, ma'am," said Roberts.

Kate felt a sudden and rough tug on her wrists.

"'At'll do, I reckon," said the voice of the other man.

Whether from the disorientation of having her head covered or from the alarming situation she found herself in, Kate's head began to spin.

Only for a moment did she wonder why she found herself being ambushed. It would be far too coincidental to believe that her discovery the night before had nothing to do with it. She had hoped that Clara was oblivious to her family's role in smuggling, but that was clearly not the case. Her strange behavior suddenly made sense.

Kate thought of Lord Ashworth and attempted a deep breath to calm the frustration she felt inside—with him but also with herself for ever believing him. Why had she not followed her intuition about Roberts? Whatever plan Lord Ashworth had claimed to have, it had clearly not been put into action. Nor would it ever be.

If there was indeed a plan.

She was left to her own devices, then, whatever those devices might be.

"Wh-what will you do to her?" Clara voiced the question which Kate had been asking in her mind.

Though she felt she would have been justified in it, Kate couldn't find it in her heart to be angry with Clara. Her voice was so pathetically full of fear and guilt, and Kate knew even without being able to see her that Clara was in tears. Self-concerned though she might be, Clara was neither ruthless nor hard-hearted. It was clear that she already regretted her role, or at least this part of it.

"Don't you worry your head over that, Miss," said Roberts. "You've done your part, now off you go."

"But, sir," Clara said in a voice tentative and pleading. "If you were to let me take her back to the manor, you wouldn't have to concern yourself with her. She won't breathe a word of it, will you, Kate?" It was a desperate attempt to save Kate from an unknown fate.

If the men were to free her, would she stay silent to save herself and the reputation of the Croftes? Were those such awful ends?

Her father's face swam before her. Not the smiling, humor-filled face of her childhood but the pulled and pale face he wore at the end of his life. She pictured returning to Wyndcross and her uncertain future. She had no reason to go back with Clara and every reason to see things through. Perhaps she would have some opportunity to stand against the men.

"No, Clara," said Kate in a calm but clear voice. "Please just go."

The shorter man let out a cackle, and Kate heard him slapping his thigh in amusement.

"Bless ye! Didn't think we'd really let ye go, did ye, Miss?" He cackled again, thoroughly enjoying himself for a moment. He became eerily silent, though, before saying in a voice devoid of any humor, "Yer a liability. And I ain't lettin' me hands off ye til all's square and tight and I got my share of them pretty yaller coins in these pockets."

There was a slight pause. "Come to think," he said, "I got a mind to help meself to some other spoils here." The sound of his footsteps moving toward Clara made Kate tense up.

"That one isn't to be touched," Roberts said in an authoritative voice.

The other man let out a huff and wrapped an arm around Kate's waist, pulling her towards him.

Her neck tightened and her skin crawled. "As ye wish. One wench is as good as another, I always say." He gave Kate's waist a squeeze, and she used her shoulders to push off him in disgust.

He swore profusely, and everything went dark.

※

"Aye. Found it in her pocket."

The words sounded muffled, and Kate's head felt heavy, full of pressure. The way her body bobbed up and down brought her aching head to the forefront of her foggy awareness. Noting a throbbing point on her head, she realized that she must have been struck unconscious. She tried to bring a hand to the spot, but her hands were tied. She groaned softly, blood continuing to rush to her head.

"Ah, finally awake," said Roberts whose shoulder she was draped over. "You may walk on your own two feet, then."

He slipped her off his shoulder.

Unprepared and effectively blind, Kate tumbled onto the grass.

The men laughed, and one of them lifted her by the arm to make her stand. The pinpricks of light shining through the sack were much dimmer than before. The day must have advanced quite far.

"Where is Clara?" The words slurred as they came out of her mouth.

"The yaller headed one?" grunted one of the men.

Kate nodded, her forehead creased in pain.

"Gone. Back home by now. Snug and safe. That'll teach ye to go nosing about where ye don't belong."

He tugged the sack off her head, and she winced at the sudden change in lighting, blinking as her eyes adjusted. Not two hundred yards away was the coast. The sun was on the horizon, nearly hidden behind long clouds, painting the sky and water hues of orange and red, just as it had the night before.

What would Clara do when she arrived back at Wyndcross? Would her guilt gnaw at her to the point of seeking help?

It mattered little. Even if Clara did go for help, how would anyone know where to find Kate?

Kate was on her own.

With her hands tied, her options were limited. She briefly examined the two men escorting her. Both were solid, the one shorter and burlier than Roberts. But the thought of attempting an escape on foot from two sturdy men, with her hands tied behind her back would have been laughable if the situation weren't so desperate. If she couldn't find a way to free her hands, there was little hope.

And if she didn't escape? She shuddered as she thought of her captor's earlier, menacing words. She was unlikely to survive with her reputation intact.

The thought that her undoing would be at the hands of free-traders brought an ironic half-smile to her face. There was something morbidly fitting in the knowledge that she should meet her end—figurative or literal—the way her father had, at the hands of smugglers. The smile faded as she realized that her own end held much less honor than her father's. Her father had been actively opposing wrong, standing for what was right. What had Kate managed to do? Nothing at all.

28

Kate's stomach growled, the rope burns on her wrists stung, and the spot on her head throbbed. From the way her hair pulled near her temple, she could only assume there was a large lump there, caked with dried blood.

The sun had finally dipped below the horizon, and the dusky sky was turning a deeper shade of blue. It meant a landscape bathed in shadow, but it also meant that the visibility of her captors would be crippled. If an escape was possible, the dark would be at once her greatest ally and greatest obstacle.

But without freeing her hands, her lack of balance would undermine any escape attempt. As if to taunt her, her recovering ankle twinged. Her body was making known its vulnerabilities, and while she couldn't resist a sardonic smile at its timing, it was better that she form a plan with her eyes wide open to the many points working against her.

As the dark crept slowly around her, she said a silent prayer of thanks for the rhythmic sounds of the ocean which would at least orient her. She mentally blessed Lady Anne for the ride they had taken together, since Kate faintly recognized the area her captors had brought her to.

A small cove lay just to their east; the path she and Lady Anne had ridden lay to their west.

Kate might have guessed that the cove would prove useful to smugglers. Between its well-concealed location and the night's near-alarming lack of moonlight, they would have little trouble moving their goods undetected.

"'Ere come the others, Roberts," barked Briggs, pointing to a spot in the direction they had just come from.

In the distance, two small spots of light appeared, gradually getting larger.

"Better be sure," said Roberts, his eyes squinting as he cupped his hands around his mouth, and the sound of a bird call erupted.

Both men stood still with an ear cocked toward the approaching lanterns.

The same call, faint but unmistakable, sailed back to them.

Within two minutes, the lantern lights were close enough that Kate was able to see a group of four men, all attired in dark coats and hats, their faces blackened so that the whites of their eyes stood out ominously. Two of the men wore coverings over their noses and mouths.

The exchange of words that took place upon their arrival was almost unintelligible to Kate who had little experience with the language of thieves. The tones told her, though, that tension was high among the group. One man seemed to have taken exception to a new face amidst them.

"He said no new blood. An' I ain't keen on rufflin' his feathers!" The man's eyes widened in a significant look as if anticipating that the others would easily take his meaning. And sure enough, two of the others chimed in their agreement.

But Roberts shushed them. "He's been vouched for. Yates knows these parts better than any of us. He's coming along."

It became clear that his comrades wouldn't take his word for it. They seemed to fear whoever had banned "new blood" more than they feared Roberts.

He talked over their objections. "You're on dangerous ground,

Jenkins. Don't think I didn't notice that you never showed your face at the last shipment."

"Me wife an' kids was sick," Jenkins exclaimed, visibly offended by Roberts's implication. A moment later, though, his brow cleared, and he added in a jeering tone, "And from what I heard, ye nearly bungled it."

"Yes," Roberts said, his voice dangerously quiet, "and if we'd had more help from you, we wouldn't have. But it wasn't Yates' fault, if that's what you're implying. It was Randall's fault, and Emmerson took care of him."

Kate stiffened, and her jaw clenched.

Jenkins grumbled a bit, but the others remained silent.

Roberts looked over the group with a slow and threatening gaze. "If any of you have a problem with Yates, take it up with Emmerson. You can tell him yourself. He's coming to ensure everything goes to plan. This is no regular shipment, and we're all done for if it's mismanaged. Emmerson will make sure of that himself, I can promise you. And I'll be right there to help him." He scanned the men one by one

A collective shudder traveled through them.

Kate closed her eyes and breathed deeply. Her jaw clenched even harder in frustration with herself. There seemed to be little doubt that the Emmerson referred to by Roberts was responsible for her father's death. If so, she had thrown away the opportunity to bring her father's own murderer to justice. And for what? A deceptively charming gentleman, if he merited the title.

"What do we do with the lady?" said a gruff voice, muffled by a handkerchief. It was asked by the only man who hadn't joined in the debates about the newcomer. Presumably Yates.

Roberts considered Kate for a moment. "We can't risk an escape, and, by the looks of her—" he glanced at her contemptuous expression "—she'd like to do us all a harm. Jenkins, you'll watch her."

Jenkins snorted. "And teach her to knit and speak them foreign languages, I s'pose?" He spat on the ground. "I ain't no governess, Roberts. I'm 'ere to send off that there gold, and I won't be fobbed off into guarding no miss." He paused and looked with a sneer at Yates. "Yates can guard her."

"She may look like a lamb," said the short, stocky man who had helped capture her, "but she's got plenty sauce in 'er. Ye saw it yerself, Roberts."

"Fine, Briggs," said Roberts. "Yates, don't let her out of your sight."

Kate met eyes with Yates across the group. The flickering of the lantern light and the man's covered face and head made it difficult to distinguish anything, but his eyes were wide and alert.

Kate's eyes held Yates's. This was the man who would have her life in his hands. She hoped that she could turn his inexperience to her benefit.

One of the men holding a lantern handed his to Yates. "Ye'll need this."

Yates's eyes dwelled a moment on Kate as he put a hand out to accept the lantern. He walked over to Kate, taking a possessive hold of her arm.

Roberts turned away, peering out over the fields as if looking for something or someone.

"Roberts," said Briggs. "What about after?"

"After what?" Roberts barked impatiently.

"After the goods is gone. What'll ye do with the lady? S'ppose she informs on us! What then?"

Roberts seemed to consider Briggs' comment. "You're right. Emmerson doesn't like loose ends. He's very particular." He looked toward the cove and then scanned the coastline. "Yates, take her to the hole and tie her up there."

Yates's hold on Kate's arm tightened. "But the tide's comin' in," he croaked before clearing his throat. "She'll drown."

Jenkins leered at him and Kate. "'E doesn't want her drowned. 'E wants 'er for 'imself. Yer too late, Yates. Briggs 'ere told me 'e's already staked 'is claim on 'er." He clapped Briggs on the back and winked. "Though 'e can be a sharing chap when 'e chooses."

Yates's body went rigid, and his grasp tightened so much that Kate exclaimed. She pulled back, looking at him beside her. Only his eyes were visible, but he was staring at Jenkins with unadulterated wrath in his eyes.

Kate blinked rapidly as she scanned his face, noting the blacking.

In such proximity to him and the lamplight, she had no trouble recognizing him.

Lord Ashworth's eyes met hers. In them she saw apology and something akin to fear. The fear, she supposed, was due to the danger he stood in if she were to betray his identity. It made her lip curl in disdain.

It might be satisfying to betray him, just as he had betrayed her. She saw in his expression the weakness and duplicity of a man who had portrayed himself as something completely opposite of what he truly was and could not face the consequences of being discovered. It brought her anger to the surface.

She pulled back, trying to loosen her arm from his grasp in disgust. Her stomach knotted, and she suddenly felt as if she might be sick. Taking in a deep, shaky breath, she struggled to calm the overpowering array of emotions swarming inside her. She felt a need to say something but was not vengeful enough to put Lord Ashworth in the danger he would face if she made his identity known.

Kate spat at him, and he reared back, blinking quickly. His jaw tensed, and he wiped the spit from his cheek as a cacophony of voices broke out.

They were swiftly silenced by Roberts.

The group, confused at the sudden display of emotion from their heretofore mute charge, began inquiring of Yates what had happened when they were all silenced by Roberts.

He strained an ear. "It's Emmerson."

Kate's emotions were at their apex, and instead of feeling the fear and enmity she had anticipated she would experience on Emmerson's arrival, the surge of betrayal and anger she had been feeling gave way to a sudden numbness and weariness. She desired nothing so much as to distance herself from Lord Ashworth, thinking for a moment that she would prefer proximity to Emmerson himself over this man.

Emmerson at least did not pretend to be something he was not.

But Lord Ashworth's hand still gripped her arm, perfunctory now rather than the urgent hold he had taken before. It, too, seemed to apologize to her with its weak hold.

But Kate wasn't fooled. She had felt the strength in the hand, and she knew that it could revert at a second's notice if she tried to capitalize on the more superficial hold he now had.

The group waited in uneasy silence as Emmerson approached with two more men. Kate's arm hung limp in Lord Ashworth's relaxed grip. Everyone else's eyes were on the approaching trio, but Kate stared blankly ahead, lost in unpleasant thoughts. Only when the three men drew near did Kate look up with a near-apathetic gaze.

Her first impressions of him left her surprised. She had expected Emmerson to be the most menacing figure of the entire group, eclipsing Roberts's intimidating manner. She was at a loss to understand what the men found to frighten them out of their wits in the diminutive form that stood before them.

But when Emmerson spoke, she understood better. His voice held authority, laced throughout his speech. It was subtle, as if it were a given that his every word would be fulfilled. Where Roberts used his stature, tone, and volume to intimidate, Emmerson exuded confidence in spite of his smaller stature.

Caught up taking in Emmerson's person, a few minutes passed before Kate realized that one of his wingmen had been stealing furtive glances at her. His face, though, was uncovered, and even with the blacking smeared around, she recognized Henry Crofte.

As their eyes met and recognition dawned on her, he seemed to almost wince—an apologetic posture even more pathetic than Lord Ashworth's pleading eyes.

Kate's anger, though, was unkindled. She had prepared herself for the involvement of the Crofte family, so even though the vision of Henry standing beside her father's killer made her feel a wave of nausea, she felt little surprise.

Emmerson began instructing the men on their roles and assignments. His instructions were precise, and each man, once his duty had been specified, walked briskly away from the group to begin immediately. Most were sent to fetch the containers for shipment while Henry was charged with preparing the boats which would be loaded up to meet the ships before crossing the Channel to France.

It was clear that Henry had gained the trust and respect of the other men.

Within a matter of minutes, the only ones who remained were Briggs, Lord Ashworth, and Kate. Emmerson turned to look at Kate, considering her apathetically for a moment. "So, this is the explorer who found us out."

He began pacing around, coming to stand directly in front of her where he raised his chin to look her in the eyes. At such a small distance, she realized that he was even shorter than he had appeared before. "What shall we do with you?"

29

Kate felt Lord Ashworth's grip tighten once again, and she took a strange and morbid satisfaction in knowing that, whatever happened to her, Lord Ashworth would have to live with it on his conscience forever, if conscience he had.

"Sir," came the tentative voice of Briggs, "Roberts was worried she might make trouble after all's said and done tonight. We found this in 'er pocket."

Kate's eyes widened in horror as she watched Briggs pass her crumpled note to Emmerson.

Emmerson considered Kate before looking down at the note. He read without any emotion and then looked up at her, his head tilted slightly.

Kate debated for a moment whether it would serve her ends to appear a cowering, frightened girl. As she met his eyes, though, any fear she felt was eclipsed by cold anger, and she knew that he saw it in her eyes.

"I think you're right, Briggs." A small smile pulled at his mouth as he continued to look her in the eye, evidence of the slight humor he found in her reaction to him.

"Aye, sir," Briggs said, his chest puffing up in pride at the validation.

"Roberts 'ad just told Yates 'ere to take 'er down to the hole before you arrived."

Emmerson looked at Kate with a touch of amusement on his face. "What have I done to deserve the daggers in those eyes of yours? And what might your name be?" Emmerson looked her over before letting his eyes return to her face.

The disdain and anger on her face were only magnified by his surveyal of her.

His brows raised as he noted her expression.

Kate had wondered about the man standing before her since her childhood. She had imagined what she would say were she to come across him, never believing she actually would. In her vision of such an encounter, she had towered over the cowering figure in righteous rage.

Never had young Kate imagined herself to be at such a disadvantage as she now was, hands tied, disheveled hair and clothing, taken by surprise at the confrontation.

Was her father one of a long list of murders for him? Had he felt anything at all when he had shot an innocent man? What could she possibly say now to him? He had only asked for her name.

"Charles Matcham," she said in the strongest voice she could muster. Lord Ashworth stiffened almost imperceptibly and turned his head to look at Kate.

Briggs guffawed. "Charles! What a name for a lady."

Emmerson put up his palm, and Briggs went silent.

"I know that name. Unlike Briggs', though," he blinked lazily, "I am not gullible enough to believe it is yours. Why, then, do you give it?"

"It is the name of a man you killed." She blinked away the stinging in her eyes, determined that she would show no weakness to the man. She could not allow her father's brave memory to be overwritten in the script of her own fear or weakness.

Emmerson's expression didn't change but for the slightest glint of recognition in his eyes. "That was many years ago," he said dismissively.

"Of that I am well and painfully aware," said Kate. She made fists with her tied hands to stop the shaking. "That man was my father."

Emmerson suddenly looked bored. "Ah, I see. You've come to

exact revenge." He crumpled the note and tossed it on the ground. "Well I am afraid you have botched it, Miss. And while I am sure we would all love to spend more time reminiscing on days past, duty calls." He began to turn away. The ease with which he seemed to put her words from his mind answered the question she had asked herself.

Her father was not the only man he had killed.

"Revenge is for the weak," pursued Kate. "Something my father taught me. He also taught me that, though life often seems unfair, the universe is ultimately a place where we all reap what we have sown. So, Mr. Emmerson, though I may not live through this night, I would still rather be in my shoes than in yours."

Briggs growled. Grasping the pistol barrel in his hand and taking two of the longest strides his short legs would allow for, he swung the butt of the pistol at Kate.

With only a split second to anticipate Briggs' sudden designs, Lord Ashworth managed to deflect the hit so that, instead of hitting Kate at her temple, the pistol butt caught her cheek.

Crying out in surprise and pain, Kate tumbled to the ground, unable to catch herself with her tied hands.

Lord Ashworth sent Briggs sprawling backwards with a swift uppercut to the jaw and moved to Kate's side.

"Are you hurt?" he said in urgent undertones.

Even amidst her pain, she looked at Lord Ashworth with brows raised. Her grazed cheek throbbed, bleeding slowly. A lump protruded from her temple where she had been knocked unconscious earlier.

Seeming to understand her expression and silence, Lord Ashworth grimaced and rephrased his question. "How badly are you hurt?" His eyes scanned her face, reaching her injured cheek. She turned her face to avoid his gaze.

That he should ask her such a question and pretend to such concern when he bore so much of the responsibility for her situation was outside of enough. It reminded her of all his prior affected concern over the past weeks.

When she responded, her voice was laced with sarcasm. "It is all quite fortunate, in fact. The pain in my face has made me forget almost entirely about the pain in my wrists and head. So, you see that all is quite well." She smiled humorlessly.

Lord Ashworth grimaced as Briggs came to.

Emmerson was observing Kate and Lord Ashworth with an impassive expression. Without turning to look at Briggs, he said, "That was quite unnecessary, Briggs."

"Aye, sir," Briggs said, rubbing his jaw.

Emmerson looked at Lord Ashworth. "Yates is it?"

Lord Ashworth rose. "Yes, sir. At yer service."

Kate's nostrils flared at the words. Hearing the gruff and raw voice he had adopted as Yates, she couldn't stifle a disdainful snort. What would Emmerson do if he discovered that Yates was Lord Ashworth, heir to the Purbeck Earldom? Would it matter to him? It must, or else Lord Ashworth wouldn't have bothered to disguise himself and adopt such language.

Kate had the power to put Lord Ashworth in danger. And though this appealed to part of her, it only did so for the briefest of moments. She was not vindictive. Had she not just told Emmerson that revenge was for the weak?

"You will take her to the hole," Emmerson said dispassionately. "There you will find a large ring attached to the cliff wall. Tie her hands to the ring. Bind her mouth." With each instruction, Lord Ashworth nodded his head.

He began helping Kate up off the ground. She desperately wished she could have stood without his aid, but any pride she salvaged by refusing his help would be wounded by the spectacle of her attempting to stand without the use of her hands.

Emmerson kept his eyes on Lord Ashworth as he said, "Briggs, you will accompany Yates and the girl. In case Yates's apparent compassion interferes with my instructions. We must not risk any errors this time."

Lord Ashworth looked up. "Sir, I can 'andle 'er on me own, I swear it! Ain't it better to use Briggs for some of the 'eavy lifting?" Despite the way his jaw had clenched on hearing Emmerson's instructions, the words were said casually enough. He even managed a chuckle as he said, "I lifted one of them barrels meself, and I fair fell over."

Emmerson smiled humorlessly. "I will take no risks. Go now. The sooner you go, the sooner you both will return to do, as you said, the heavy lifting."

The three of them turned to leave, and Emmerson's voice sounded a final time. "Oh, and Briggs?" Briggs turned around. "If Yates falters, shoot him."

30

Though Lord Ashworth's grip on Kate's arm was guiding rather than compelling, Briggs insisted on taking her opposite arm in a vice-like hold. He seemed determined to do everything in his power to exceed Emmerson's expectations.

The three of them walked towards the coast, Kate attempting deep breaths to still the nerves which were beginning to overcome her. Briggs set the pace for the group, pulling along not only Kate but Lord Ashworth with his zeal.

Kate had spoken to Emmerson with the conviction and assurance borne of being in the right, but the exhilaration had faded and left her with the prospect of an imminent death. And despite her general recognition of the area, she had no knowledge of the hole they had spoken of. She imagined a sort of well which they might drop or lower her into. From Lord Ashworth's words, though, she gathered that the rising tide should be of chief concern to her.

She cursed the ropes which chafed her skinned wrists with each harried step they took. The thought of sea water on her abrasions made her wince.

The cringing expression was followed by an ironic smile. How ridiculous that she should concern herself with salt on her wounds when death itself was knocking more loudly on her door with every pace.

The lantern held by Lord Ashworth illuminated an approaching precipice, and Briggs slowed his pace, ordering Lord Ashworth to give him the lantern so that he might determine whether the hole lay to the east or west. He released Kate's arm to inspect the surrounding area.

The smell of seaweed and damp rock was heavy in the night air.

Lord Ashworth leaned his head closer to Kate's ear. "Do you trust me, Kate?" he said in an urgent whisper.

Kate reared her head back to look at him in utter disbelief. "That depends. Am I speaking to Yates or to Lord Ashworth?"

She paused for a moment but cut him off before he could answer. "It was meant rhetorically, my lord." The last words were said in contempt. "The answer should be quite obvious, I imagine."

The lantern light which had been moving along the cliff edges stopped a moment, throwing its beams out over one part of the cliff. Briggs turned and began walking toward them again.

"There is no time for your outrage or vengeance," Lord Ashworth said with more anger and impatience than she had ever seen from him. "Trust me."

She snorted softly.

"Over here," Briggs cried to them.

As they approached the cliff edge, it became clear to Kate that the edge was not, as it had appeared to be, a steep drop into the water below. It was rather a ravine leading down to a small cove, surrounded on all sides by large rock formations. At the base of the rocks nearest the ocean gaped a hole. As each wave approached, water broke around the openings, spilling through the hole and wetting the small rocks inside.

Kate peered down at the base of the ravine. How long would it be until water began pouring into the cove with the rising tide? It was unlikely that such a small cove would take much time to fill with sea water. She swallowed and breathed deeply, knowing that time was rapidly running out.

The only way down to the hole was a steep slope, a perilous descent even for a person privileged with the use of their hands. Not being thus privileged, Kate was obliged to rely on her captors to assist her. Her ankle ached, and she gritted her teeth as they made their way down.

Briggs seemed to have a fear of heights and was chiefly concerned with his own safety, as evidenced by his blatant disregard for Kate's welfare each time his or her footing became doubtful. Had it not been for the care and adroitness of Lord Ashworth, Kate had to grudgingly admit to herself that, bedraggled and injured as she felt, she would have fallen any number of times.

On more than one occasion, Lord Ashworth was required to catch Kate's tottering form in the crook of one arm as he crouched and balanced himself with his other hand. On those occasions, Kate thanked him almost inaudibly, too trained in civility to omit doing so, but upset enough with him to resist it. But after a second and sizable piece of fabric tore at the hem of Kate's dress due to a clumsy misstep of Briggs, causing all three of them to slide precariously, Kate could bear it no longer.

"Oh, for heaven's sake," she cried. "Untie my hands before we all fall to our deaths!"

Lord Ashworth pursed his lips, but Kate noted how they had twitched. "I reckon she's right, Briggs."

Briggs shook his head vehemently. So much so, in fact, that he was required to stabilize himself to prevent a fall. "I don't trust 'er."

"And just where do you suppose I might go?" Kate said in exasperation, indicating with her head the unforgiving landscape surrounding them, with water and waves on the one hand and a steep, rocky climb on the other.

Briggs made a noncommittal "hmph" before agreeing to untie her hands. "Only til we reach the bottom, mind ye."

Lord Ashworth took the rope in his hands, deftly undoing the knot and unwrapping Kate's wrists. He slowed as he undid the last loop and swore softly.

But Kate was not in the mood for fruitless sympathy or pity. She tugged her wrists away from his hands. "There," she said, ignoring the stinging through a forced smile full of clenched teeth. She demonstrated the good sense her captors had used in freeing her by using her hands to brace herself as she descended further toward the bottom without them.

As her feet met the pebbles, she tried not to think of how quickly the water would cover her feet and then reach her waist, her neck, and her head. With her hands temporarily free, the time to think of escape had come. But how was she to escape when surrounded by unpredictable ocean currents and a steep ravine?

Escape by water she hastily discarded as an option. She was not sure she could swim and guessed that her dress would complicate the attempt, to say nothing of the wild current. A quick look at the violent crashing of the waves on the surrounding rocks confirmed the ineligibility of such an option. As for an escape up the ravine they had just descended, the men were dressed in a manner much more conducive to scrambling up rock, not to mention the fact that she was outnumbered.

The only avenue open to her seemed to be the one she had only recently condemned to Emmerson: violence. And though she disliked Briggs intensely, she was shrewd enough to admit that, if his clumsy descent was any indication, he would be the less formidable foe to run from if she had to choose which of her two captors to leave uninjured.

She felt annoyance as her conscience recoiled from doing Lord Ashworth an injury. If they were keeping tally of intended injuries to one another, the injury she did him would come nowhere near to evening the scale. If she submitted to the fate he had prescribed her, it would be the last thing she did.

She was unsure she possessed the fortitude to follow through with her plan. But the door of opportunity was quickly closing, so she hunched over on the pretext of removing a pebble from her shoe.

Briggs was still occupied in traversing the final stretch of ravine, and Lord Ashworth was readjusting his hat, his mouth cover pulled down.

A large rock rested near Kate's feet, small enough that she could hold it in one hand but significant enough that she felt sure, unversed though she was in the ways of violence and brutality, that it might at least stun him long enough to give her the head start she required. She was fairly certain that the only person she had managed to injure in her entire life was herself, and that was always quite unintentional, of course. Her hands shook.

Kate watched, trembling, as Briggs reached the bottom of the ravine. He eyed the water entering the cove uneasily. Standing water was already visible in the lower areas.

"Tie 'er up, then, Yates, and let's be on our way."

Kate and Lord Ashworth met eyes for a moment, apology written on both their faces. Seeing his apologetic gaze gave Kate a greater determination to carry out her plan. His apology was hollow. The hypocrisy was unfathomable. It was surreal to her that this man—one who had laughed with her, cared for her when she was injured, drew her out of her protective shell—stood before her, prepared to send her to her death. And he had the gall to look apologetic as he did it?

He approached her, and his gaze became pointed, as if he were willing her to understand something.

"Be quick about it," Briggs yelled. "I ain't of a mind to drown with 'er, ye clod!"

Lord Ashworth held Kate's eyes. "Right ye are," he said, never taking his eyes from hers. He pulled the rope from his coat.

Kate took a breath, steeling herself against the prospect before her. Never having tested her strength to injure, she was suddenly struck with the fear that she might do greater harm than she intended. She had heard stories of men being killed by a single strike, and though she doubted she had the strength for such a thing, she could never forgive herself if the damage she caused was lasting or, heaven forbid, fatal.

Her only consolation and hope was that, if she were indeed strong enough to do great harm, Lord Ashworth's hat might act as a small buffer.

His most recent words to her sounded once more in her head. *"Trust me."* She knew a moment of doubt, wondering if perhaps he still had some plan that truly did merit her trust.

With such a struggle taking place inside her, she raised the rock high above her head, bringing it down upon the head of Lord Ashworth. And though her will to injure him had instinctively weakened at the last moment, resulting in a contact more wavering and weak than she had intended, Lord Ashworth fell to his knees and then onto his side, motionless.

Eyes wide with disbelief and fear that she had indeed killed him, Kate dropped to her knees next to him.

She had killed him.

31

"Oh dear!" she gasped.

The moment for her escape had arrived, but she had no thought of leaving the lifeless form which lay before her. She suffered an inexplicable pang of guilt as she realized that, not only had she done injury to his head with the weapon she had used, but he had then fallen head first onto the uneven and hard pebbles below.

She gently lifted his head and placed it in her lap. Removing his hat, she ran a hand through his hair and felt softly along his scalp for the inevitable bump which would be forming. Had she drawn blood? Was there a crack in his skull from the blow?

"'Ey!" there was both surprise and anger in Briggs' voice as he rushed over.

Gently but quickly laying Lord Ashworth's head onto the ground, she picked up the stone again. She knew a moment's panic as she realized that she was left alone and essentially defenseless with a man who had earlier expressed an intent to compromise her reputation. A man who had a gun.

"Stay away." She held the rock above her shoulder, ready to defend herself. "I am much stronger than I appear!"

Briggs cackled. "Well that's not sayin' much, is it? Don't feel bad, though. Pretty figures like yours ain't made for cruelty, Miss." His eyes surveyed her in a way that made her skin crawl. "Though I do prefer my wenches feisty."

It seemed to Kate, as she looked at the abhorrent man Briggs, that her situation could hardly have been worse. Death seemed preferable to the prospect Briggs had suggested at, to say nothing of the guilt she would have to live with, having killed a man.

"You see that I have killed Lor—Yates," her voice broke, "and I am quite willing to help you to the same fate if you take one step closer."

Briggs had begun walking towards her with purpose, but on hearing her words, another cackle erupted from him, and he slapped his thigh.

"Killed 'im?" He held his round stomach in enjoyment. She thought he might weep with mirth.

Kate glanced behind her and did a double take. Lord Ashworth, holding his head with one hand, and supporting his weight on the other, was sitting up.

Disbelief and relief filled her. Relief that she was not the murderer she had thought herself, that she was not to be left at the mercy of Briggs. Depraved as Lord Ashworth might be, at least he would not allow Briggs to compromise her.

She dropped to her knees, wrapping her arms around Lord Ashworth and saying, "Oh thank heaven!"

Though he was quite obviously startled at the unexpected embrace, for a moment it almost seemed to her that he settled into it. No sooner had the thought crossed her mind, though, than he broke free of her hold, rising to his feet, and leveling a pistol at her.

Briggs reached for his pistol as well, pointing it at her. He stood next to Lord Ashworth, his face a strange mixture of delight and wrath.

"I told Emmerson she weren't no fainting miss," he said with a gleeful sneer. "Didn't I warn him, Yates? Give 'er an inch!" He shook his head as though in Kate he saw all women. "Tried to murder you, she did. But she didn't 'ave the strength on account of being a wench." He leaned back and guffawed at the thought.

In a scramble of movement, Kate watched as Briggs' pistol was knocked from his hands by Lord Ashworth.

"Don't move." The voice had lost its gruff quality. He spoke as Lord Ashworth, and he pointed the pistol at Briggs' temple.

"What the devil?" Briggs hands were up in defense, and he looked as though he wasn't sure whether his companion was having a laugh at his expense.

Lord Ashworth reached for Briggs's pistol and handed it to Kate who stared down at it with wide eyes.

It felt cold and smooth in her hands. And terrifying.

"Miss Matcham," said Ashworth. "Shall we make use of the torn hem of your dress?" He kept his eyes and pistol trained on Briggs, but he motioned with his free hand for her to bring the dress fragment which was hanging on by only a few threads.

Still at a loss to understand the increasingly strange situation in which she found herself, Kate placed the pistol carefully in her pocket and rose to her feet, feeling it knock against her thigh, then bent over to tear the very tattered hem of the riding dress Fanny had gifted her.

"Yes," said Lord Ashworth, glancing over at the sound of the tearing. "Briggs' clumsiness made that much easier than it should have been. Thank you, Briggs. As delightful and stimulating as your conversation has been, my friend, I'm afraid we really must do away with it for the remainder of the evening. Miss Matcham, with the fabric in your hand, you will please fashion a gag around Briggs' mouth."

Kate hesitated. What game Lord Ashworth was playing at? Did this mean he was on her side? Was this part of his plan for her? Or was it part of his own selfish plan?

She walked toward Briggs, giving him a wide enough berth until she was well behind him so that he had no opportunity to reach for her.

Having never fashioned a gag before, Kate needed a bit of direction from Lord Ashworth, though she felt she had done quite a tolerable job, all told.

Lord Ashworth complimented her work, adding afterward, "I have no desire to hear him talk, but my greater fear is that he might make an attempt to alert others to our position. Now we will make our way back up the way we came." He looked at Briggs through narrowed eyes. "If the world were just, Briggs, we would tie your hands behind your back, but as I have no desire to heft your less-than-coordinated personage up this ravine, selfish mercy wins the day."

Gagged as he was, the only mode of expression available to Briggs was his eyes and brows. They told quite a story, though, and Kate was grateful she was not destined to spend any more time as his captive. Her only concern was whether a gag would be enough to keep him in check as they scaled the hill.

As if reading her thoughts, Lord Ashworth added, "I would remind you, Briggs, that I will have my pistol, which I have no compunction whatsoever in using if you attempt anything at all. You will walk in front of us at all times. And I have no need to remind you that Miss Matcham is quite capable of doing you harm with even the most commonplace of rocks."

Kate blushed, lowered her gaze, and bit her lip in embarrassment. She was immeasurably grateful that she had not, as she had feared, killed Lord Ashworth. But the fact that he knew she had done her best to maim him made things awkward. That, and the impromptu embrace she had subjected him to.

She stole a glance at him.

He was smiling at her reaction. But an instant later, his gaze moved toward the ocean, and his demeanor shifted, any signs of humor or enjoyment replaced by decisiveness and gravity.

He directed the three of them to begin moving, his manner urgent. And though Kate didn't understand what was happening, the knowledge that she had only nearly escaped a miserable death made her anxious to put distance between herself and the small cove where the water continued to rise.

32

Briggs seemed to be in awe at his lordship's manner and to trust his threats enough that he obeyed Lord Ashworth's orders, staying in front of the group. And Kate, though her wrists burned as ever and the skin had begun to tighten painfully, pushed her way up the hill with gritted teeth. Her ankle and cheek throbbed.

"I don't mean to press you," she said caustically, "but might I be informed what it is you plan to do with me?"

Lord Ashworth looked at her with a strange expression as though he failed to understand her.

"Well?" she said. "What is the meaning of it all? Are you staging a coup of some sort? To take over as Emmerson's replacement, perhaps." She slipped on some loose rock and tried to regain her balance.

Lord Ashworth put out a hand to help steady her, but Kate pulled away.

"A coup?" he said blankly.

She swallowed, feeling very silly as he stared at her with disbelief.

"I free you," he said between breaths, "and arm you with a pistol, and you assume that it is part of my plan to stage a coup? Did you think you were to be my accomplice?"

They reached the top, and Kate tried to catch her breath, relieved that she had made it, despite the constant protestations from her aching body.

"You say that," Kate said breathlessly, rubbing at her throbbing wrists as if she might rub the pain away, "as though it is a strange assumption. Might I gently remind you that your behavior and words have been contradictory in the extreme?"

Lord Ashworth chuckled, grabbing Briggs' arm in his. "This from the woman who hit me over the head with a rock and then embraced me?"

Kate flushed, and Lord Ashworth took the lantern from Briggs before stepping up beside Kate.

His smile had faded, and he gave her a searching glance.

"I will explain it all, I promise," he said. "But there's no time right now. Not much longer. Have your pistol at the ready."

Kate looked at him with wide eyes, the thought crossing her mind that, if she had failed to use a simple rock as a means of violence, her use of a pistol could be catastrophic.

Lord Ashworth guided them onward with confidence, and it wasn't long before Kate saw small pricks of light appear in the dark expanse before them. As they approached the dim lights, Kate's eyes began to make out the shape of men, walking next to horses loaded with the same large barrels she had seen in the stables. They were moving in the direction of the large cove.

A muffled sound came from Briggs, and Lord Ashworth stopped a moment.

"It will be better if you keep your thoughts to yourself, Briggs." Lord Ashworth paused a moment, looking at him. "I must remind you again of the pistols we carry and insist that you not try anything you might have cause to regret."

Eyes narrowed angrily, Briggs nodded his understanding, and they pushed forward.

Soon they were close enough to distinguish the individual men in front of them. Did Lord Ashworth intend to forge a path straight through the trail of men carrying barrels?

But he stopped. Standing a few feet away in the dark, Kate noticed a man watching the procession of barrels. He turned as he heard them approach.

It was Emmerson.

He looked momentarily taken aback, an expression not at home on his otherwise-stoic face. But before he could say a word, a shot rang out.

Kate jumped at the unexpected noise, her hand flying to her pocket in an acutely anxious moment of worry that the pistol in her own pocket had fired. She glanced at Lord Ashworth whose pistol was in the air.

Kate scrambled to pull her own pistol out, leveling it at Emmerson with trembling hands.

"You'll forgive me, Emmerson, for the disruption," said Lord Ashworth, the gruffness of his voice from earlier absent.

Emmerson's eyes were wide, but his brows were drawn together in anger. "What the dev—"

His exclamation was cut short by another shot, not quite so near, but in the vicinity. Moments later, the distant sound of hooves pounding on the ground met their ears, growing louder. The four of them watched the approach of a group of at least ten men on horseback.

On hearing the hoofbeats, the line of men stopped. There was a brief silence and then mayhem as horses and barrels were abandoned, men running in the opposite direction as the approaching riders. Briggs ran as quickly as his short legs would carry him toward the other escapees, the gag still fastened around his mouth.

Emmerson himself seemed tempted to flee, but Lord Ashworth had anticipated his intention and, in a swift gesture, reached for the pistol in Kate's hand and pointed it at Emmerson.

"Not a step." His voice was cold and hard, unfamiliar to Kate. Even in the grave situation they had faced in the hole, there had been some humor in Lord Ashworth's manner. But here, no trace of it was left.

"Run, Emmerson," he said, "if you wish to be shot dead in your tracks. I would not suggest it, but I will not try to stop you myself. I leave that to the riding officers approaching. Whatever you decide, your tyranny is over."

For a moment, Emmerson looked as though he was still considering an attempted escape, but his composed demeanor returned, and he stood his ground. His eyes held no fear, only a sort of apathetic stare.

Kate had been listening in rapt attention, her eyes wide as she looked at Lord Ashworth beside her. Was this the man she had been sure would be the cause of her own death, not an hour before? The one she had attacked?

Her thoughts whirled around in her head, memories flitting through her mind to make sense of it all. Everything which had made her suspect him took on a new hue with the events of the night. Could it really all have been part of this end game?

If so, her original, charitable reading of his character had been correct. And, so far from being the treacherous criminal she had come to think him, he stood beside her, bringing to justice the man Kate had desired to see pay for his crimes for so long. Curiously, the fulfillment of seeing Emmerson apprehended was matched by the relief she felt to know the true character of Lord Ashworth.

The riding officers slowed their horses, and a few of them dismounted, informing Emmerson that he was under arrest. A man sat upon his horse at the front of the group with the unmistakable air of a leader. He looked at Emmerson.

"I warned you of this day."

Even faced with arrest, Emmerson wore a derisive half-smile. "You'll forgive me, Officer, if I don't find myself impressed. It was so long ago I find it hard to remember." He tipped his hat in a mocking gesture.

"Yes," responded the officer. "Long enough for you to engage in sufficient crimes to put you to death a hundred times over. I knew one day you would go too far. This is where your greed has led you. Men like you are never content to enjoy spoils. You always want more. But we always catch up with you in the end."

He nodded to his officers on the ground who had been surrounding Emmerson awaiting their captain's orders. They began tying his hands.

The captain turned to Lord Ashworth, doffing his hat as a show of respect.

"Your lordship, I'm sure I have no need to tell you that the entire county is beholden to you. The country, even. You've prevented Bonaparte's army from acquiring strength and support from the very people working to defeat him." He inclined his head to Lord Ashworth in gratitude. "As you heard the man say, we have had our eye on him for nearly two decades now, but never with more than hearsay evidence from villagers who always later retracted their claims. Bullied and threatened by Emmerson's men, no doubt. Now that we have him, though, and now that the people know that you won't hold with such dealings on your land, we will have no trouble at all finding people to testify against him, including yourself. Thank you."

Lord Ashworth only nodded, looking somewhat discomfited by the encomiums of the sober captain.

The captain gathered the reins in preparation to leave, and Lord Ashworth reached a hand to the saddle.

The captain looked down, his brows raised expectantly.

Lord Ashworth paused a moment before speaking in a solemn voice. "Captain, that man is responsible for the death of this lady's father, Mr. Charles Matcham. If he pays for nothing else, please make sure he pays for that."

The captain looked at Kate who held his gaze, her eyes stinging. He nodded. "You have my word." He turned to his men, giving a few final commands before the group rode off with their prisoner.

The light of the lantern flickered, and Kate realized that only she and Lord Ashworth remained.

She looked at him, but he seemed to avoid her gaze.

"Miss Matcham," he said, pulling the handkerchief from around his neck, "you have had the most trying of nights. I wish it were not necessary to require any more of you, but I'm afraid we must now walk a bit further. I am sure your ankle is in an awful state." He clenched his jaw and grimaced at her. "Lancelot is tied up not far from here." He indicated the way in front of them with his head.

Kate nodded and followed. She thought for a moment of Wyndcross. Had Henry escaped? How would she face the Croftes after such a night? Had Clara expected Kate to come out of it all alive?

She had no greater desire than to climb into her bed and sleep away all her thoughts and fatigue, but the idea of doing so in the home of those who had sacrificed her to maintain their deceit made her feel sick inside.

As if reading her thoughts, Lord Ashworth said, "Ashworth Place is much closer than Wyndcross Manor, and my sister Anne insists that you come to visit for a few days." He paused a moment, and then bethinking himself of something, added with a half-smile, "If you are wishful. There is no obligation."

Kate smiled at the reference to their previous conversation. "Insistence but no obligation?"

His eyes danced with humor as he nodded.

She doubted whether Lady Anne had insisted on any such thing, but she was grateful for Lord Ashworth's fabrication. It enabled her to accept the invitation.

The gratitude she felt was marred only by the awareness that not two hours ago, she had hit this same man over the head with a rock. And yet he was treating her with thoughtfulness despite that.

It was all very strange. But whatever awkwardness she might feel on the subject, he seemed not to regard it. It would be best to put off an encounter with the Croftes until she had sorted out her thoughts and feelings. A short stay at Ashworth Place would allow such reflection.

"Thank you, my lord," she said, looking over at him next to her. He didn't meet her eyes, only looking ahead and nodding with a polite smile. Did his head ache from where she had struck him? "Why didn't you tell me?" The words left her mouth before she could check them.

He stopped, finally looking at her. His eyes scanned hers under a pair of brows drawn together. "I wanted to," he said. "Believe me."

And she believed him.

He started slowly walking forward again, shaking his head. "I couldn't take any risks. It was too dangerous. This was the opportunity the officers had been waiting for, and no one who was not directly involved could know of our strategy. For years, Emmerson has been the man behind the curtain, arranging and ordering everything, but never allowing himself to be seen as an active participant in the trade. He risks the least but profits the most, always playing it safe.

"Tonight, he strayed from that. The shipment was too valuable for him to trust to his men, and I was sure we could catch him red-handed. And we did."

He inhaled deeply. "I knew you wanted to be part of bringing about justice, but I couldn't let you, not when I knew Emmerson himself was so involved. He is even more dangerous than you know. But had I known that not telling you would result in what you experienced tonight..." He shook his head, stopping again.

Kate was silent, thinking on his words. She shook her head, thinking of all that had transpired. "You should have told me. I could have been trusted with your secret."

"And *you* should have told *me*." There was an angry inflection to his voice.

"Told you of what?" she said incredulously. "All my plans were frustrated, thanks to you."

"Then how did you come to be taken by Roberts?" he said.

Kate huffed. "Quite innocently, I assure you. Clara convinced me to go for a ride. Little did I know that it was part of some elaborate plan to keep me from informing the authorities of what I saw in the stables last night."

Lord Ashworth looked at her with a pained expression. "I had no idea." He shook his head. "I was so angry and so terrified when I saw you there with Roberts and Briggs. I was sure that you had ignored my note and then been taken in an attempt to frustrate the free-traders' plans."

"Well," she admitted in a reasonable voice, "I suppose I can't fault you for coming to such a conclusion. It is not out of the realm of possibility, had I found the opportunity to do it. What of Henry, though? Was he involved in your plan?"

Lord Ashworth's brow creased. "No, he was not. In fact, I didn't know he was involved until last night, before I met you in the courtyard." He shook his head. "I considered confiding in him and asking for his assistance, but I believe I did right in resisting the idea. His fear of Emmerson would have eclipsed his trust in my ability to execute the plan. And then he would be in greater trouble with the law than he now is."

"What will happen to him?" Kate asked.

Lord Ashworth exhaled sharply and gripped his lips together. "My hope is that he will be shown leniency. His part in it all was foolish and naïve—I believe that he would have stopped had he known that he was aiding and abetting Bonaparte's army by his involvement. That he didn't know will, I hope, lead the powers that be to judge him less harshly. I will do whatever I can to mitigate the damage to him and his family."

He looked up at her. "Kate," he said. "Please tell me in all honesty, can you ever forgive me for tonight?"

The sensation of her heart racing had become a more common occurrence during her acquaintance with Lord Ashworth, but it still surprised her each time it happened. Hearing him dispense with the formality of "Miss Matcham" had not only caused such a reaction but also made it difficult to swallow. Her nerves brought on a strange desire to laugh.

"Forgive you?" she said incredulously. "When I very nearly killed you?"

A laugh escaped him, and she couldn't help but smile, relieved at his reaction to a situation she had been hesitant to bring up.

"My dear Kate," he said in utter enjoyment, causing her to swallow at his form of address, "I am afraid that I have given you an overinflated sense of strength."

"Not so," she said with an impressive attempt at gravity. "I was quite sure that I had murdered you using nothing but my own brute force. You can't imagine the relief I felt to see that the case was otherwise!"

He threw his head back in laughter. "I hesitate to do damage to your ego, but I am afraid you have no business hitting anyone over the head. The blow was shockingly feeble, which made my pretended fall that much more difficult to carry out convincingly. If Briggs weren't such a fool, he would have seen through it immediately."

Kate's eyes were wide, and she batted at his arm. "You lie!" She paused and looked at him. "You truly only pretended?"

He nodded and began walking forward again. "When you hit me, I figured that you had a plan of your own. And so I trusted you and went along with it." He looked at her with a censuring gaze. "A novel concept for you, I know."

"Well," said Kate in a voice of deep offense, "that is quite the most deflating thing anyone has said to me in recent memory. I was certain that I possessed hitherto-unknown superhuman strength, but I see that is not the case."

"I am afraid not." He smiled at her and, for a moment, and their eyes met in shared enjoyment. But his smile faded slowly, the troubled brow returning.

"I promise you I would never have let you come to harm under my care." He stopped, looking down to her wrists. He reached for her arm, gently pulling it into the light of the lantern he carried. He closed his eyes and exhaled through his nose, shaking his head slowly at the sight of her red and torn skin.

Unused to such attention being paid to her pain and wishing to change the subject, she said, "My lord, if we stop every ten paces, I don't believe we shall ever reach Ashworth Place."

"You are right, of course," he said with a half-smile. His eyes lingered on her wrists, though as he guided her arm back to its place at her side. "Lancelot is just beyond this thicket."

Hearing the name of his horse put Kate in mind of something which had escaped her memory during the fast-paced events of the past day.

"My lord?" she said with some hesitation, wondering if perhaps Fanny had been mistaken somehow.

"Yes," he said, pulling a branch back to let her pass through.

"Why did you not tell me that you were responsible for bringing Cleopatra to Wyndcross?"

One corner of his mouth turned up. "You know, when I wrote to Lady Hammond, I requested her quite plainly not to tell you of my involvement."

Kate laughed. "You betray your unfamiliarity with Fanny, then. I don't think she ever kept a secret in her life." She smiled as she thought of her aunt, but her head tilted to the side as she realized he hadn't answered her question. "Why should you not wish for me to know?"

He inhaled deeply, and she watched his face. He looked to be debating within himself but soon chuckled. "After inspecting Lady Crofte's horse myself, I felt far too much sympathy with you to consign you to riding—Cinnamon, was it? —for the duration of your visit."

Kate couldn't resist a smile, but she raised an incredulous eyebrow. She wanted to press him more but felt it would be uncivil to do so, particularly since he seemed intent on deflecting her questions with humor, but she understood his use of the tactic since it was one she herself was partial to.

"Well, I can't say that I believe you," she said with a twinkle. "Particularly given that, left to your plan, my visit would have come to an abrupt end this evening—" he made as if to reply, but she talked over him "—*if* I hadn't channeled my hidden and considerable strength to frustrate it."

A loud laugh erupted from him, and he looked at her with such warmth and enjoyment that she felt light-headed for a moment.

"Your show of strength, as you very inaccurately call it," he said, "was unnecessary. While I applaud your initiative, it is only fair that I call your attention to the many times that I told you that you could safely trust me."

"Oh," Kate tapped a finger on her lip, feigning an epiphany. "You are referring, I presume, to the times when you *ordered* me to trust you, despite the fact that you were leading me to my death. Yes, I see. It was quite silly of me not to have believed you."

He bit his lip to keep from laughing and said, "Did you really believe I would allow you to be harmed?" He said it as if it were unthinkable.

Kate opened her mouth to talk but instead closed her eyes and breathed in deeply, mustering patience. "Yes, I did." Before he could remonstrate, she continued. "I suppose I can be forgiven for assuming such a thing, given that you were about to tie me up in an enclosed space where I would drown with the incoming tide?"

She raised her brows, but he shook his head as she spoke.

"Before you struck me—with what I can only describe as the force of a small child—" he added as her twitching lips belied her indignant expression, "I was trying to convey to you that I would leave your ropes loose. Then you could escape back up the hill where I would return to you after I ensured that Emmerson had been caught. We had to have him in the act of managing the entire affair." Again, he spoke as though he were pointing out the obvious.

"An admirable plan," Kate acknowledged, "but I fail to see how I was expected to divine it, given the circumstances. Yes," she nodded decidedly after a moment of thought, "I think my plan served just as well."

He looked ready to debate more, but she said with sincerity, "I am grateful to know that you did indeed have a plan, and I am sorry that I didn't trust you. Let us simply agree that all's well that ends well."

He smiled at her and grasped her hand briefly in a gesture of agreement just as they reached Lancelot, making her feel strangely lightheaded. He insisted that she ride while he walked beside.

"If I had known how things would go, I would have brought a second horse," he apologized.

"Yes, and if I had known, I would never have come," she said with a roll of her eyes, softened by a smile. "Call me impatient or forward or whatever you like, but I am quite unwilling to go at the pace of your legs when Lancelot is capable of carrying us together in much better time."

Lord Ashworth considered a moment. His hesitation lasted too long for Kate who let out an impatient huff and pulled him by the arm toward Lancelot, insisting that he ride in front and she behind him.

"How overbearing you are." The corner of his lip trembled.

"You have no idea," she said.

Once they were both situated on Lancelot, Kate gripping the back of the saddle behind to steady her, they started on their way, riding in silence, swaying in synchronicity with the steps of Lancelot.

Her thoughts turned to her own situation. While the knowledge that Lord Ashworth had not betrayed her had been terrifically welcome, it had also rekindled the romantic feelings she had been smothering by reminding herself of Lord Ashworth's duplicity.

With such a glaring flaw no longer at her disposal, she was forced to face the reality of her desires, elusive as those desires might be. Many barriers remained unmoved.

Clara had seemed to be coming around to the idea of following her own wishes instead of her mother's. But if history was any indicator, she might very likely be swayed when under her mother's influence again. Lady Crofte wouldn't trade Lord Ashworth for Mr. Bradbury without a fight.

Perhaps more importantly, Lord Ashworth's feelings were still a mystery. Did he have feelings for Clara? Did he wish to marry her for practical reasons? Even removing Clara from the equation by no means made a connection between Kate and Lord Ashworth a foregone conclusion.

Lancelot stumbled, startling her out of the lax hold she had adopted on the saddle. She grasped Lord Ashworth to stabilize herself only to remove her arms from around his waist in embarrassment, apologizing. She was interrupted.

"Lancelot, old boy," Lord Ashworth said in a chiding voice, "what ails you? I believe he's falling asleep on us. Or under us, rather. That won't do, will it, Miss Matcham?"

She tried to ignore that he had reverted to a more formal form of address and feigned a sigh. "Actually, I have quite given up on ever getting to Ashworth Place."

Lord Ashworth chuckled appreciatively. "She mocks us, Lancelot! Tsk tsk." He shook his head and readjusted himself in the saddle. "As you wish, Miss Matcham. I would recommend holding on tightly." He signaled Lancelot, and they lurched forward.

Kate found herself once again obliged to grab Lord Ashworth around the waist. The wind whipped her face, making her tired eyes sting so much that she turned and ducked her head, burying it in his back. She had always enjoyed a good gallop, but never had she experienced it as a second rider. She found it to be a much more thrilling experience and was quite sure that the circumstance of Lord Ashworth being her companion or the fact that she had to hold him tightly to keep her seat had nothing to do with the pleasure she took from it.

33

At the pace they rode, Ashworth Place was attained in a matter of minutes. The courtyard was shrouded in darkness. Kate had no idea what time it was—only that it had been dark for hours.

"I think we made quite good time in the end, don't you?" he asked as he helped Kate off of the horse.

She replaced her smile with a look of hauteur and smoothed out her skirts, the hem of which was both torn and filthy. "It was adequate."

He laughed and looped Lancelot's reins onto a nearby post, turning to encounter a yawn from Kate. "Yes, quite so. You must be exhausted."

She sighed. "I can't deny it."

A smiled peeped at the side of his mouth. "I believe I know what you would say right now."

She raised her brows, wincing slightly as the gesture reminded her of the wounds on her cheek.

"*Weary with toil,*" he quoted, "*I haste me to my bed, the dear repose for limbs with travel tired.*" He smiled and raised his own brows, as if questioning whether he was right.

She smiled, recognizing the lines, and tilted her head to the side in thought. Her smile grew wry as she remembered the rest of the sonnet and just how à propos was his choice.

Seeing her ironic smile, he looked a question at her. "What is it?" he asked, full of curiosity.

She gave a quiet laugh and shook her head. "I was only remembering the rest of that particular sonnet."

His eyes squinted in an attempt to remember, but after searching for a moment, he shook his head. "I confess it is the only part I remember."

She smiled, unsure whether she was grateful or disappointed that he didn't recall the rest. "Well you are quite right in your assumption, my lord. I'm not sure when I have looked forward with so much anticipation to a bed."

He seemed still to be trying to remember the lines.

"My lord?"

He looked up.

She inhaled deeply and then exhaled in a quick rush of air. "Thank you."

He smiled slightly at her gratitude, but shook his head, looking down as he moved a pebble with the toe of his boot. "How you can forgive, much less thank me, is beyond me. It was a roguish thing to deceive you. I'm more sorry than I can express to be the cause of it all. I wish I could redo it."

"What," Kate said in pretended offense, "and deprive me of the greatest adventure of my life? How very selfish. If you had given up catching Emmerson only to save me some paltry scratches, now *that* is something I could never forgive you for."

His gaze rested on her, warm and appreciative. In an action that seemed a natural complement to the way he was looking at her, he reached his hand toward her own, taking it gently, ever-aware of her injuries, and moving in closer.

She swallowed the sudden lump in her throat and tried to continue smiling despite the way her heart thumped uncomfortably inside.

His brows drew together, and he dropped her hand gently.

"You need sleep. Forgive me for keeping you. We should go." He turned to lead the way into Ashworth Place.

Kate, taken off guard both by his sudden familiarity and by the restraint which followed it so abruptly, was too distracted by the confusion she felt to take in her surroundings. She was aware of Lord Ashworth ringing a bell after which a maid was brought to show Kate to a room.

Lord Ashworth wished her a good night's sleep, glancing out one of the large windows lining the hallway where the skyline was beginning to lighten with the first signs of morning. He told her to sleep as long as she was able, bid her good night, and left her to the maid.

Kate's limbs seemed to be sluggish with exhaustion. Anxious as she was for rest, she dreaded the battle between the fatigue which consumed her body and the desire to analyze all she had just experienced which consumed her mind.

Her feelings were, for better or worse, not in question. To spend more time on them was to waste both time and energy in a cause already decided. Everything she had learned in the last few hours had reconfirmed and magnified her regard for Lord Ashworth ten-fold.

His own feelings were another matter. At times he seemed to reciprocate on some level; at others, to distance himself from her. She didn't doubt that he enjoyed her company. But the way his warmth had cooled so suddenly underlined what she already knew—Lord Ashworth had much more than love to consider in making a match. Even if he had not, enjoying her company did not equate with love or a desire to marry her.

Kate's realistic nature forced her to accept the unlikelihood of her hopes being realized, but it also forced her to acknowledge that, were Lord Ashworth to desire to marry her, she would not refuse him. She desired his happiness, and if by some miracle their happiness was intertwined, she would not sacrifice that simply to satisfy those who wished to see him make a good match. Her selflessness did not extend so far as to deny herself joy and fulfillment based on an arrogant presumption of knowing what was best for Lord Ashworth better than he himself did. Her reason would not let her act in such a foolish or patronizing way, even if it appeared noble on the surface.

But the insignificant place she held in society permitted her to place little stock in the opinions of others. Most of society was indifferent to her—something that was not true for others like Lord Ashworth. He was heir to an earldom, and whatever decisions he made would be hashed and rehashed in social circles for as long as society's voracious appetite would allow.

Whatever his future held, the successes and failures he might experience would forever be tied up in his decision to marry. Kate had seen it often during her seasons in London, and she recognized it in her own parents' marriage.

Her mother had been deemed too far below her father to be an acceptable choice. As a result, anything Charles Matcham did which was disapproved of was attributed to his unwise marriage. The ills in her father's life were looked on without sympathy, viewed as the natural byproduct of an unwise marriage. Kate couldn't wish such treatment upon someone she loved as well as Lord Ashworth.

KATE FOUND HERSELF WAKING AT AN ADVANCED HOUR OF THE DAY, momentarily confused by her unfamiliar surroundings.

She made a motion to pull back the bedcovers only to find that the skin on her wrists was painfully stiff. A flood of memories from the night before explained her discomfort, and she examined a wrist for a moment, pursing her lips at the ugly sight of her scabbed and red skin.

A knock sounded on the door. Kate rose from the bed and cracked the door, expecting to see the kind maid from the night before. She found herself facing her own maid, Lindley.

"Lindley!" she exclaimed, opening the door for Lindley to pass through.

"Miss!" Lindley said, her eyes darting to Kate's cheek.

Kate put a hand to her sore cheek and shook her head with a reassuring smile. "It's nothing. I am well, Lindley. But how do you come to be here?"

"Yes, you may well ask." Lindley sniffed. "And it's no thanks to you that I am here. Worried sick is what I've been!" She sniffed loudly, setting down a portmanteau full of Kate's belongings.

"Oh, indeed I am so sorry, Lindley, but I can tell you that there hasn't been even a moment when I could have written to you. How in the world did you know to come?"

"His lordship was good enough to send word over early this morning, and my mind couldn't rest until I'd seen you myself." The words came out as a strange mix of chastisement and hurt, interspersed with sniffs and huffs.

Realizing how upset her maid was, Kate led her to the window seat where they sat together while Lindley gave vent to her emotions.

She recounted her hours of concern over Kate's whereabouts when Cleopatra was found wandering the grounds riderless; the return soon thereafter of Clara who was too hysterical between fits of crying and terror to speak a coherent thought; and finally the intervention of Sir Richard who was forced to pour the nearest vase of water over his daughter's head and talk sense into her before she could be brought to tell what she knew.

But even once Clara had recounted all, they had no way of knowing where Kate might be found. Too much time had passed since Clara had last seen her. Sir Richard had sent out two servants to search for Kate, but Lindley hadn't slept a wink for worry. She herself had been very near going out to search when she had received the missive from Lord Ashworth.

When Lindley spoke of the note and of his behavior to her on her arrival at Ashworth Place, she always referred to him as "that angel of a man" or "your guardian angel." She became noticeably calmer as she spoke of her conversation with him and did it with such a light in her eyes that Kate was made to wonder if her own maid hadn't fallen victim to his charms as well.

Lindley had much to say when the subject of Clara and the Crofte family arose. "Saving Sir Richard, if you please, Miss, for a more decent man I've never met, even if he was dreadfully oblivious to what was happening under his own roof, which I do believe he was. When he discovered what his children and wife were about, there was such a fire in his eyes as you never should wish to encounter."

Once Lindley had exhausted her stream of talk, she insisted on attending to Kate's mutilated wrists, all the while detailing the events of the preceding day.

Kate listened patiently but was relieved when Lindley pushed her out of the bedroom door to go see to her hosts. She was met in the hallway by Mary, the maid from the previous evening, who informed her that the ladies were partaking of a luncheon outdoors.

Kate thanked her and breathed deeply, wondering what to expect from her hosts. The circumstances of her stay were so peculiar, after all.

But Lady Anne and Lady Purbeck were all consideration, expressing surprise that Kate should already be awake and dressed after such an evening as she had passed.

Lady Purbeck's eyes fell on Kate's cheek and then her bandaged wrists.

"Good heavens!" she said, her eyes wide and horrified. "William mentioned that you had been injured, my dear, but—." She let out a gush of air, and her mouth drew into a tight line. "I should very much like to box his ears!"

Kate smiled appreciatively, aware of the way her heart felt light at Lady Purbeck's concern for her. "I hope you will not," she said, "for I assure you that I feel nothing but gratitude to your son. Bruised wrists would have been the least of my worries, had he not come to my rescue."

Lady Purbeck seemed gratified by Kate's professions of appreciation, though she continued to glance at Kate's injuries and shake her head in mute disapproval.

Kate couldn't help thinking that Lady Purbeck was everything one could hope for in a mother. Her genuine concern for someone she knew as little as Kate was a clear manifestation of her nurturing nature.

Kate partook as politely as she could manage given the ravenous hunger she felt. As the three of them were finishing the luncheon, Lord Ashworth approached from the house.

Inhaling a deep breath to stabilize her nerves, Kate focused on the sandwiches. She wasn't at all sure how to act in front of Lord Ashworth, given the events of the night before.

He greeted them, kissing his mother on the forehead and commenting on how well she looked before asking if he might have a word with Kate regarding a few items of business.

Kate thanked Lady Anne and Lady Purbeck before excusing herself to join Lord Ashworth.

They walked slowly toward the small pond on the east side of Ashworth Place, Kate admiring her first views of the grounds. They came upon a small pond, covered in large lily pads whose white flowers were open and soaking in the early afternoon sun.

Lord Ashworth inquired after Kate's rest, wondering if she had been able to sleep after such a disturbing evening. She allayed his fears on that score and thanked him for his thoughtfulness in sending word to Lindley. He brushed her thanks aside, insisting it had been no trouble.

"Miss Matcham," he said. "The timing of all this has obviously been less than ideal in that your visit to the Croftes has coincided with this entire affair. I think that it will be best if you remain here at Ashworth Place for the present. The Croftes will be much occupied for some time with the mess they are in. I don't think—and your capable maid agrees with me—that it is a suitable situation for you. I am exercising the small influence I have to soften the blow to the Croftes, but I'm afraid it will take time for everything to be ironed out." He watched for her reaction as they strolled.

Kate inhaled and nodded her understanding. "Thank you for your kindness and trouble." She smiled up at him, hoping he would understand that she meant it. "I appreciate your willingness to entertain a visitor who has been as good as thrust upon you. But I shan't impose upon you. I am sure my Uncle John would be happy to welcome me at Coombe Park until I go to Brighton."

The words were said in a confident tone, but Kate thought it just as likely that her uncle would shut the door in her face. She would take the mail coach to Fanny in Brighton if she had to, but she would not oblige Lord Ashworth's family to host her indefinitely, however awkward her situation might be.

Lord Ashworth's eyebrows knit together, and he stopped walking, pushing down an errant patch of grass with his boot toe before looking at Kate and quoting,

"But then begins a journey in my head
To work my mind, when body's work's expir'd:
For then my thoughts—from far where I abide—
Intend a zealous pilgrimage to thee,
And keep my drooping eyelids open wide."

Kate felt her cheeks redden in embarrassment, but she attempted an air of nonchalance when she spoke. "Ah, you have remembered the lines," she said, seeking out the small ripples in the pond to avoid looking him in the eye.

He smiled wryly. "I'm afraid that memory played no part in it. I was far too curious, though, to leave it to memory, and I sought Shakespeare out before I did haste me to my bed, as the sonnet says."

Kate was silent, so unsure what he had inferred from their interaction the night before and from his reading of the sonnet that she could think of nothing to say that would not give her feelings away entirely.

"Kate," he said, stepping closer to her and causing her heart to thud with such force that she was sure he could hear it. "I must ask you. When you smiled in such a way while thinking on those words last night, were you thinking of Mr. Hartley?"

Kate looked up at him, the surprise visible on her face. "Simon Hartley?" The nerves she had been feeling, the relief she felt to know he had cared enough to seek out the sonnet even before sleep, and the hope she felt at his question collided, eliciting a shaky laugh from her. She looked up to his eyes where she thought she recognized the same doubtful hope she herself had been feeling for an age. Was that what he was feeling?

"I had no thought of Simon Hartley," she said, looking back to the pond. She couldn't bear to see his reaction. She felt his eyes trained on her, as if he were waiting for her to finish.

Quiet reigned, and she turned to meet his eyes, willing him to break the silence; to take her meaning without requiring her to speak the words. But he would not. She laughed again, "You will insist that I say it, won't you?"

His half-smile appeared, and the accompanying twinkle replaced the doubt which had been so apparent before.

She looked down, smiling, as she gathered the courage to speak. She could lie or try to conceal the truth, but then, she might always wonder what he would have said had she been completely honest.

But lying and telling all were two ends of a spectrum, with an infinite number of choices between. And he had not asked her to tell all. He had asked a simple question, and only a simple answer was required of her. When she looked up, her expression was sincere and devoid of its customary humor. "I thought only of you."

He took in a slow breath, never losing eye contact with her, and placed a hand on her uninjured cheek, smoothing her cheekbone with his thumb as he looked in her eyes. She found it hard to breathe. Was there enough air for two to breathe in such proximity?

He lowered his head so that their foreheads touched, and she closed her eyes, bringing her hand up to rest on his cheek.

"I can't tell you," he said in a voice so soft she had to strain to hear it, "what hope I felt as I read those words last night. Or of the doubt which accompanied it."

She swallowed, all too familiar with the sentiments he was expressing. Then she smiled softly as another verse of Shakespeare came into her thoughts.

"*Doubt thou the stars are fire,*" she quoted, "*Doubt that the sun doth move...*"

"Now that one," he interrupted her, "I am familiar with."

He wrapped an arm around her waist, pulled her toward him, and guided her chin up with a finger. Their lips met, and there was a pause before he pressed his to hers, kissing her gently. Her skin tingled, and she wrapped her hands behind his neck. His hand moved from under her chin, and his fingers slid into her hair, cradling her head from behind.

After several minutes, Kate broke away with a sigh, leaning her nose up against his. "You know," she said, "I believe the blow would have been quite fatal if my own very *admirable* hesitation at the last moment had not weakened it pitifully."

Lord Ashworth threw back his head in a mix of amusement and

aggravation. "Persistent Kate! Still fixed on that, are you? Do you wish it had been a fatal blow?"

"Well, of course not. But I do think it important that you are aware of my extraordinary strength." She ran a hand softly through his hair, finding the small bump she was searching for. She raised her brows at him and clucked her tongue. "What a blow!"

He grabbed at her hand playfully, pulling it away from his head and holding it between his own hands. "Despite what you believe, love, I am rather glad to know that my wife will not be capable of killing me with her bare hands, even if she should wish to do so."

Kate considered his words for a moment with a furrowed brow but ended by shaking her head. "But I'm convinced it could be quite an asset."

"If you insist upon speaking such nonsense," he said, pulling her closer, "I have no choice but to put a stop to it in the only way available to me." He kissed her again through laughing lips.

"Well," she said, smiling back at him until the skin around her eyes wrinkled, "That is hardly an inducement for me to stop speaking nonsense, is it?"

READ THE NEXT IN SERIES:

Isabel: A Regency Romance (Families of Dorset Book Two)

ALSO BY MARTHA KEYES

If you enjoyed Wyndcross, make sure to check out my other books:
Families of Dorset Series:
Isabel: A Regency Romance (Book Two)
Cecilia: A Regency Romance (Book Three)
Hazelhurst: A Regency Romance (Book Four)
Phoebe: A Regency Romance (Series Novelette)
Other Titles:
Goodwill for the Gentleman (Belles of Christmas Book Two)
Eleanor: A Regency Romance

Join my Newsletter to keep in touch and learn more about the Regency era! I try to keep it fun and interesting.

OR follow me on BookBub to see my recommendations and get alerts about my new releases

AFTERWORD

Thank you so much for reading *Wyndcross*. The story of Kate and William had its beginnings long before I had ever stepped foot in Dorset, England—and before I had the slightest clue how to write fiction. I had a very blurry vision of one scene of the novel and picked a spot I had never been to in England on Google Maps, hardly dreaming how much I would come to love the area.

When I finally got the chance to go to Dorset myself, I was enthralled. But I knew that I had been telling the wrong story. I scrapped half of what I had written (and later heavily revised the rest). I am so grateful for all I've learned in the process of writing Kate and William's story

I've done my best to be true to the time period and particulars of the day, so I apologize if I got anything wrong. I continue learning and researching while trying to craft stories that will be enjoyable to readers like you.

If you enjoyed the book, please leave a review and tell your friends. Authors rely on readers like you to spread the word about books you've enjoyed.

If you would like to stay informed about my upcoming releases and

AFTERWORD

other wonderful sweet romance books, sign up for my newsletter! You can connect with me on Facebook and Instagram as well. I'd love to hear from you!

ACKNOWLEDGMENTS

This novel has been a labor of love and time. It bears only a little resemblance to the story when I first began writing it in 2015. There were so many times I wanted to give up on *Wyndcross* and leave it on the "shelf," but my parents encouraged me enough to help me push through. Thank you, Mom and Dad, for believing in me even when I didn't know how to believe in myself.

A big thank you to Dan Hogan who read the manuscript and provided constructive feedback and a dose of much-needed hope.

Thank you to my husband, Brandon, for picking up my slack at home as I've worked on this story since long before we even had kids.

Thank you to my boys who keep me grounded while inspiring me to reach for greater heights.

And, as always, thank you to all my fellow Regency authors and to the wonderful communities of The Writing Gals and LDS Beta Readers. I would be lost without all of your help and trailblazing!

ABOUT THE AUTHOR

Martha Keyes was born, raised, and educated in Utah—a home she loves dearly but also dearly loves to escape whenever she can travel the world. She received a BA in French Studies and a Master of Public Health, both from Brigham Young University.

Word crafting has always fascinated and motivated her, but it wasn't until a few years ago that she considered writing her own stories. When she isn't writing, she is honing her photography skills, looking for travel deals, and spending time with her husband and children. She lives with her husband and twin boys in Vineyard, Utah.